The first time Aaron had seen Lily had been a cloudless day, and he'd paid the price for staring at her.

Looking at Lily was like looking directly into the sun. You could get blinded. In his case, he'd had a detention.

He'd been sneaking back into school after slipping outside to have a smoke. He'd listened for the bell and then inched open the door to ease back into the flow of students moving from sixth-period class to seventh. But then he'd glimpsed Lily emerging from the art room. She was so beautiful she'd practically sparkled, and he'd stopped to stare—with the door still open, in full view of the art teacher, who'd dragged him down to the prinicpal's office to report him.

Lily hadn't even noticed him.

She didn't notice him now. He turned in time to see her near the front of the church, sliding into a pew with her parents. She didn't look shattered to him. She looked just as perfect as ever.

Dear Reader,

Welcome to Superromance, where we aim to give you varied, dramatic, emotional and satisfying stories.

Our NINE MONTHS LATER story comes to you from talented author Rebecca Winters, who also writes shorter novels for Mills & Boon. *The Family Way* is a strong story where a much too attractive mysterious man comes to the aid of a family without a father, but of course he isn't quite what he seems to be...

Wonderful New England writer Judith Arnold kicks off a five-book series set in a town called Riverbend, where everyone does know everyone's name, and where a group of friends are living and learning about love. *Birthright* is available now and the other books are coming monthly up until Christmas.

The Commander is a fabulous action-packed read by Kay David about the leader of a police SWAT team in Florida, and this Commander is a woman about to be assigned to protect her former fiancé. This is the second in a trio of novels, THE GUARDIANS, but it stands alone as a marvellous, dramatic read.

TWINS is a theme we all find fascinating and which offers wonderful possibilities to writers who can't resist thinking *'What if...'* And Bonnie K Winn's *The Wrong Brother* explores how an identical twin finds himself in trouble when his brother goes missing and he takes his place!

Enjoy them all,

The Editors

Birthright
JUDITH ARNOLD

SILHOUETTE® SUPERROMANCE™

*Silhouette, Silhouette Superromance and Colophon are
registered trademarks of Harlequin Books S.A., used under licence.*

*First published in Great Britain 2002
Silhouette Books, Eton House, 18-24 Paradise Road,
Richmond, Surrey TW9 1SR*

© Barbara Keiler 2000

ISBN 0 373 70924 2

38-0802

*Printed and bound in Spain
by Litografia Rosés S.A., Barcelona*

Dear Reader,

Every time a writer writes a new novel, she creates a world.

For *Birthright*, the first book of the RIVERBEND series, I got to create the world of Riverbend, Indiana, with four other authors. I live in Massachusetts, so I really needed their help in getting a feel for small-town Mid-Western life. Riverbend's terrain is quite different from the hilly New England town where my family and I live; the architecture, the types of businesses, the scents and sights and sounds are all different.

But people are people, no matter what world a writer creates for them. Men are men and women are women. Our struggles, our laughter, our yearning for love… No matter where we live, whether it's a real New England village or a fictional Indiana town, the essence of our humanity is universal.

I hope you enjoy spending time in Riverbend as much as I enjoyed living there in my imagination, creating this special world where my hero and heroine, Aaron Mazerik and Lily Holden, find themselves—and each other.

Sincerely,

Judith Arnold

Birthright is dedicated to my wonderful, talented
Riverbend collaborators:
Pamela Bauer, Laura Abbot,
Marisa Carroll and Kathryn Shay.

RIVERBEND

Birthright by Judith Arnold
August 2002

That Summer Thing by Pamela Bauer
September 2002

Homecoming by Laura Abbot
October 2002

Last-Minute Marriage by Marisa Carroll
November 2002

A Christmas Legacy by Kathryn Shay
December 2002

CHAPTER ONE

AARON AND CHURCH didn't get along. His mother had urged him to go a few times when he was a kid, but he'd known that the people who sat in church each Sunday feeling pious and pure were the same people who spent Monday through Saturday glaring at him with a mixture of disgust and contempt. Whatever they were learning in church, it didn't seem to have much to do with love and generosity.

So he stayed away from church, figuring that if he had anything to say to God, he could say it from his own back porch.

But his mother had wanted to be here today, and here they were, standing in the doorway of the Riverbend Community Church. The aisle ahead of them was clogged with people, and the pews were filling up. All of Riverbend, it seemed, had decided to pay their last respects to Abraham Steele.

"Over there, Aaron—there's a couple of seats," his mother said, pointing to a half-empty pew just inside the door.

"I see plenty of seats closer up."

She shook her head. "Back here is fine. We don't belong up in front."

They didn't belong at the memorial service at all, but his mother had insisted on coming, and she couldn't walk all the way from her apartment to the church. She couldn't drive, either, given that her right leg wasn't reliable. Reluctantly, Aaron had agreed to take her.

He was worried about her leg. She'd gotten a lot back after the stroke, but not enough. She was lazy about her physical therapy. She was still smoking, too. It infuriated him that he'd rearranged his whole life so he could help her out, yet she'd done so little rearranging of her own life. She'd given up her car and switched from waitressing to running the cash register at the Sunnyside Café, but she'd refused to move out of the second-floor flat she'd been living in since before Aaron was born. Every day she tottered up and down the stairs, insisting she was perfectly all right, she wasn't dizzy, the railings were sturdy and, damn it, she wasn't going to move out of her home.

And she wasn't going to quit smoking until she was good and ready, either.

He could smell the faint familiar scent of cigarette smoke in her hair. It mixed with the smell of her cologne, which in the June heat seemed heavier than usual, and the fragrance of the huge flower arrangements at the front of the chapel. She was wearing a pistachio-green linen suit that she'd bought for Easter a few years ago. It was inappropriately cheery.

But then, people in Riverbend had always considered Evie Mazerik and her son inappropriate. If they whispered about her outfit, it wouldn't be the first time they'd ever whispered about her.

At least Aaron was dressed for the occasion, in a dark-gray jacket and lighter-gray slacks, a white shirt and a plain burgundy tie. Dressing correctly was the least he could do in Abraham Steele's memory. He'd hardly known the guy, but he'd played basketball with Abraham's son, Jacob, and he remembered seeing Jacob's old man at every game, watching every play, sitting straight and proud on the bleachers and hollering whenever the Riverbend boys scored. Even after Jacob graduated, Abraham Steele had continued to attend the games.

Aaron's mother had never come to a single one.

She was edging past the people already seated in the pew and apologizing repeatedly as she made her way clumsily over their feet and around their knees. Aaron eased along the pew with more grace. He held her cane as she lowered herself onto the hard white bench, then sat next to her. Organ music filled the air, some hymn that sounded vaguely familiar. If Aaron attended church, he might have recognized it.

People continued to stream into the building. Abraham Steele's twin sisters entered, their heads bowed, one of them clinging to the other's arm. Behind them trailed Kate McCann, the young woman who managed their bookstore, which was just across the street from the café where Aaron's mother worked. The Steele sisters seemed to have aged a lot in the weeks since Aaron had last seen them. They had to be in their seventies, but they'd always seemed strong and spirited.

Not today.

"It's breaking their hearts," Aaron's mother whispered, her gaze following the sisters down the aisle as the crowd parted to let them through. "I don't know how they'll survive this." Her voice caught in her throat and her eyes glistened as she wallowed in the drama of the moment.

"They're tough," he whispered back. They'd always treated him courteously, even when he'd been just a kid hanging out in the streets and looking for trouble. If they found him loitering near their store, they used to ask him not *what* he was doing but *how* he was doing. They'd tell him to give their regards to his mother, as if the Mazeriks were just like anyone else in town. To acknowledge him when he'd been nothing but a punk on the fast track to bad news proved just how tough they were.

More people entered the church, the men in dark suits, the women in somber dresses. In her bright green outfit, Aaron's mother stuck out like a shoot on a tree, a sprig in need of pruning.

Aaron noticed Mitch Sterling entering with his son Sam. Mitch had been a classmate of Aaron's and a fellow member of the high-school basketball team. Now he ran the town's hardware store and lumberyard. When Aaron had bought his house, which hadn't been much more than a glorified fishing cabin when he'd taken title to it two summers ago, he'd spent a lot of time and money at Mitch's store, purchasing supplies to expand the rear deck and insulate the attic.

Aside from basketball, Mitch hadn't had much to do with Aaron at Riverbend High. Mitch had been part of a group that had called themselves the River Rats. Aaron wasn't sure where that name had come from. All he'd known was that they were the insiders, the popular kids, the leaders. They'd known who they were and where they belonged.

Aaron hadn't been in their group. He hadn't belonged anywhere back then.

He watched Mitch move down the aisle with his son. The kid was about ten, trapped in that awkward state between childhood and adolescence. Mitch had enrolled him in Aaron's summer program, which was fine with Aaron, except that the boy was seriously hearing-impaired. Aaron didn't know sign language. He wasn't sure how he was going to communicate with Sam.

"Kate is such a sweetheart," Aaron's mother was murmuring, her gaze still on Kate McCann and Ruth and Rachel Steele as they sorted themselves out in a front pew. "She comes to the Sunnyside for lunch sometimes. But her daughters are wild. Adorable as hell, but wild. I don't know how she manages the two of them all by herself."

Some single mothers managed better than others, Aaron thought. His mother had done the best she could. Unfortunately her best had been lousy.

"And I'll tell you what's really breaking Ruth and Rachel's hearts," his mother continued in a low voice. "Jacob didn't come home. How could someone not come home to pay his last respects to his father?"

Aaron shrugged. The relationship between the most powerful man in Riverbend and his absent son wasn't his business.

Apparently it was Evie's business, though. As the Sunnyside Café's cashier, she considered everything in town her business. "Even if there's bad blood there, what kind of son would stay away at a time like this?" She shook her head.

Aaron hoped his lack of response would discourage her. He didn't like gossip, especially since he'd been the subject of so much of it in his life.

Surveying the crowd, he spotted Charlie Callahan taking a seat across the aisle, a few rows ahead. Charlie had been another classmate of his, and another River Rat. After Aaron had bought the cabin, Charlie had offered his expertise as a carpenter, helping with the rehab work. No one seemed to care much about who Aaron used to be fifteen years ago, or which group he hadn't been a part of. They weren't in high school anymore.

"There's a rumor floating around that Jacob left the country," his mother confided. "He got real rich, set up one of those bank accounts in the Bahamas and now he's living there. And obviously doesn't give a damn that his father is dead."

"He was a good guy," Aaron whispered. "He wouldn't do that."

"Then where is he? He left town years ago and never came back. He broke his father's heart—his aunts' hearts, too. You know those aunts just about raised him after his mother died. And now he won't even come to the memorial service."

"Maybe he couldn't come back. Maybe—"

"He's dead? That's what Lucy said. She was willing to bet money on it, but I told her that's too ghoulish, betting on the death of a young man like Jacob."

Apparently it wasn't too ghoulish for his mother and the other Sunnyside waitresses to conjecture about, Aaron thought with a wry smile.

Evie reached for his hand and gave it a squeeze. "Everyone knows *you* came home when I needed you. Quality isn't about how wealthy you are. It's about how you act, how you take responsibility. Jacob Steele didn't come home. *My* son did.''

Aaron hadn't come home because he'd wanted to. Riverbend had never been a happy place for him. If he'd thought about it, he might have moved his mother down to Indianapolis, instead of the other way around.

But he hadn't thought about it. He'd quit his job, broken up with Cynthia because she'd refused to accompany him to ''that closed-minded little town that you hate, anyway, Aaron, so I don't know why you're going there,'' and come back to Riverbend.

He noticed Frank Garvey entering the church right behind the mayor and her husband. Clad in civilian clothes, Garvey wasn't immediately recognizable. He'd aged, too, and added a good twenty pounds of paunch. But Aaron would never forget the cop who'd locked him up. At the time he'd loathed Garvey. Now he'd matured enough to understand that maybe Garvey had saved his life. Garvey and Coach Drummer, one hauling Aaron in and the other bailing him out.

Behind Officer Garvey was another man Aaron knew well: Dr. Julian Bennett, tall and fit, his chestnut hair streaked with gray. He was older than Aaron's mother but looked ten years younger, his face barely lined, his posture straight and confident. Aaron had mastered the skill of looking at Dr. Bennett without wincing, but his gut always tightened with rage when he saw him.

His gut always tightened when he saw Dr. Bennett's daughter, too.

She entered the aisle after her father, and Aaron felt his innards clench with more than simple rage. Resentment was a part of it, along with frustration, regret and the cold understanding that some things could not be changed.

He hadn't seen her since they'd all graduated from high school fifteen years ago. She'd been beautiful then and she was beautiful now, slim and elegant in a gray silk suit, her straight blond hair dropping loosely past her shoulders. Viewing her today was as wrenching an experience as it had been the first time he'd glimpsed her in the hallway at Riverbend High.

"Look, there's Lily," his mother murmured. "She's so pretty."

He focused on the stained-glass window behind the altar, unwilling to acknowledge how pretty Lily Bennett was. Sunlight filtered through the slivers of color, making them glow ruby and amber and royal blue. If he stared at the window long enough, maybe the colors would hypnotize him and he'd lose track of Lily and her father.

"She's Lily Holden now," his mother added.

As if he cared that Lily had gotten married.

"A terrible tragedy. She married a millionaire, a big-shot attorney in Boston, and then he died in an automobile accident. The poor girl hasn't gotten over it."

As if he cared.

"Rumor has it she was so shattered by his death she still hasn't gotten over it. She came home last March. Lucy says Lily just rattles around her house—she bought that old Victorian on East Oak Street, with the wraparound porch. Must've paid a fortune for it, but that rich husband of hers left her mighty comfortable. Not that money can buy you happiness. She hides in the house, won't socialize, won't get out and do things. It's tragic.''

Aaron shifted his attention from the stained-glass window at the front of the room to the narrow side window at the end of his pew. Through it he could see unrelievedly blue sky. It was a perfect day for stretching out in the hammock on his refurbished deck, a beer in one hand and John Grisham's latest in the other. It was a day to avoid worrying about the summer program he'd planned, about scraping up the funds to maintain it, about how the hell he was going to get through to Mitch Sterling's hearing-impaired son. It was a day to avoid thinking about his mother's health and the death of the town patriarch—and definitely about Lily Bennett, or Lily Holden, or whatever her name was now.

The first time he'd seen her had been another cloudless day many years ago, and he'd paid the price for staring at her. Looking at Lily was like looking directly into the sun. You could get blinded.

In his case he'd gotten detention. He'd been sneaking back into the school building after slipping outside to have a smoke. He'd wedged a piece of paper into the doorjamb so the door wouldn't lock behind him, and after he'd finished his cigarette, he'd listened for the bell and then inched open the door to ease back into the flow of students moving from sixth-period class to seventh. But then he'd glimpsed Lily Bennett emerging from the art classroom. She was so beautiful she'd practically sparkled, and he'd stopped to stare—with the door still open, in full view of the art teacher, who'd grabbed him by his collar and dragged him down to the principal's office to report him for cutting a class and smoking. Aaron had stunk of cigarettes.

Lily hadn't even noticed him.

She didn't notice him now. He turned from the window in time to see her near the front of the church, sliding into a pew with her parents. She didn't look shattered to him. She looked just as perfect as ever.

It was her father Aaron ought to hate. But he hated *her*—because she was gorgeous and smart and poised, because she glowed with confidence, because she'd fed an unruly young teenager's wildest fantasies, and those fantasies had frightened the hell out of him.

The Bennetts took their seats. Despite the crowds, he spotted the back of Lily's head, her hair pale against the gray-blue of her jacket.

"If you're looking for money for your program," his mother suggested, "you ought to ask Lily. She's got more than she'll ever spend in this lifetime."

He would never go to Lily for anything. "Maybe her father's still giving out money," he muttered under his breath, recalling Dr. Bennett's regular visits to the Mazerik apartment when Aaron had been a kid. The good doctor would sit in the kitchen with Aaron's mother for a while, talking quietly, and then he would find Aaron watching TV or reading a comic book, and he'd ask stilted questions like "How are you doing in school?" Or, "Do you have any hobbies?" Or, "Boy, you're growing fast. Do those sneakers still fit you?" Aaron would mumble a response, and Dr. Bennett would return to the kitchen, hand Aaron's mother an envelope filled with cash and leave.

Aaron wasn't supposed to know about the cash. He was supposed to think Dr. Bennett had come only to eyeball him so his mother could save the expense of taking him in for an official physical examination. But from the living room, he could see through the doorway that Bennett was giving his mother money.

Lynn Kendall, the minister of the Riverbend Community Church, stepped up to the pulpit and the organ music ceased. "Thank you all for coming here today," she said. "For joining together as friends and neighbors to remember Abraham Steele."

A hush as thick as fog settled over the crowd. Aaron glanced behind him and noticed people standing three deep at the rear of the chapel. Turning forward, he again caught a glimpse of sleek blond hair, as if a hundred people weren't jammed into the pews between him and Lily. He clenched his jaw to keep from swearing.

"Everyone in Riverbend knew Abraham," Lynn continued.

Settling herself against the hard wood back of the pew, he stretched his legs. Clearly the pews hadn't been designed for the comfort of anyone over six feet tall. He banged his shin against the pew in front of him and stifled another curse.

"You all know that Abraham's great-grandfather Gideon founded Riverbend, and that the Steele family has always been the heart and soul of this town. Many of you knew Abraham as the president of the bank. He helped you to finance your homes and businesses. He helped you to teach your children how to save their allowances. Abraham also supported our community through his patronage of our stores. You never saw him driving out of town to shop at one of the big chain stores near the highway. No, if he needed penny nails, he bought them from Mitch Sterling. If he needed socks, he went to Killian's. If he was in the mood for a cup of coffee, he'd head right on over to the Sunnyside Café.''

Aaron glanced at his mother. Fat tears rolled down her cheeks and her lower lip trembled, as if Steele had been her dearest friend and not just someone who used to stop in at the café for a hit of caffeine.

"I've invited several people who knew him to share their memories with us today," the minister said. "If any of the rest of you would like to join in, please step forward and let us reminisce with you. Ruth?" She gestured toward one of the Steele sisters, who rose slowly and crossed to the pulpit.

Looking solemn but determined, Ruth adjusted the microphone, then cleared her throat and squared her shoulders. "My brother could be a pain in the rear end," she began, and the room filled with laughter.

Aaron made another attempt at straightening his legs, this time sparing his shin a bruise, and listened as Ruth Steele described her brother in his youth, relating his escapades, his stubbornness, his arrogance—and the generous heart that lurked beneath his imperious demeanor. She declared that no one in Riverbend worked harder or loved the town more than Abraham; no one felt closer ties to their community. She mentioned Abraham's profound grief at the death of his wife thirty years ago, and the pride he took in his son, Jacob, who grew up to be a top student and a star basketball player.

And didn't bother to come home for his father's funeral. It went unsaid, but Aaron suspected the entire congregation was thinking it.

Ruth Steele sat down. Her sister leaned her gray head against Ruth's shoulder.

One of the tellers at Abraham's bank got up and talked about how kind Abraham had been to her when she was having a difficult pregnancy. "The doctors said I had to stay off my feet for the duration of the pregnancy. Not only did Mr. Steele hold my job for me for all those months, but he bought a crib for my baby." Her eyes shimmering with tears, she sat down.

Officer Garvey took the mike to let everyone know that years ago, when Abraham Steele had been serving as mayor, the police department had asked for funding for new uniforms, but the town's budget was too tight. Abraham had personally paid for new uniforms for the entire department, but had asked Officer Garvey not to go public with this donation because he didn't want people to think that he owned the police in any way.

As Garvey returned to his seat, Lily stood up and walked to the pulpit. She moved like a dancer, her posture regal and her shoulders straight, as if she was balancing a book on her head. She leaned toward the microphone. In a soft crystalline voice, a voice Aaron had never forgotten, she said, "When I was four years old, Abraham Steele gave me a tin box of watercolor paints, and he opened up an entire world to me.'' Then she turned away from the mike and glided back to her space on the pew.

That was it? A box of watercolor paints?

He recalled that Lily Bennett had been the class artist, always painting the posters for the school plays and the dances. She'd designed the cover of the yearbook. That first time Aaron had seen her, she'd been coming out of the art room. So maybe the box of paints *had* been significant.

More people stood up and spoke about Steele. Aaron's attention drifted back to the side window, to that clear open sky, a blue as vivid as Lily Bennett's eyes.

Lily Holden. The young widow. The *rich* young widow he could hit up for money, if he found the nerve. He'd already made money-raising pitches for the summer program to the school board, the town council, the Rotary Club. Just last month he'd paid a call on Abraham Steele himself. They'd sat in Steele's office at the bank, a paneled high-ceilinged room so stately Aaron had thought they ought to be enjoying cigars and brandy, not talking about donations and loans. He'd described what he had in mind: a sports program for kids in town whose parents couldn't afford summer camp. They'd learn skills, and more important, they wouldn't spend the summer being bored and getting in trouble, he'd explained.

''That's something you've had some experience with, Aaron, isn't it?'' Steele had said.

Aaron had been surprised that Steele knew about his background. But Riverbend was a small town. ''Who better than me to know that sports can keep kids out of trouble?'' Aaron had replied. ''The high school is providing the facilities—we've got the gym, the tennis courts and the pool. But I can only teach basketball. I'm not a certified swim instructor, and tennis…" He'd snorted. Tennis was a sport for rich kids. He'd never learned to play.

"How much do you plan to charge for participation in the program?"

"Thirty dollars a week per kid."

"That's a bargain."

"This is for kids whose families can't afford camp," he'd emphasized. "If I charge more, it'll price people out of the program. I've already got a list of families interested in enrolling their children. The fees will pay for the use of the school building, insurance and equipment."

"Your salary?"

Aaron had grinned. "Let's just say I'm deferring it."

"I like your grit, Aaron," Steele had said. Usually brusque, he'd seemed almost sentimental, Aaron recalled now, revealing that generous heart his sister spoke of from the pulpit. "I admire the things you've accomplished in your life. Leave your proposal with me and I'll see what I can do for you."

Unfortunately, Steele had died before committing any funds to the program. So Aaron was back to grubbing for donations.

Why not ask Lily Holden? Just because she'd been a source of pain to him in school, just because she'd unknowingly driven him crazy in too many ways to count, didn't mean she couldn't put some of her late husband's millions to good use helping the kids of Riverbend.

He'd never been short of guts. He could pay a call to the grieving widow and see if she would bankroll his program. She probably had no idea how he felt about her... Then again, maybe she did know. Maybe she knew why. And maybe if she helped him out with the funding, he would resent her a little less.

"WAS THAT TRUE?" Charlie Callahan asked, sidling up to Lily as she stood in the shade of a silver maple on the lawn beside the church.

She'd removed her jacket. The dry June heat made her arms sting, but the air was a good ten degrees cooler under the tree, and the leaves spread a dense mesh of shadows around her.

Her parents, she knew, would take forever to make their way to the car. They had to stop and chat with everyone who'd attended the service, starting with the Reverend Lynn Kendall, then sharing some private words with Ruth and Rachel Steele, then working their way slowly through the crowd, greeting everybody.

If Lily had come to the memorial service on her own, she could have driven herself home. Instead, like an idiot, she'd agreed to attend with them, and now she had to wait.

She'd hoped no one would notice her hiding under the protective arch of the tree. But if anyone had to find her, she was glad it was Charlie. She'd known him since childhood. He was a River Rat, practically a brother to her. When he looped his arms around her and kissed her cheek, she felt safe.

"Was what true?" she asked back.

"Steele gave you your first watercolors?"

"Yes. My father was his doctor. Abraham used to bring me presents when he had medical appointments. Most of it was stuff I didn't want—dolls, little bead bracelets—but the paints were wonderful. I loved them."

Charlie grinned and nodded. She adored his grin—it was so familiar. Lord, it was good to be home.

He dug his hands into the pockets of his trousers. "It's great seeing you, Lily," he said, his gaze so intense she couldn't meet it. She searched for a glimpse of her parents in the throng of people who milled around the broad front steps of the church and let Charlie's voice wash over her. "I can only guess how awful it was, losing your husband that way. I know you're still broken up about it. But you've got friends here. You don't have to hide."

"I'm not hiding," she said quietly, sifting all the emotion from her voice.

"You've been back, what? A couple of months, right? And this is the first time I've seen you."

"I know." She wanted to look at him, wanted to tell him the truth: that she was embarrassed for her friends to see her in such ghastly shape. They all knew her as Lily Bennett, the Girl Who Could Do No Wrong. And she'd blown it. She couldn't bear to be around all those people who'd believed she had so much promise, didn't want to see their faces when they learned she was such a failure.

"I'm still healing," she said, pleased that it was the truth. Let them all think she was healing from the agony of having lost Tyler. They didn't have to know she'd really lost herself. "I appreciated the card you sent, Charlie."

"It was the least I could do. When I heard about the accident, I felt so bad for you being all alone in Boston."

"I wasn't all alone. Tyler's family was there," she said, hoping she didn't sound as bitter as she felt. Her in-laws had been horrible to her after Tyler had died. They hadn't been much better when he was alive.

But she didn't want to think about that. Today was a day for remembering Abraham Steele, the town's patriarch and her father's friend. She'd had less trouble believing Tyler was dead than believing that Abraham was. He'd been the beating heart of Riverbend for so long. "I was sorry Jacob didn't come back for the service," she said.

"He hasn't been back in years."

"I can't understand why he would have just disappeared like that. Maybe if he'd known his father was going to die…"

"We're all going to die sooner or later," Charlie said. "If he'd wanted to make up with his father, he would have."

"You're right. Still…I miss him." Jacob had been one of the River Rats, as well—their leader, in fact, mostly because he'd been the oldest of the group. He'd been a devoted son, always respectful of his father, kindhearted and fair. What a shame that he'd never had a chance to reconcile with Abraham. Now it was too late.

"Tom didn't come back, either," she noted. Abraham's nephew, Tom Baines, had spent his childhood summers in Riverbend, hanging out with the River Rats. But now he traveled the world as a journalist, and Lily hadn't really expected him to come back to town for the memorial service.

"It would have been nice to see him," Charlie murmured.

She noticed a twosome working their way slowly down the church's front steps. The woman was thin but determined in a bright green suit, her hair a shade of red Mother Nature had never intended. One hand manipulated a cane and the other clutched the arm of a tall younger man in a dark gray jacket and pale gray trousers. His hair was brown and in need of a trim. His chin was sharp, and his eyes, she remembered now, were a mix of blue and green, gold and gray, the color of the river on a stormy morning.

Aaron Mazerik.

She hadn't thought about him in years. One quick glimpse of him, though, and she couldn't imagine why she hadn't. He'd been startlingly handsome in high school, dangerously handsome, handsome like a panther. The kind of handsome that could spring at you and leave you bleeding.

She'd been scared to death of him back then. Scared, but intrigued.

"Isn't that Aaron Mazerik?" she asked, keeping her tone casual.

Charlie glanced toward the church steps. "Yeah. All grown-up, just like us."

She shook her head in amazement. "I never would have guessed he'd be here in Riverbend. The cops would have run him out of town if he hadn't had the good sense to leave on his own."

"He wasn't *that* bad," Charlie said.

She shot Charlie a skeptical look.

"Okay," Charlie conceded, "so maybe he had a few run-ins with the police. That was a long time ago."

"What's he doing in town now? Who's that with him?"

"His mother. She had a stroke a couple of years back. He came home to help her out."

Lily resisted the urge to laugh. Aaron Mazerik, the troublemaker, the kid who defied authority, who wore tight black T-shirts to school and spent half his time in the detention room, who seemed to know so much about life, so many dark nasty things, had come home to take care of his mother?

Evidently Charlie sensed her disbelief. "It gets better," he added. "He's the basketball coach at the high school."

"You're kidding!"

"Coach Drummer retired and Aaron took over the team. And the high school put him on the staff as a counselor or something, working with kids on the edge. He's got a master's degree."

"Aaron Mazerik?" Her head ached. From the sun, she told herself, from the parching heat. From anything other than the shock of learning that the boy who used to send a delicious shiver of fear down her spine whenever she saw him had a master's degree, of all things. "How do you know this?"

"He bought Old Man Miller's place up on River Road and renovated it. I lent him a hand."

"Wow." She tried not to stare as Aaron helped his mother into the passenger seat of an old Pontiac parked in a handicapped space. "Riverbend has certainly changed."

''Not much,'' Charlie argued.

Lily should have been relieved. She didn't really want her hometown to have changed. She'd come back to Riverbend because she wanted her old life back. She wanted to regain her faith in herself and her judgment. She wanted to trust her instincts again. She wanted to know she was a good person, not someone who harbored fear and hatred in her heart. She wanted to be the innocent, optimistic girl she'd been when she'd graduated from Riverbend High School and embarked on life's grand adventure.

If Riverbend hadn't changed too much, maybe she would be able to find that girl somewhere here, somewhere inside her.

But if Aaron Mazerik, the baddest bad boy in town, was working at the high school, coaching the basketball team and helping his mother, Lily knew that Riverbend couldn't be the same place it used to be.

CHAPTER TWO

THE HOUSE WAS much too big for one occupant—three stories, with gables and sloping eaves and a rounded corner that rose towerlike to a cone-shaped roof. It sat on a huge, impeccably landscaped lot. The trees were mature and leafy, the shrubs bordering the porch dense and green. The front walk was paved in red brick and bordered by flowers some gardening service probably charged a fortune to maintain.

Aaron supposed it made sense that Lily Bennett Holden was living in a house that could pass for a castle. She'd always been a princess. Even as a teenager, she'd carried herself with imperial confidence, the knowledge that she was a doctor's daughter, pure of breed and positioned near the top of the social ladder. She hadn't been arrogant, just supremely self-assured.

He wasn't envious of her newly inherited wealth. Envy was no longer a part of his life the way it had been when he was a kid, growing up in a cramped second-floor flat and knowing that other kids in Riverbend had nice homes with yards big enough to play in. He used to pedal his rickety old bike across town to Dr. Bennett's house just to stare at it. But he hadn't even known of Lily's existence then.

Dr. Bennett's home had seemed mighty grand to

Aaron, but it was modest compared to the house Lily
Holden had bought for herself. She might be devas-
tated by the loss of her husband, but she was clearly
making the best of a bad situation.

Aaron had decided to pay her a call to see if he
could convince her to make a donation to his summer
program. It would be starting tomorrow, and he had
enough cash in his budget to cover the basic costs of
getting it off the ground. But he needed funds to hire
more staff—and it would be nice if he could pay
himself a salary, too.

Aaron climbed the three steps to the porch and
approached the front door, a thick varnished slab of
oak with brass fittings and a small leaded-glass window. Through it he could see the entry hall. The
walls were white and the stairway had a railing of
polished wood and a fancy carved newel. To one side
a pedestal table held a vase filled with fresh flowers.

He rang the bell.

No response.

He should have phoned before coming, to see if
she was home. But for some reason he'd thought it
would be easier to talk to her in person than on the
phone. Face to face, he'd have living breathing proof
that she wasn't the leading lady of his tormented adolescent dreams. She was just a woman. A very
wealthy woman.

He rang the bell again and waited. Nothing.

Sighing, he turned to head back down the stairs,
then changed direction and headed along the front of
the wraparound porch and then down the side. If she
wasn't home, she wouldn't object to his taking a
peek at her property, would she? The house was so

big and imposing, he was curious to see what it looked like in back.

He halted when he reached the corner where the porch continued along the rear of the house. Lily sat on a folding metal chair in front of a bridge table, ignoring the more comfortable-looking wicker chairs near by. Clad in old jeans and a baggy white T-shirt, she had one bare foot tucked beneath her. Her hair was woven into a sloppy braid that hung down her back.

She was painting. A small easel held a sheet of stiff paper on which she'd painted half a jug and most of a pear. Beyond the bridge table he noticed a jug and a real pear perched on a stool, the models for her creation. Along with the easel, the bridge table was cluttered with jars of murky water, small cakes of paint in a palette, paintbrushes, a box of tissues and a rag.

She was so immersed in her work, she apparently hadn't heard his approach. He stood silently, watching her as she swirled a brush in a jar of water and wiped the bristles on the rag. Then she dipped it in the water again, dabbed the bristles against one of the cakes of paint and applied a few careful delicate brush strokes to her painting.

It was a good rendering, although Aaron couldn't imagine why anyone would want a painting of a jug and a pear. The jug was fat, and she gave it dimension in the painting, using areas of white and shadow to make the jug seem to bulge out of the paper. Her hand moved with exquisite deliberation, and after each dab she sat back and studied the picture.

Her fingers, he noted, were slender, her wrists and

forearms slim. Her back was perfectly straight. The white cotton of her shirt draped in a way that hinted at the angular grace of her shoulders, the sleek lines of her body.

She was, if anything, more beautiful now than she'd been in high school. More beautiful, and just as unattainable.

If he stood watching her much longer, she'd be really upset when she finally noticed him there. He hadn't meant to sneak up on her—he supposed shoes like his were called sneakers for a reason.

He cleared his throat. She flinched and spun around in her chair. The paintbrush slipped from her hand and dropped onto the table, clinking against one of the glass jars.

Her mouth popped open and then shut. She gripped the back of her chair with one hand and stared at him. He couldn't tell from her expression whether she was angry or alarmed, whether she was about to charge him with trespassing or flee into the house and bolt the door.

"I'm sorry," he said quickly, hoping to avoid either possibility. His apology seemed to puzzle her, and he added, "For startling you like that."

She took a deep breath. Her cheeks grew pink. It occurred to him that she was shy, and the realization almost made him laugh. Lily Bennett, the dignified, self-possessed, most-likely-to-succeed girl from his high-school class, was shy.

"I rang your bell," he continued after her silence stretched a full minute. "I guess you couldn't hear it out here."

"No." She turned, lifted the rag and wiped her

hands on it, then uncoiled from her chair and stood up.

"Anyway, I don't know if you remember me, but—"

"Aaron," she said.

It was his turn to be startled. He had never heard her speak his name before. They'd never talked to each other in school. He'd known who she was, but she'd had no reason to know who he was.

Whether or not she'd known who he was in high school was irrelevant. They were fifteen years older now, and she knew his name. He had to focus on the reason he'd come, not on the fact that even in an extra-large T-shirt and fraying jeans Lily Bennett Holden was the most beautiful woman in Riverbend, if not the entire world.

"That's right," he said, extending his right hand. "Aaron Mazerik."

She slipped her hand into his. Hers was fine-boned and smooth. He stood a good six inches taller, but she tilted her head and looked directly into his eyes. The blush remained in her cheeks, and her faint smile really did look shy. But not so shy she couldn't meet his gaze squarely.

"I didn't mean to interrupt you," he said.

She shot a quick glance at the paper on the easel and shrugged. "That's all right."

"It's very nice." He gestured at the painting.

"Thank you." She glanced at it again, as if to make sure he wasn't lying. Actually he was, sort of. The painting *was* very nice but, hey, it was a jug and a piece of fruit.

He wondered if he could discreetly put some distance between her and himself. She wasn't crowding him, but her scent was. She smelled of summer, warm and tangy.

It irked him that all these years later, he was still affected by her. It irked him even more because he knew how wrong it was to be affected by her. He'd grown up thinking there was something bad inside him, something evil that made him desire her, but he hadn't cared. Being so damned attracted to her was still bad, only he *did* care now.

He pushed those thoughts away. He'd come here on a mission. The sooner he embarked on it, the better. "I was wondering if we could talk for a few minutes."

She took a step back, then twisted to study her painting, as if deciding whether she could leave it alone and give Aaron the few minutes he was asking for. "Sure," she said, lowering her gaze to somewhere in the vicinity of his chest. She shoved a loose strand of hair back from her cheek and shaped another shy smile.

He recalled that she was in mourning. Shattered, his mother had said. She didn't seem shattered, though. Only distracted and a bit skittish.

"Would you like to sit down?" she asked, indicating the wicker chairs with a wave of her hand. He nodded, then waited until she'd sat in one before lowering himself into the other. It was stiff, the seat cushion thin and hard. Just as well; no point in getting too comfortable.

"I'm surprised you knew who I was," he said, then grimaced inwardly. Not a good start.

Her smile grew warmer. "We were classmates, Aaron. It wasn't such a large class."

"I didn't know most of the kids in it."

"But you knew who I was?" she asked.

God, yes, he thought. "Everyone knew who you were," he said. "You were at the center of things."

She shook her head. "I'm not so sure about that. But I'll concede that you and I traveled in different circles."

"I didn't travel in any circle at all," he said, then let out a long breath. He wasn't managing this encounter well at all. If he'd believed reminiscing about the good old days was the way to get money out of her, the conversation would be fine. But for some reason, with absolutely no evidence to go by, he suspected that Lily was the sort of person who appreciated a direct approach.

"I'm running a summer basketball program at the high school," he told her. "Originally it was supposed to be for the high-school team to stay in shape and keep sharp over the summer. But younger kids wanted to participate, and they wanted teams and skills training, and there are a lot of kids whose parents can't afford summer camp. So I thought it would be a good idea to offer a low-cost program of basketball and swimming at the high school." He took a deep breath. He was talking too fast.

She shook her head. He hadn't asked her for money yet, so he knew she couldn't be saying no to that. "Charlie Callahan told me you were the basketball coach at the high school," she said. An amazed laugh escaped her.

Granted, the notion of him working at Riverbend

High School would have seemed pretty funny to him, too, if he hadn't lived it. "Wally Drummer—remember him? The old coach? He was ready to retire and he recommended me for the job. I guess someone must have misplaced my school records, because they hired me."

"I'm sure they hired you because you're a good coach."

"They hired me because Wally told them to."

"Well, Coach Drummer always seemed to know what he was doing." She drew her feet up onto the seat, hugged her knees and rested her chin on them. She looked almost girlish, not like a woman who'd been married and widowed, who owned this enormous house. He could more easily see her as a four-year-old getting her first set of watercolor paints than as a bereft widow.

"I shouldn't have laughed," she said contritely. "I bet you're an excellent coach. Better than Coach Drummer."

"No one was better than him," Aaron said, meaning it. "It's out of respect to him that I'm working so hard trying to get this summer program off the ground."

A breeze wafted across the porch. She glanced toward the bridge table to make sure nothing had been disturbed. Following her gaze, he studied the painting. Pears ought to be eaten, not painted, he thought.

"Did you come here to talk to me about basketball?" she asked.

"Yes, in a way." He leaned forward, resting his forearms on his knees. He'd worn khakis and a tailored cotton shirt. He'd figured he couldn't show up in his usual Sunday garb—old T-shirt, denim cutoffs and ratty sandals—and hope to make a good impression on her. "The program needs funding. I've gotten some money from the Rotary Club, a little from the school board and some from private donations. The kids pay thirty dollars a week to participate. Abraham Steele had implied that he would help bankroll the program, but he died before we got anything down on paper."

She turned back to him. "You came here for money?" she asked, sounding suspicious.

"Yes." No sense trying to sugarcoat it.

She regarded him for a long silent moment. "Why?"

Because your husband left you drowning in cash, he wanted to say. Instead, he relied on tact. "I've talked to lots of people about making donations. It's a good program, but with adequate financial support it could be great."

"Thirty dollars a week from the participants isn't enough?"

"No."

"Then why don't you charge more?"

"Like I said, this is for kids whose parents can't afford expensive summer programs."

"They can't afford it, and yet you're charging them thirty dollars."

"Because if we didn't charge anything, they wouldn't value it as much," he explained. "If their parents pay thirty dollars, they're going to show up every day and appreciate it. If it was free, they'd come now and then, when they remembered. It means more to them if it costs money, even if it's just a nominal amount.''

She nodded. Then she turned from him and gazed out at her backyard. A detached garage stood in one corner at the end of the driveway. A trellis on the side of the building held climbing yellow roses. The lawn was as uniformly green as in front of the house, but it was broken up with little patches of flowers. An apple tree stood close to the porch, its blossoms long gone.

She was thinking, and he let her. A bird chirped somewhere nearby, and the breeze rustled the leaves of the tree. He returned his attention to her painting, wondering why she'd chosen to paint that jug, instead of the tree, or the flowers, or anything else on her well-cultivated property.

She finally met his gaze once more and broke the silence. ''Did someone tell you I was rich?''

He used to be a pro when it came to lying, and although he was out of practice, he didn't think he'd lost his touch. But he couldn't bring himself to lie to her, not about this. He sat up straight. ''I heard about your husband dying,'' he said. ''I'm real sorry.''

She turned away again, her gaze traveling from her painting to the screened back door, to the porch's freshly painted white railing. ''Thank you,'' she said in such a dull, flat voice he almost questioned her about it. Did she think he was just paying lip service to her loss? Did she think he was happy her husband had died? Even when he'd been spending the better part of every night dreaming about her, he'd known she was never going to be his, so her marrying someone else didn't matter to him. If her husband had been poor, his death would have been sad. As it turned out, he'd been rich and it was still sad.

So why did her eyes appear so hollow? Why was she looking at him as if he wasn't even there? All he'd done was offer his condolences. Nothing unusual about that.

Unless there was more to her husband's dying than he knew.

He didn't *want* to know. All he wanted was for the life to come back into her eyes.

"All right," he said, leaning forward again as if he could will her to cheer up. "Yes, I've heard rumors you inherited some money. This is a small town. People talk."

His candor brought a spark back to her eyes. "No kidding," she muttered, evidently not pleased that people talked—even though he couldn't imagine anyone ever saying anything bad about her.

"So I thought I'd give you a try. It's a terrific program, and if I can get a little extra money, I can hire an assistant and handle more than ten kids a week. I also want to hire a certified water-safety instructor so the kids can use the pool when they aren't playing hoops. Right now I can't budget any of that into the program."

She appraised him, her gaze steady and mildly intrigued. "You have only ten children in this program?"

"Ten a week. That's all I can handle at one time. I've got around forty kids signed up, and I'll be rotating them from week to week. I wish I could take more into the program, but I can't with the funding I've got."

"Aaron Mazerik," she murmured, a faint smile tracing her lips once more, assuring him that she had, indeed, come back to life. "Who would have thought?" She tapped her fingers on her knee, then got to her feet and shrugged. "How much do you need?"

"A hundred thousand dollars would be great," he said, then flashed a grin. "I'd be thrilled by a thousand. Even a few hundred. Right now I've got coffee cans in the Sunnyside Café, the IGA, Sterling Hardware and a few other places. I'm collecting nickels and dimes. Paper money would really turn me on."

She laughed again. It wasn't a big boisterous laugh, or even a frothy, charming laugh. It was low and…rusty-sounding somehow, as if she hadn't laughed in a long time—which was probably the case, given that she was supposedly shattered. "At the risk of turning you on, Aaron, I'm going to think about this. I'm not saying yes or no. I'm saying I'll think about it."

"Great." If she wanted to risk turning him on, all she had to do was laugh again. Or smile. Or just look at him.

He gave himself a shake. He wasn't going to *let* her turn him on. Even if she wrote him his dream-come-true check, he wouldn't let her turn him on. The money, yes. Lily, no.

Not wanting to overstay his tenuous welcome, he rose to his feet. "I appreciate it. The program starts tomorrow. If you have any questions, you can reach me at the high school. The gym office is extension 407."

"All right."

He extended his hand to shake hers, this time in farewell. But she seemed distracted by her painting. "You strike me as an honest man," she said.

He wasn't sure what to say to that, so he merely shrugged.

"Tell me what you really think of the painting."

He sensed that this was some kind of test. If she wanted her ego stroked, she'd come to the wrong person. If she wanted honesty, though… "The truth? It's too safe."

"Safe?" She eyed the painting, her head tilted to one side. "What do you mean?"

"I mean, it's *good*, but… Look, I'm no art critic."

"I asked your opinion, Aaron. I'm not going to hate you for giving it."

Maybe she would, maybe she wouldn't. "A jug and a pear don't mean anything to me," he admitted. "And you've painted them so—" he struggled for the right word "—precisely. It's so neat and pretty and…I don't know, safe."

She stared at the painting for a minute longer, obviously dissatisfied—with the painting or with him, he couldn't say. For all he knew, his critique might have screwed his chances for getting any money from her for the program. It had probably screwed his chance to be anything more than a former classmate to her—if indeed that chance had ever existed. And it hadn't. It wouldn't.

Her silence continued, unsettling him. It occurred to him that he was never going to see a penny from this meeting, and he was never going to feel anything but uncomfortable around Lily. "Anyway, thanks for hearing me out," he said, edging toward the side of the house. "I won't take up any more of your time."

She turned from the painting. Her eyes had come fully back to life, he noticed, glittering like stars in a night sky. "Safe, huh?"

"I shouldn't have said anything." He didn't care about the money. He just didn't want her to feel offended. "When it comes to art, I don't know what I'm talking about."

"I'm not so sure about that." An enigmatic smile flickered across her face. "I'll think about your program, Aaron."

"Thanks." He nodded, pivoted on his heel and walked away, one long resolute stride after another. The farther he got from her, the more certain he was that she wasn't going to donate to the program. He'd been a fool to ask her for money, and a fool to speak the truth about her painting. That was more than enough foolishness for one day.

AARON MAZERIK scared her.

He always had and he still did. It didn't help to remind herself he was no longer a rebel with a wicked reputation. Fifteen years after they'd graduated from high school—she near the top of the class, he by some miracle that had kept him out of reformatory—he still sent a sensation down her spine, ice and heat, something that left her feeling oddly breathless. He was still tall and lean and teeming with barely checked energy. He still had the most dangerously beautiful eyes she'd ever seen.

And he was still so reckless he'd criticize a painting by a woman from whom he was trying to wrest a charitable contribution. Reckless but honest. He was right about her painting. It was too safe.

Sighing, she entered the kitchen through the back door. She was thirsty—and restless. She needed to take action, although she couldn't think of anything to act on besides her thirst.

The kitchen was too large. The entire house was too large. She'd managed to furnish most of its spacious rooms because the house she and Tyler had owned in Cohasset, outside Boston, had also been absurdly large. Once she'd sold the place, she'd had the furniture shipped to Riverbend.

Her gaze circled the sun-filled room. Potted herbs lined the windowsill above the sink. To either side, glass-fronted oak cabinets displayed neat stacks of dishes and rows of glasses. She pulled down a glass and hiked across the room to the refrigerator, where she filled the glass with lemonade.

She didn't care that the house was too big. She'd fallen in love with it when she'd been a child, cycling past it on her way to meet her friends down by the river. She hadn't known anything about the house or the family living in it then; all she'd known was that it seemed grand and magical, with its porthole windows and angled roofs and the rounded tower. It was the sort of house that spiced a girl's imagination. She could imagine fairies living beneath the eaves, and a ghost in the cellar—a friendly ghost, of course—and the scent of gingerbread in the air. When she'd returned to Riverbend and discovered the house for sale, she'd bought it without thinking.

She didn't regret her impulsive purchase, but she acknowledged that a woman living alone couldn't possibly fill it. It was a good place to hide from the world while she attempted to pull herself together, to come to terms with the tragic mistakes of her life. She liked ambling through the generously proportioned rooms, sitting wherever she wished, turning the stereo up loud or watching television at two in the morning.

Carrying her lemonade, she headed for the front door. A peek through the window there revealed that Aaron was gone.

Did he still have a police record? Or had it been expunged once he turned twenty-one? Why was she even wondering about it? She'd never had anything to do with bad boys.

During his wild adolescence, Aaron Mazerik had been a source of curiosity, not just to her but to all her friends. When he'd suddenly made the varsity basketball team—as a sophomore—they'd all been stunned. Why on earth had Coach Drummer taken a chance on a punk like Aaron Mazerik? Everyone knew he sneaked out for cigarettes and worse. Everyone knew he cruised the streets late at night, without a curfew, and there were rumors that he stole things, although Lily wasn't sure she believed that. Or maybe she just didn't want to believe it.

She'd heard he'd been arrested, though. She'd heard he'd been picked up for vagrancy, that he'd hot-wired cars and smoked pot and filched a knife from the hardware store, though no one had ever found the knife on him. She'd heard that Frank Garvey had arrested him and he'd spent a night in a holding cell at the police station. His mother had never married. There was no Mr. Mazerik. Just Evie and her son. The loner. The troublemaker. The outsider.

Lily was uncomfortable about his coming to her for money. Yes, Tyler had left her quite wealthy, but she would gladly have traded every last nickel for some happiness and relief from the crippling guilt that continued to plague her. She knew that coming back to Riverbend had meant everyone would be talking about her inheritance, because everyone talked about everything here.

Still, she didn't want people to assume she was an easy mark. She didn't want them looking at her and seeing dollar signs. In time she would probably wind up giving a lot of her money away. But she wasn't going to be stupid about it.

She stood in the arched doorway of her living room, surveying the embroidered sofas, the brick fireplace with its polished mantel, the framed oil painting above it. It was a seascape. Nothing special, but it had appealed to her when she'd spotted it at an art festival one summer. Tyler had hated it—he'd called it a cliché—but the house had been *her* realm, and she'd fixed it up the way she liked it, paintings and all. The seascape had caught her eye because it had mirrored the view of the ocean from their patio. But she'd also been drawn to it by its motion—the white spuming spray, the eerie shadows in the waves, the ominous clouds riding the horizon. It wasn't a "safe" painting.

Her little watercolor was. Aaron had been right about that. He might be a reformed thug—or a not-so-reformed one—but he'd spoken the truth about her painting. It was a still life, not a moving life. It was tight and tidy and safe. She hadn't dared to paint outside the lines.

Well, who could blame her for wanting a little safety now? She'd grown up feeling safe, loved by her parents, accepted and respected by her friends. Riverbend had been a safe place to grow up, a town where people looked after one another and the river never moved so rapidly that a swimmer could get swept away. Lily had thought that after eighteen years of safety she was ready to take risks.

She'd taken them, leaving home to attend college in New England, then marrying a man so different from anyone she'd known before. She'd taken risks and failed so miserably she was afraid ever to take a risk again.

Talking to Aaron Mazerik had been a risk, though, and she'd survived. She wasn't sure she was going to write him a check for his summer basketball program, but she'd sat with him, and shaken hands with him, and dared to ask him to tell her his honest opinion of her painting.

Maybe she *was* ready to start taking risks again.

Or maybe Aaron, with his mesmerizing eyes and his inexplicable charisma, had gotten her to take a risk she would rather not have taken.

CHAPTER THREE

LILY HADN'T KNOWN much about being rich before she married Tyler.

She'd known about being comfortably middle-class, about living in a nice home in a nice neighborhood and never going to bed hungry. Every August she and her mother would shop for a new school wardrobe without any hand-wringing, and she'd always owned more than one pair of shoes, even when her feet were growing a size every few months. She took piano lessons, ballet lessons and art lessons. More often than not, her family went out to a restaurant for Sunday dinner, and no one thought twice about the cost.

When she'd been accepted at a small private college in Massachusetts, her parents hadn't said it was too expensive or she'd need to get a scholarship. Not only had they sent her there, they'd paid the airfare so she could fly home for Thanksgiving, winter recess and spring break.

But until she met Tyler, she hadn't known what it was like to be rich the way the Holdens were rich.

It had been hard for her even to conceive of a family having so much money. Tyler had seemed like a member of an alien species to her, a precious stone buffed to a high gloss, radiating not just beauty but an almost overwhelming attitude of entitlement. On their first date, he'd thought nothing of driving her up to Boston in his Porsche, taking her to a restaurant where the cheapest appetizer was ten dollars—he'd insisted that she order a complete dinner—and then driving her back to her dormitory, kissing her and departing with a promise to call.

She'd been dazzled.

He'd called.

She never gotten used to his spending so much money on her—ironic, since his parents had assumed she was a gold digger. When she and Tyler had gone shopping for her engagement ring, she'd chosen one of the smallest diamonds on the jeweler's tray, but Tyler had rejected her selection and insisted on buying the largest. She hadn't cared about his wealth—which, he'd told her, was one of the things he loved about her. Apparently he'd dated too many women who were attracted more to his wallet than to him. He'd trusted Lily, though. He'd loved her beauty and her quiet intelligence, and her honest insistence that she loved him for himself.

They'd lived in Boston for a few years, in a spacious apartment in a ritzy Back Bay neighborhood. By the time he was well established at his law firm, the marriage was already beginning to show hairline cracks, and he'd decided they could mend those cracks by buying a palatial house with ocean views in Cohasset. She'd assumed the reason he wanted a five-bedroom house was that he was finally ready to start a family, but no, he wasn't. He'd just thought that moving out of the city would make things better.

It hadn't. Things had gotten worse. She'd become

active on some local boards and volunteered at a nearby hospital, but those efforts hadn't fulfilled her the way a career might have, or a baby. She'd been trained to teach art. She'd been born to become a mother. Living in Cohasset with Tyler, she'd seen neither goal realized.

"No wife of mine is going to work," Tyler had declared. "You can't take a good job away from someone who needs the money." As for children, well, they could talk about it after he made partner at his law firm.

By the time he'd made partner, she knew she would never bring a child into their world. Not unless Tyler changed. And he'd shown no interest in changing.

So she'd filled her days with library-board meetings and stints delivering flowers to patients at the hospital. She'd filled her evenings with Tyler and his parents and all their elite Boston friends at galas and symphony concerts and benefits. She'd filled her nights with tears and recriminations and prayers that Tyler would somehow turn back into the man she'd fallen in love with, the smart, witty, imaginative guy who used to listen intently to everything she said, who used to ask her opinion about things and surprise her with silly gifts and unplanned outings, who'd seemed as devoted to her as she was to him.

No one in Riverbend had known the truth. She couldn't have borne it if they found out how dreadfully her life had turned out. Phoning home regularly, she'd assured her parents that everything with Tyler was wonderful. She'd written letters to her old friends and told them she was happy.

She had always been perfect. She'd done everything she was supposed to do, and everyone had predicted that she would live a golden life, married—and why not?—to a handsome wealthy Harvard Law School graduate like Tyler Holden. How could she admit she'd failed? How could she let everyone down?

Tyler's parents had been appalled by the amount he'd left Lily in his will. She'd tried her best to be a good daughter-in-law to them, but they'd never accepted her. They'd always been condescending toward her, putting forth a great effort to make sure she knew she wasn't one of them. When she'd tried to talk to them about her concerns regarding Tyler, they'd told her she was exaggerating. Surely enjoying a couple of martinis before dinner was merely being civilized, they'd insisted. Perhaps if she saw a problem, it was within her, not within him.

That was what Tyler had said, too: "If you think I'm drinking too much, then maybe you ought to think about *why* I'm drinking. Maybe you don't make me happy. Maybe my home isn't as pleasant as it ought to be. Maybe my wife doesn't love me enough."

She'd really, really tried to love him enough. But by his fifth martini of the night, every night, she couldn't bear to be near him.

After he died, she took her inheritance, sold the house and left. Now she was back home, where apparently the entire town knew she was rich, if not precisely *how* rich. They probably all saw her inherited fortune as more evidence of how perfect her life was. A beautiful marriage, a tragic death, and she was still the golden girl, the wealthiest widow Riverbend had ever seen.

One thing she'd learned from Tyler was that when you were rich, you had to be cautious around people who weren't as rich, because nine times out of ten, their interest in you was actually interest in your money. Their attentiveness, their ingratiating behavior, their kindness—it usually meant they simply wanted to get their hands on your assets.

She was by nature a generous woman, but she had to be careful. She had to think before she acted. And right now she was thinking and having doubts about donating money to a summer sports program run by Aaron Mazerik, of all people.

She wasn't sure she *didn't* want to donate to the sports program. The amount Aaron sought was a mere drop in the bucket to her. But she wasn't going to write him a check just because she could. First she wanted to figure out exactly what the money would be used for, and she wanted to get a sense of what, if anything, he might want from her besides her money.

She had pretty much avoided going into town since she'd moved back to Riverbend. She feared having to make small talk with all the people she would run into. She hated having to try to guess whether what she saw in their eyes was pity or envy. She hadn't seen either in Aaron's expression, which might be why she was considering contributing to his program. Maybe that wasn't a good reason, but it was the only one she had so far.

She needed to have a look at the program first. She needed to find out what it had, what it lacked, how her money would be used. For all she knew, Aaron harbored grandiose visions of setting up a semipro basketball training program, with topnotch facilities and members of the Indiana Pacers coming to town to teach master classes. She didn't want to subsidize something overblown like that.

More importantly, though, she needed to learn whether she could trust Aaron.

So, at around noon on Monday, she climbed into her BMW convertible and pointed it in the direction of the high school.

She was going to have to get a new car. There was nothing wrong with the BMW except that it was a BMW. Tyler had picked it out for her, claiming that it would retain its value, and she had to admit she liked driving a convertible. Plenty of people in the Boston area had driven BMWs.

But in Riverbend the pricey coupe seemed pretentious. Foreign cars were a rarity. She had no idea where she'd be able to take such a car for servicing, or who would buy it from her if she decided to get rid of it. She'd probably have to advertise in the Indianapolis newspapers.

But until she sold it, she could enjoy driving it on a lovely day in late June, with the sun warming her face and the wind whipping her hair. She could enjoy glancing up to see nothing but trees and sky.

She didn't enjoy the stares her car received from people as she turned onto Main Street. Maybe if she put the top up she'd be less conspicuous, but it was too late for that. Pedestrians and shoppers darting from their cars to stores had already noticed her.

At least she had her sunglasses on. She didn't have

to meet anyone's gaze, wave at people she recognized or acknowledge the attention her car attracted. Besides, she was in mourning. No one expected her to be friendly.

Up ahead, she spotted her mother emerging from Jones's Drugstore. Even from half a block away, Eleanor Bennett looked beautiful in a crisp white blouse and a denim skirt. She was as slim as she'd been the day Lily's father had met her, and her complexion was still creamy. It was from her that Lily had learned the importance of good posture and proud bearing. "If you carry yourself like a queen," her mother used to tell her, "people will treat you like a queen."

Lily wished she'd learned more than that from her mother. But her father had been the dominant presence in her life. Her mother had never seemed to mind that Julian Bennett was the earth and she was his moon, revolving around him. She'd always been a quiet, almost passive woman, willing to smooth the edges for everyone else, willing to supply whatever was needed and then step back and join in the applause. Thirty-three years old, Lily still didn't feel she knew her mother very well.

She did know, however, that her mother was looking tense and grim as she exited the drugstore, a small shopping bag clutched in one fist. Lily cruised up the street until she was alongside her mother and then called, "Mom? Need a lift?"

Eleanor Bennett turned, and her face broke into a bright smile. "Lily! I'm so glad you got out today. It's just gorgeous, isn't it?" She approached the car, spreading her arms as if she could embrace the day.

"It is," Lily agreed, pulling to the curb and untangling her windblown hair with her fingers.

"What brings you into town?" her mother asked.

Lily couldn't guess what her mother would think about her possible investment in Aaron's sports program. If her mother remembered Aaron at all, it was probably as a troubled young man whom she prayed her daughter would never date.

In any case Lily wasn't about to have a lengthy car-to-sidewalk discussion with her mother about Aaron's visit to her house yesterday. "Are you busy now?" Lily asked, feeling spontaneous. "Why don't we have lunch?"

Her mother appeared first bewildered, then pleased by the invitation. "I don't see why not. Find a parking space. We can pop right down the block to the Sunnyside Café."

Lily's misgivings set in as soon as her mother waved her toward an empty parking space a few cars down. She wanted to have lunch with her mother, mostly to find out why she'd looked so solemn when she'd left the pharmacy. But not at the Sunnyside, the most public place in town.

Everyone ate at the Sunnyside: professionals, truck drivers, shopkeepers, city workers, farmers from outside town. The place was a hive of gossip. Once Lily entered the café with her mother, word would spread throughout Riverbend: The rich widow is out and about, tooling around town in her snazzy car. The recluse has *un*-reclused. She's ready to glide back into the flow of life.

But she wasn't. Not because she was in mourning, but because she'd left Riverbend as a young woman

blessed with luck and hope and she'd returned tainted
by what had happened to her, shamed by it, practically smothered by the weight of her guilt. She
wasn't ready to glide back into anything.

Too late now. Her mother was waiting at the corner for her, her expression a mask of good cheer.
Lily would simply have to don a similar mask and
get through lunch.

They entered the bustling restaurant. Its cheerful
yellow walls would have hurt Lily's eyes if she
hadn't left on her sunglasses. The din of conversation
and rattling plates would have given her a headache
if stress hadn't spawned a headache first.

"There's a place," Eleanor said, pointing to the
only empty booth in the room. She led the way
around the tables, waving at someone she knew, and
Lily followed, keeping her gaze lowered. She didn't
want to recognize people and wave. All she wanted
was to spend this time with her mother.

They slid into the booth facing each other, and
Lily reluctantly removed her sunglasses. To keep
them on might offend her neighbors; they'd think she
was putting on airs. She tucked the glasses into her
purse and discreetly scanned the room.

The woman occupying a stool behind the cash register near the door looked familiar. Her hair was an
odd auburn shade and her face was striking, full of
angles and hollows. She was chatting with a beefy
fellow in overalls and a John Deere cap, grinning up
at him all the while.

Suddenly Lily remembered where she'd seen the
woman before: leaning on Aaron as they'd left the

church after the memorial service for Abraham Steele. Aaron's mother, Evie Mazerik.

Lily had never met her, but she vaguely recalled being told that the woman worked the day shift at the Sunnyside. As a high-school student, Lily hadn't had much reason to eat breakfast or lunch here. At night sometimes, she and her friends would head to the café for ice-cream sundaes, but in the evenings the cash register was run by a man.

She'd heard more about Aaron's mother than just where and when she worked, of course. People talked. Evie had had Aaron without the benefit of marriage. Out-of-wedlock children were a lot less common thirty-three years ago, and they'd been practically unheard of in Riverbend. Certainly girls must have gotten pregnant back then, but they wouldn't have stayed in town and had their babies. They would have been sent to serve their nine-month sentences at a relative's place in another state, and their offspring would have been put up for adoption.

But Evie Mazerik—Lily had heard her name whispered, usually accompanied by an arched eyebrow or a knowing nod—hadn't hidden her pregnancy from the town; nor had she given her baby away. She hadn't moved to Indianapolis, where an out-of-wedlock child might have been accepted more readily. No, she'd stayed right where she was. It had been a courageous decision, Lily supposed, although Aaron had paid the price, as if it had been his fault his mother was unmarried. He'd been labeled a bastard, and he'd done what he could to live up—or down—to that label.

He didn't seem so easy to label now. Yesterday,

when he'd come to her house, closed his hand around hers, told her about his program, critiqued her painting…he'd unsettled her. He was just a little too forthright. A little too blunt. A little too sexy.

What a peculiar thought. Lily had no interest in sex. She was still getting over Tyler. And anyway, it would be next to impossible for someone like her even to contemplate a love affair in Riverbend, the Land of No Privacy.

And besides, Aaron was *Aaron*. The bad boy. Most Likely to Do Time. Not her type at all.

"What a wonderful idea this is," her mother said, snapping Lily back to attention. Her mother looked animated, no trace of her earlier distress in her expression.

Her hair was a breezy bob, shorter than the last time Lily had seen her. "Did you just get your hair done?" she asked, admiring the cut.

"This morning. I told her to go a little shorter. What do you think?"

"I like it." It wasn't just shorter. It was lighter. The dusting of silver that used to glitter through the dark-blond strands was gone, replaced by paler-blond highlights. "You lightened it?"

Her mother laughed bashfully. "You must think I'm a vain old woman," she said.

"No. It looks great. Dad's going to love it."

"Do you think so?" Her mother looked hopeful.

Lily did think so. But even if her father didn't love it, would that be such a terrible thing? Eleanor was less than a year away from her sixtieth birthday. Surely she'd earned the right to fix her hair any way she liked, not worry about pleasing her husband.

A waitress approached and handed them laminated menus. "Hi, Mrs. Bennett," she said to Lily's mother.

"Hi, Tina. How are you?"

"I'm good." The waitress turned to Lily. "You must be Lily."

Lily had no idea who the waitress was. She looked to be in her early twenties at the most, a skinny pixieish girl with curly brown hair barely contained by an array of silver barrettes. Lily knew better than to be surprised that this total stranger knew who she was, though. She forced a polite smile, said, "Hi," and then buried her nose in the menu.

She wasn't terribly hungry. But since lunch had been her idea, she felt obliged to order something. She asked for a tuna sandwich, and her mother requested a spinach salad with the dressing on the side.

As soon as the waitress was gone, Lily gave her mother another look. "Dressing on the side?" she asked, not bothering to conceal her surprise.

"I'm trying to cut back on my fat consumption," her mother explained. "Cholesterol and all that."

Lily recalled the shopping bag that now sat on the banquette next to her mother. She'd bought something at the drugstore and she'd looked worried. "You don't have a cholesterol problem, do you?"

"No, not at all." Her mother brushed Lily's concerns away with a flick of her hand. "It just doesn't hurt to eat sensibly."

"Did Dad tell you to watch your cholesterol?"

"Well, no, but you don't have to be a doctor to know about the importance of a healthy diet, Lily. I don't need him to tell me I should watch my fat intake.''

Lily detected a hint of defensiveness in her mother's voice, a hint others weren't likely to notice. She'd learned at one of the Al-Anon meetings she'd attended that people who lived with alcoholics usually developed a special radar about their loved ones. They sensed trouble before trouble arrived, the way some people could sense an imminent storm from the pain in their joints. They learned to read the signs, even invisible signs, so they could protect themselves when the storm clouds opened up.

A storm was brewing inside her mother. Lily felt badly about being so caught up in her misery and self-loathing that she'd neglected to notice what was going on beyond her own little world. ''Mom, are you all right?'' she asked, leaning forward and searching her mother's face for an answer she suspected her mother might not be willing to share.

''Of course I'm all right,'' her mother said even more defensively. ''I'm fine.''

''I saw you coming out of the drugstore, and now you're not eating salad dressing.''

Her mother chuckled—unconvincingly, Lily thought. ''I've discovered that skipping salad dressing makes me feel better. And for heaven's sake, I think I'm allowed to go to the drugstore without being sick.''

''What did you buy?'' Lily asked, her laugh as forced as her mother's had been. ''Something wonderful? Chocolates to reward yourself for skipping the dressing?''

This time her mother's laughter was genuine.

"Actually, I bought this cream." She pulled an elegant porcelain jar from the bag and showed it to Lily. "Gloria Hoff told me about this moisturizer. She said it's really lovely."

Erases visible lines, the fancy gold script on the jar read. *Makes you look years younger.* "Anti-aging cream?"

"It's a moisturizer," her mother emphasized. "With a sunscreen. Gloria says it makes her skin feel very soft." She tucked the jar back in the bag.

A new hairstyle. Moisturizing cream. No salad dressing. It dawned on Lily that her mother had decided to tackle her impending sixtieth birthday aggressively.

Before she could question Eleanor further, she felt a tap on her shoulder. Twisting around, she saw Grace Pennington leaning over the back of the banquette, a huge grin on her face. "Lily!" Grace exclaimed, reaching around to give Lily a hug. "I can't believe it! It's so good to see you! How are you?" Without waiting for an invitation, Grace dropped onto the seat next to Lily and gave her a less contorted hug.

Lily hugged her back. Grace was a dear friend, one of the River Rats. A year older than Lily, Grace had always been an inspiration to her. Unlike Lily, she'd never cared what anyone else thought of her. She used to say Lily should be flattered that everyone had such high expectations of her, but Lily used to argue that life was a whole lot easier when no one expected anything.

Not that Grace had disappointed anyone's expectations. She was happily married to a fellow River

Rat, Ed Pennington, and they had three children. Life had worked out sweetly for her.

"I've been dying to call you," Grace went on, "but I wanted to respect your privacy. We all did. Everyone wants to see you, though. Hi, Mrs. Bennett," she said belatedly, then gave Lily another exuberant hug. "God, your mother looks prettier every time I see her."

"Maybe your eyesight is getting worse every time you see me," Lily's mother joked. "How are you, Grace?"

"I'm fine. Better than fine," Grace told her. "The kids are visiting with my in-laws for the week. It's like a little honeymoon for Ed and me." Abruptly her smile faded and she glanced anxiously at Lily. "I'm sorry."

"No, don't be. I think it's great that you and Ed are able to get some time alone." She and Tyler had had plenty of time alone, but it had never seemed like a honeymoon to her.

"Well, look…" Grace slid out of the booth, stood up and squeezed Lily's shoulder. "I didn't mean to interrupt your lunch. Just tell me you won't hate me if I give you a call, okay, Lily?"

"Sure." Lily gave her a genuine smile.

"How could anyone ever hate that girl?" Lily's mother murmured as Grace headed toward the front counter, where her lunch companion was waiting for her, another young woman, who looked vaguely familiar to Lily. Probably another old schoolmate.

It was strange to be back in Riverbend. So much had changed, and so little.

The waitress arrived with their lunch, and Lily tore her gaze from the front counter. She realized her attention had shifted from Grace and her companion to Aaron's mother. Evie Mazerik had a face as angular as his, but her eyes were a pale hazel, not the rich blend of colors in Aaron's eyes. Her mouth had a slightly lopsided cast to it, even when she smiled. Perhaps that was a result of the stroke she'd had.

Who'd have thought Aaron would come home to take care of her?

As if aware of Lily's thoughts, her mother said, "Now, tell me what brought you into town today."

Lily wasn't ready to inform her mother that she'd been on her way to check out Aaron's sports program. If she told her mother she was considering making a contribution to it, her mother would become suspicious—not about Lily's wanting to give her money away but her wanting to give it to someone like Aaron, who'd had run-ins with the law as a teenager and would never win any awards for civic responsibility. Until Lily decided for sure what she was going to do, she saw no reason to discuss it.

"It was a nice day," she fibbed. "A perfect day to drive around with the top down."

"Obviously I'm not the only person thrilled to see you out and about." Her mother dabbed her fork into the paper cup of salad dressing, then touched the coated tines to the spinach leaves.

Turning the spotlight on her mother would be a good way to keep the spotlight off herself. "Grace was right, Mom—you really look terrific. I don't know why you're wasting money on anti-wrinkle cream."

"It's not a waste of money. The cream is going to protect my skin, keep it healthy. When I saw how wonderful Gloria looked at her niece's wedding, I just had to give this stuff a try.'' She launched into a lengthy description of the wedding, the reception, everyone who'd been there and what they'd been wearing. Lily ate her sandwich and listened. Her mother seemed animated and happy. Whatever had made her look so grim when Lily had first seen her on the sidewalk was gone now.

Eleanor was clearly relieved that Lily didn't mind discussing a young bride's joy. Lily had been a joyful young bride once, too, full of hope and high spirits. She still had fond memories of her wedding day, even if Tyler's wealthy relatives had seemed out of place at the modest Riverbend Community Church. She hadn't cared. She'd fought them on the venue for the wedding—they'd wanted it in Boston, but she'd insisted that it be held in her hometown—and they'd acquiesced. After she and Tyler had returned to Boston from their honeymoon, his parents had hosted a reception for them at a posh hotel, and it had been nowhere near as much fun as the wedding party she'd had here, surrounded by all her friends.

It was nearly two o'clock by the time she and her mother left the Sunnyside Café. Once Eleanor had finished dissecting Gloria's niece's wedding, she'd described her garden-club work, the floats that would be appearing in the July Fourth parade and the efforts of the River Valley Historical Society to repair an old bridge a few miles west of town, rather than tear the bridge down and replace it with something modern and ugly.

As far as Lily could tell, her mother was too busy to worry about looking old—or getting old. The best way to stay young, as far as Lily was concerned, was to stay active, not to buy expensive anti-aging creams.

She and her mother parted ways outside the café. She got into her car, checked her watch and grimaced, wondering whether she would even find Aaron at the high school at two o'clock. She had no idea how late in the day his program ran.

Donning her sunglasses, she eased out of the parking space and headed down Hickory Street toward the school. Many of the shops hadn't changed since when she'd been a little girl. The trees were taller, and the benches along the sidewalk were new and spiffy, but the pet shop was just as she'd remembered it, and the Clip-Curl-and-Dye, and Killian's Department Store. She used to get her bangs trimmed at the Clip-Curl-and-Dye, and all her school clothes had come from Killian's. It didn't carry anything like the clothing sold in the high-fashion boutiques of Boston's Newbury Street, but what would anyone do with a twelve-hundred-dollar dress in Riverbend? Lily had a few twelve-hundred-dollar dresses in her closet right now, and she couldn't imagine an occasion in town where they'd be suitable.

She hadn't been back to the high school since she'd graduated fifteen years ago, but it, too, hadn't changed. The driveway was the same, the flagpole standing like a mast before the front doors, the rows of windows as straight as a grid. She steered past the football field to the back parking lot. The gym door stood open. An old Pontiac was parked in one of the spaces. Good. Aaron must be there.

She parked in the adjacent space and turned off the engine. Through the open door she heard the squeak of sneakers on polished wood, the brief shrill of a whistle, the rhythmic thump of a basketball being dribbled. The sounds were so familiar she had to grin. Basketball was practically a living entity in Riverbend, the constant thump of balls its pulse.

She got out of her car and crossed the asphalt to the open door. In the gym, a gaggle of kids maybe eight or nine years old raced back and forth on a small court. They wore sneakers, shorts and white T-shirts with Riverbend Hot Shots in red lettering across the front. Half of the kids wore red pinnies over their shirts, but Lily could see the lettering through the red mesh.

Like a tree planted amid a garden of shrubs, Aaron towered over his charges. He, too, wore a white Hot Shots T-shirt, but his was glued to his torso by perspiration. He had on athletic shorts and high-tops, and a whistle hung on a cord around his neck. His purpose seemed to be to present an obstacle as the kids brought the ball down the court. "Pass it, pass it!" he shouted to one, who kept dribbling doggedly down the court until Aaron swiped the ball away. "Gotta pass sometimes, Jimmy. Try again." He handed the boy the ball and positioned himself to block him again.

The kids laughed. They ran. They stumbled and shoved and screeched, "I'm open, I'm open!"

A girl took a shot and Aaron batted it away. "Gotta pass," he reminded her. "Don't hog the shots. If I'm in your way, pass to someone else. Try it again."

The gym was warm, although the open door let in a breeze. But the kids looked hot, and Aaron looked hotter. He had such long legs, muscular and taut, covered in a fine mesh of dark hair. She lifted her gaze to his chest, outlined by the clinging T-shirt, and then moved higher, to his glistening face and his unruly hair. "Come on, Stacy, pass the ball!" he shouted to a girl. She passed it and he gave her a huge grin. "There you go! That's the way! This is a team sport, everyone!"

He blew his whistle and scooped the ball into his hand. "Okay, guys—water break." He led his charges to the bleachers, where several large insulated jugs of water stood. After handing out paper cups, he proceeded to fill the cups for the kids. "Sip it, guys, and then take seconds. Remember what I said this morning?"

"Drink lots of fluids," one of the boys called out.

"That's right. Always drink lots of fluids when you're doing heavy physical activity. That may be the most important thing I can teach you." He paused. Then, "How much fluid should you drink?"

"Lots!" the kids chorused. Aaron smiled.

Lily smiled, too.

She felt like a trespasser, lurking unnoticed in the doorway, dressed in a floaty pale-blue jumper with a matching blue shirt under it and a pair of rope-soled sandals. She didn't belong here, yet she couldn't walk away. Not when Aaron was grinning so magically at his scruffy band of athletes. While they sipped their water, he lifted a smaller water bottle to his lips and took a swig. Then he lifted the hem of his shirt to wipe his face, offering Lily a view of his abdomen, a sculpture of lithe muscle shiny with sweat.

God, what a body.

The thought stunned her. She blinked and fell back a step, surprised that she could be turned on by a fleeting glimpse of a man's midsection, surprised that she could be turned on by anything at all. It had been so long since she'd felt any sort of sexual stirring. She'd been married to Tyler, and once she was married she'd never even looked at another man. But Tyler had come to bed drunk too many times, and when there was sex, it had been ugly.

There was nothing ugly about Aaron Mazerik. Absolutely nothing.

Lowering his shirt, he reached for his water bottle again, then spotted her hovering in the doorway. He smiled, this time not the broad grin reserved for his kids but a quiet, questioning smile. She smiled back, feeling suddenly shy and uneasy. Was he aware that she'd been ogling him? Could he tell what one quick look at his bare abdomen had done to her? Was she blushing?

"Keep drinking," he ordered the children, then jogged across the court to the door. She wanted to shrink from him. Heaven knew, if he got too close to her, she might not be able to control the urge to touch his skin, to lift up his shirt and run her fingertips over the hard, sleek surface—

She must be insane even to think such a thing! This was Aaron Mazerik, an admittedly handsome man but one with whom she had nothing in common.

He loomed in front of her, his hands on his hips, his breathing heavy from all his running and his eyes glittering like emeralds set in silver and gold. And she felt something. Something scary. Something dangerous. Something unforgivably tempting.

Something she hadn't felt in a long, long time.

CHAPTER FOUR

AARON TOLD HIMSELF he was standing in the open doorway of the gym, grinning like an idiot at Lily Holden, because her being there implied that maybe she was going to donate money to his program. He told himself the awareness buzzing through him, as fierce and physical as an electric shock, had nothing to do with her personally, her beauty, her eyes the color of her dress, her hair the color of the sun. He told himself the reason he was having trouble catching his breath was that he'd been running pretty much nonstop for the past half hour.

After a moment his breathing finally began to get more regular. His eyes adjusted to the bright outside light, and once they did she looked more like a human being than an apparition out of his dreams.

Money, he thought. *Money is the only thing Lily Holden can give me.*

"Have you been standing here long?" he asked.

"Just a couple of minutes. I hope you don't mind." She gave him that shy smile that said she wasn't quite as self-assured as he assumed.

"No problem." He glanced over his shoulder at the kids, who were beginning to look bored. Another few seconds, and they'd be hurling cups of water at each other. "I've got to get back to work," he said, then gestured toward the bottom bench of the bleachers, which were folded shut along one wall. "If you want to sit and watch, feel free. We've got about an hour still to go here."

"Thanks." She entered the gym and arranged herself neatly on the end of the bench, smoothing the skirt of her dress over her knees.

He returned to the children, who were gathered across the gym from where Lily was seated, and told himself not to think about the fact that she was there, watching him. "All cooled off?" he asked them.

"Yeah!"

"Okay. I want each of you to take a ball." He loosened the drawstring on the mesh ball bag and passed basketballs around until each child had one. He took one for himself and tossed the bag aside. "Everybody spread out a little so you won't be in each other's way. Now what we're going to do—" he waited until they'd arranged themselves around the gym "—is dribble with your right hand. Everyone raise your right hand." Jimmy raised his left hand. "Jimmy?" Aaron prodded. Jimmy quickly switched hands and smirked. "Okay. You're all going to dribble with your right hand while singing 'Happy Birthday.'"

This prompted roars of laughter. "Happy Birthday to *who*?" Jessica wanted to know.

"To me. Coach Maz. Okay? Let's—"

"Is it your birthday?"

"No. We're just singing to Coach Maz because Coach Maz is the boss. Okay? Ready, set, go." He started dribbling and singing, all the while surveying the children. The task, which had obviously sounded silly when he'd described it, was actually quite challenging. The kids kept stopping and starting the singing as they struggled with their dribbling. By the third line of the jingle, no two kids were singing together. By the end, they had all dissolved in laughter, except for Andy, whose ball had gotten away from him and rolled to the far side of the gym.

Once Andy had returned with his runaway ball, Aaron settled them down and said, "Now we're going to do it again, only this time you have to alternate hands—one dribble left, one dribble right, left, right." He demonstrated. "Got it?"

"Are we still singing?"

"Still singing. Ready, set, go!"

This time both Andy and Stacy lost their balls, and everyone was giggling well before they got to "Happy Birthday, Coach Ma-a-az…"

Aaron didn't mind. This wasn't a voice lesson. It was an exercise designed to help them learn how to focus, and once the children calmed down he told them so. "The idea," he explained, "is to reach a point where dribbling is so natural to you, you don't even have to think about it while you do it. You can be dribbling and thinking about something completely different—like, is the rest of your team set up for a play? Do you have an opening for an inside shot? Is your forward ready to receive the ball? Will Coach Maz love me because I sang 'Happy Birthday' to him?" The kids laughed. "You don't even want to be thinking about dribbling. So we're going to take this one step further. Everyone get in a line—that's right—and follow me. We're going to walk and dribble and sing 'Happy Birthday' all at the same time."

"Walk or run?" Jimmy asked.

"You guys can hardly do this standing still, and you want to run? No, we're just going to walk."

He led them in a serpentine parade around the gym, listening to their off-key warbling. Every few dribbles, he'd spin around and walk backward, facing them, so he could make sure they were all following him. They were—sort of—but the task clearly wasn't easy. Most of them still looked down at the ball a lot more than they looked ahead at where they were going. Collisions ensued, stumbling and jostling. The song got massacred along the way.

Aaron didn't care. He didn't even care that the kids were all over the gym, losing balls, chasing balls, bellowing the song off-key. What he cared about was that they were having fun and learning a new skill.

He ended the day with a relay race, partly to work on their running speed but mostly to burn them out. They were all replenishing their supply of fluids when Stacy's mother arrived to pick her daughter up.

Over the next few minutes he greeted a string of adults—mostly mothers, but one uncle and one older sister—who had come for the children. He answered questions, said goodbye and waved everyone off. Only when the last of the kids was gone did he allow himself to look at Lily.

He hadn't had to look at her earlier to feel her presence. He'd deliberately avoided the corner of the bench where she sat, but he'd never lost his awareness of her. Like white noise, she'd been there, a constant hum in the room, in his mind. He'd inhaled her, felt her on his skin, sensed her along his nerve endings.

If taking money from her was going to be so distracting, maybe he ought to thank her for considering a contribution to his program and send her and her checkbook away. But damn, the money wasn't for him. It was for Andy and Stacy and Jimmy and Jessica, and the other thirty kids who wouldn't be starting the program until next week or the week after because he couldn't take them all at once. It was for kids who had nothing to do with their time, nothing to keep them busy on a lazy summer day, nothing other than Aaron to prevent them from wandering the back alleys behind the Main Street shops scavenging for cigarette butts, or stealing money from their mother's purses for marijuana, or—in the case of the younger kids—sitting mesmerized in front of their TV sets, watching shows filled with violence.

It was for the kids that he would tamp down whatever conflicted feelings he had about Lily and try to woo a little money from her.

Using the hem of his shirt to wipe the excess sweat from his face again, he crossed the gym to where Lily was sitting. She rose to her feet and smiled hesitantly. "Towels," he said, letting his shirt drop back down over his shorts. "If you donate some money, I can buy towels."

Her smile faltered slightly, as if she wasn't sure whether he was joking. In truth, he wasn't sure whether he was, either. The physical-education department used a laundry service that provided towels during the school year, but he couldn't afford that. He would have worn a headband and brought his own towel if he'd realized that he was going to be running around and sweating as much as the youngsters.

He gestured toward the gym's rear door, which led to the phys-ed offices. His office was so small the desk and file cabinets nearly filled it, but he'd managed to wedge a compact fridge into a corner. He pulled out a couple of bottles of iced tea and extended one to Lily, who shook her head.

Of course she wasn't thirsty. She hadn't been sprinting around a gym for the past several hours. Her skin was dry, her dress unwrinkled. Looking at her refreshed him almost as much as taking a swig of iced tea.

He indicated for her to sit in the guest chair. Then he circled the desk and settled into his creaky swivel chair. He took another swallow of iced tea, screwed the cap onto the bottle and leaned back, waiting for her to speak.

She didn't seem to know what to say. She met his eyes fleetingly. Then her gaze darted around the small office, pausing at the file cabinets, the computer on a small table next to his desk, the clipboards hanging from hooks beside the doorway and finally the team photos lining the walls. Aaron was in the most recent one, as coach, and he was in three old ones in uniform, as a player. When he looked at those photos—especially the first one, taken when he was a sophomore with one foot still in the world of petty crime—he hardly recognized himself. The features were the same, the lean build pretty much the same. But the eyes…God, his eyes had looked angry back then. He didn't want to think he still had that much anger in him.

Lily's gaze lingered on the old photos for a while, and then she turned back to him. "You were right," she said, breaking the silence. "My painting was too safe."

Her comment surprised him. He'd thought she'd come to discuss his summer program. But hell, if there was a nice fat check at the end of the conversation, he'd talk about her painting.

As if he could think of anything to say on that subject. He could identify the *Mona Lisa* if he had to, and that painting of the skinny old farmer with a pitchfork and his wife, but that was about the extent of his knowledge of art.

Lily was looking directly at him now, her gaze almost a challenge. He had to say something. "I was just talking off the top of my head when I said that."

"No, you were absolutely right. Everyone always says my paintings are nice and pretty. But I've been thinking 'nice and pretty' might not be such a good idea."

"You think nasty and grotesque are better?"

She laughed. "Maybe they are. My problem is that I wouldn't begin to know how to do that."

"Good," he said automatically, then grinned and shrugged. He had a feeling they were talking about two different things. The only problem was, he didn't know what she was talking about. He wasn't sure what he was talking about, either.

"The nice, pretty thing for me to do would be to give you money for your basketball summer school," she said.

"Well, then, I'm all in favor of nice and pretty."

She laughed. He watched much too intently as her laughter faded and her smile grew quiet. She could never be anything but pretty, he realized. Even if a terrible accident befell her, leaving her disfigured, she would still be pretty. Her prettiness didn't come from her features, even though they were lovely. It came from something inside her, something tender and sweet and vulnerable. Not even losing her husband in an auto accident could make her interior grotesque. She was doomed to be pretty forever.

"Nice" was another matter, though. "Nice" was within her power to change. Aaron had learned how to be nice, more or less, over the past fifteen years. If he could learn that, he supposed even the nicest person in the world could learn how to be nasty.

"Do you have a budget for your program?" she asked.

"I've got several." He opened a drawer in his desk and pulled out his budget folder and passed it across the desk. "I've got a reality-based budget, a dream-based budget, and everything in between."

She opened the folder and began to read. "This must be the reality-based one," she guessed as she skimmed the numbers on the top sheet.

"Yeah."

"Where's your salary?"

"What salary?"

She gave him a hard look. "Aren't you paid a salary to run the program?"

He shrugged again. "There's no money for it."

"Then how can you afford to do this?"

"I'm a school counselor," he reminded her. "We

get paid enough during the school year to cover the summer months. In theory, anyway.''

Frowning, she resumed her study of the budget plans he'd written up. Lacking anything better to do, he watched her read. It didn't seem fair that he found her so attractive. Mother Nature should have designed things so that people would be attracted only to people they could conceivably hook up with.

Yeah, Mother Nature had been slacking off when she'd worked out the chemistry between Aaron and Lily. Seated in the tiny office with her, he felt the same crazy sensations he'd felt the first time he'd glimpsed her—sensations that could drive a screwed-up adolescent not to care if he got detention yet again for staring at her and forgetting the incriminating open doorway.

For four long years of high school, he'd had a near-fatal infatuation with her. Even after he'd learned she was Dr. Bennett's daughter, he'd felt the zap of desire whenever he saw her. He'd never had any classes with her, but he would see her—in the hallways, at the assemblies, in the stands during basketball games, in the cafeteria on those rare occasions he ventured into that room to buy a bottle of apple juice.

He'd avoided the cafeteria most of the time. It was a place for the kids who belonged, not him. Once Coach Drummer had taken him in hand, he'd been allowed to eat lunch in this very office where he and Lily were sitting now. His lunches were invariably leftovers his mother brought home from the café. Coach Drummer must have understood that Aaron would have felt embarrassed if he'd unwrapped a lunch consisting of half an omelet, a slab of meat loaf and a pickle spear in front of his classmates.

But when he did go into the cafeteria to buy a drink, he'd search for Lily. She was always at a table with other pretty girls or with those River Rat kids. They'd all be laughing and sharing confidences, nudging each other or crumpling their napkins into balls and tossing them at each other. Amid the crowd, amid the din, she was like a beacon to Aaron, snagging his attention. He would stand by the beverage machine, turning his quarters over and over in his palm while he stared at her and wished she was his—and hated himself for wishing.

He didn't hate himself now. He'd learned over the years that self-hatred wasn't good for much. Still…life would be a little easier if merely gazing at her as she flipped through the various budgets he'd printed out didn't make his blood run hotter than normal.

He drained the bottle of iced tea and swiveled away from her, searching for something to occupy himself while she perused the budgets. Grabbing the clipboard on his desk, he jotted some notes on the different drills and games he might have the kids try tomorrow. He managed to stay reasonably absorbed in that until she cleared her throat.

He swiveled back to face her. "So you want to add a swimming component to the program?" she asked.

"It would be great if I could break the day up with a little pool time. It would cool the kids down. The school has the facility, but it's open only in the evenings, when adults can come in to use it. It seems like a waste to have it sitting there empty during the day, while I've got a bunch of kids who'd really enjoy it."

"But you need a certified water-safety instructor for that?"

"Absolutely."

She gestured at the budget file. "You've suggested it would cost at least a hundred dollars?"

"They may be teenagers, but they're highly trained," he explained. "It's not like bringing in some of my team guys and asking them to help me run drills with the kids. Water-safety has a lot more responsibility."

"I see." She skimmed the top sheet of the budget file for a moment longer, then folded it shut. Without meeting Aaron's gaze, she pulled a checkbook from her purse. "Whom should I make this out to?" she asked.

"Hot Shots Summer Program," he said, amazed and pleased that he'd won her over so easily. Abraham Steele could have whipped out a checkbook and written a donation when Aaron had visited him last month, but he'd wanted to think about it awhile before deciding—and then he'd died.

Maybe Lily knew her mind better than Abraham had known his. Or else it was that Abraham had been considering donating the bank's money, not his own, whereas Lily had no directors or investors to answer to.

She wrote out a check and handed it to him. He looked at it, then looked again. *Ten thousand dollars.* He swallowed, looked once again and found that the number hadn't changed.

"Um, I think you've put too many zeros here," he mumbled.

"No."

He lifted his gaze to meet hers. She was wearing that mystifyingly shy smile of hers, but there was a certainty in her eyes. "This says ten thousand dollars."

"I know what it says."

"Are you sure you want to give that much?"

"I want you to hire a water-safety instructor. And another teacher so you can have more children participating. And maybe you could use the rest as seed money to carry over till next year. That way you'd have something to build on."

He opened his mouth and shut it. He hadn't expected this. When he'd left Lily's house yesterday, he figured he'd blown any chance of getting a contribution from her. He'd told her her painting was too safe, hadn't he? And now she thought he was a brilliant art critic? Was that why she was handing him ten thousand dollars?

"Does this summer program have a board? Because if it does, I want to be on it," she said.

"It didn't have a board," he told her, "but for ten thousand dollars, if you want a board we'll have a board. *You* can be the board, all by yourself."

"Well, it's just...I don't want the money squandered."

"You don't trust me, huh?" He grinned to take the sting out of the words.

Her smile was much more reserved. "I hardly know you, Aaron, and what I know..." Her words drifted off as if she was unwilling to say something rude.

"I'm no longer the punk I was in high school," he reminded her.

"There was a rumor in high school that you were arrested." She stared past him at the screen saver on his computer monitor, apparently unable to look at him when she dredged up his sordid past.

"It wasn't a rumor. I had a police record."

His candor drew her gaze back to his face. She appeared startled and dismayed, and he braced himself for the possibility that she was going to ask for her check back.

"Vagrancy," he told her. "Underage drinking. Possession of a controlled substance. Chronic truancy. Suspicion of shoplifting. More vagrancy."

"A controlled substance?" Her eyebrows pinched together in a frown.

"Pot."

She nodded gravely.

"Frank Garvey gave me some warnings and I ignored them. He arrested me a couple of times, and the judge gave me continuances and yelled at me to shape up. Finally Garvey locked me behind bars for a night. He thought it would be a good idea to scare the sh—the stuffing out of me," Aaron said, editing himself so as not to offend her even more.

"That was for possession of pot?"

"Public intoxication. Beer. I was fifteen."

"Where in the world did you get beer?"

Her naiveté amused him. At fifteen, she probably hadn't had any idea of how to get beer. For him, it had been a no-brainer. "The refrigerator," he said.

"You just took beer from the refrigerator? Didn't your mother say anything?"

"No." He let out a sigh. He used to drink beer at night while his mother was out partying. Sometimes he went out, too. His mother hadn't noticed him missing; she certainly hadn't noticed the missing beer. Unlike Lily, he hadn't been blessed with parents who actually cared enough to keep tabs on him.

"I'm sorry," Lily said abruptly. "You must think I'm terribly nosy, but—"

"But you just handed me a big check. If you're having second thoughts—"

"No. Not at all. I think you're running a worthwhile program, Aaron." She tucked her checkbook back into her purse. "But I do like the idea of being on some sort of board that can monitor how the money is being spent."

"Fine. Set up a board, whatever you want." As long as she didn't think she'd bought the right to tell him how to organize his drills and games, he didn't care what she and her one-woman board did.

She snapped her purse shut and stood. Aaron sprang to his feet, too. "I'll be in touch, then," she said, extending her hand.

He shook it and smiled, but his mind was revving. She'd be in touch? About what? Board meetings? God help him if she turned his simple program into something formal, like the garden club or a church auxiliary, with meetings where members would expect him to stand at the front of the room and justify his every decision. He could scarcely stand all the bureaucracy involved in his counseling work at the school, but at least in that case, the mental health of

Riverbend's students was at stake. This was just a summer recreational program.

Besides, if there were regular board meetings, he'd have to see Lily all the time. He could handle that if he had to, but he'd prefer *not* to have to. She was too tantalizing. Too troubling. Just glimpsing her seemed to reduce him to the hormone-driven adolescent he'd been the last time their paths had crossed.

Ten thousand bucks could buy an awful lot, he admitted grimly. It could buy a board, the opportunity to monitor his expenditures...the ability to throw his equilibrium out of whack.

But ten thousand bucks could also buy a water-safety instructor and an assistant coach for the kids. "Thanks," he remembered to say. "The money will be put to good use."

"I hope so." She turned and left his office. He should have walked her through the gym and out, but he was feeling a little shell-shocked.

Ten thousand dollars—more than he'd ever dreamed—was his to spend on the program. Not only could he hire assistants and work some pool time into the schedule, but he could even pay himself a small stipend, if there was anything left.

Yet he couldn't squelch the niggling fear that this was going to turn out to be the most costly gift he'd ever received.

WHAT WAS SHE, crazy?

Yes. She was crazy. Certifiable. Ready for immediate installment in the nearest padded cell.

She slumped in the leather bucket seat of her car, which had baked to a scorching temperature in the midafternoon sun, and shook her head at the two most insane things she had ever done in her life: donating ten thousand dollars to Aaron's summer program and insisting on having some sort of input into how the money was spent.

The money she wouldn't miss. But the input... Did she actually want to see Aaron on a regular basis? Even on an *ir*regular basis? The man still scared her, not because she was an innocent young girl, ignorant of what all his sexual energy implied, but because she was an experienced woman who knew exactly what all his sexual energy implied.

She'd been aware of his sexual energy even as a teenager, when she'd never dared to speak to him as they passed each other in the school's corridors. She and her friends used to whisper about him. "Did you see him play last night? He always looks kind of wild when he's running down the boards—like he's being chased." Or "I heard he got arrested. He spent the night in jail. Can you believe it?" Or "Have you ever noticed his eyes? They're bedroom eyes. If you look directly into them, he'll *own* you."

Aaron had never seemed to own any girl in school, but Lily had assumed that was because he knew things none of the schoolgirls knew. She'd figured he wouldn't waste time with girls. He'd be with women.

She was a woman now, but she still felt lost whenever she looked into his eyes. They took more than they gave. They hinted at deep turbulent emotion but didn't reveal what that emotion might be.

They were impossibly sexy.

Damn. She had to be the world's biggest fool, giving money to a man like him. Why had she decided to write that check? If not because of his dazzling eyes, then because he'd criticized her painting?

No, not because he'd criticized it. Because he'd spoken the truth. Because unlike everyone else, he hadn't treated her with kid gloves, afraid to ruffle the poor widow's feathers. He'd offered his opinion and she'd recognized its honesty. Her painting was too safe. *She* was too safe.

The truth was, she'd given Aaron so much money because it wasn't safe, because she didn't want to be safe. She'd learned safety wasn't all it was cracked up to be, and she was eager to try something new.

Definitely, she ought to be locked in a padded cell and heavily medicated until she came to her senses. She was nuts, nuts, nuts.

Yet as she backed out of her parking space and steered slowly past the football field and around to the front of the school, she was grinning. Her life was about to get very interesting, and for the first time in months, she was looking forward to turning the page and finding out what was going to happen next.

CHAPTER FIVE

SEVERAL CARS were already parked along the grass's edge in front of Grace and Ed Pennington's house when Lily arrived. She'd spent days debating whether to attend the informal barbecue they'd invited her to, and she'd spent hours that afternoon debating what to wear. Her wardrobe seemed divided into painting clothes and everything else, everything else being all those overpriced Boston ensembles she wasn't sure she'd feel comfortable wearing to a party with her hometown friends.

She'd finally settled on a long sleeveless shift of unbleached white cotton, with a matching crocheted sweater for the chill that would inevitably arrive after the sun set. Once she was dressed, her hair brushed and pulled back into a tortoiseshell clasp and her lips shiny with a tinted gloss, she'd engaged in yet another debate about whether she was ready to be social.

Yes, she was ready. She was ready to step out, to start living her life again, to stop alternately feeling sorry for herself and hating herself. She was ready to play it just a little less safe.

Not that she would be anything but safe at the Penningtons' house. These were her friends, after all, River Rats and other people she'd known forever.

They liked her. They cared about her. They would never judge her harshly—at least not as long as they didn't know all her secrets.

Sighing and wishing she felt courageous—and wishing she didn't need courage simply to walk around to Ed and Grace's backyard and join the party—she climbed out of her car.

Voices and laughter drifted through the evening air as she strolled around the side of the house. The grass tickled her bare toes through the straps of her sandals, and its scent filled her nostrils. When she turned the corner she saw a dozen people gathered on the broad deck, chatting and laughing, holding cans of beer or plastic stemware glasses filled with something frothy and orange, a pitcher of which sat on a table covered with a bright plaid cloth. The table also held platters of fresh vegetables and dip and bowls of chips—typical pre-barbecue fare.

Lily scanned the crowd, quickly identifying everyone. Mitch Sterling was there, clad in khaki pants and a short-sleeved shirt. Erin Wilson, in shorts and a striped maternity blouse, was engrossed in a conversation with Susie Rousseau; they'd both been in a bunch of high-school classes with Lily. She spotted Charlie Callahan digging a beer out of a cooler and smiled. Charlie's ex-wife, Beth, was Ed Pennington's sister. Beth had been a River Rat, and she and Charlie had always been friendly—until they'd gotten married. If their marriage had been a surprise, so had their divorce.

Obviously the divorce hadn't damaged Charlie's friendship with his former in-laws. Or else maybe the

River Rats had such strong bonds that even divorce couldn't sever them.

Lily wished Beth could be at this party, too, but apparently she no longer lived in town. At least Lily knew everyone else here.

And they knew her. Susie spotted her first and raced over, arms outstretched. "Lily! It's so good to see you!"

Within seconds she was engulfed by friends, embracing her, touching her, beaming at her. She felt loved. She felt smothered. She told herself that if she survived this party, she would know she was truly ready to rejoin the world.

Everyone asked her how she was and no one gave her a chance to answer. A glass of the foamy orange drink was pressed into her hand, and she was led to one of the upholstered deck chairs. Erin pulled up a chair on one side and Grace pulled up a chair on the other. They proceeded to tell Lily all about Erin's pregnancy.

She was delighted. She'd much rather hear what her friends were up to than discuss what she'd been up to. What could she tell them? That after spending two and a half months holed up in her house on East Oak Street, she'd finally ventured out because Aaron Mazerik, of all people, had presented her with a challenge? That she'd spent an entire hour last Monday watching children run back and forth in the high-school gym? That she'd written a big charity check, as if she was some sort of society matron? That thanks to Aaron, she was no longer sure she wanted to keep working on pale decorous watercolors?

She'd wandered into the crafts store in town that

morning and found a wide array of knitting, need-lepointing and doll-making supplies, but nothing she was looking for. Then she'd returned home and ordered some canvases and an ample assortment of acrylics through an Internet site. She had her old paintbrushes in a carton in the cellar, and she was sure they'd come back to life after a good soaking and scrubbing. The supplies she'd ordered would arrive early next week, and then she would decide if she was daring enough to abandon her watercolor paints.

She wasn't sure whether she should thank Aaron or curse him for what he'd spawned with one simple comment about her painting. But the order was already in, and she wasn't going to cancel it.

"I've got some munchies in the oven," Grace said, shoving away from her chair once she was done lecturing Erin on the importance of eating high-quality protein. "And I've got to get Ed to start the grill. If people keep drinking orange blossoms and not eating anything, everyone will be passing out drunk."

One thing Lily didn't want to see was everyone drunk. Her beverage was a delicious blend of orange juice and other flavors and something potent—vodka, probably, since it didn't have much of a taste. She'd stopped drinking completely during the last few years of her marriage, because alcohol had developed such dreadful associations for her by then, but since Tyler's death she found she could enjoy an occasional glass of wine.

This orange blossom, though... She lost her thirst

for it. "Let me help you," she offered, rising to her feet.

"Oh, you don't have to," Grace said.

But Lily didn't want to sit in her chair like a guest of honor on display. She felt too conspicuous, aware that even though no one was talking about her, they were all watching her, probably wondering how fragile she was, how long she would stay, whether their old friend Lily was back in spirit or only in body. She followed Grace through the sliding screen door into the kitchen, where more people were gathered, chatting and nibbling on pretzels from a massive bowl on the center island.

"What can I do to help?" she asked.

Grace looked on the verge of shaking her head, then relented and donned a pair of oven mitts. "See that empty platter over there?" She motioned with her head toward a large cut-glass dish. "In two minutes I want it filled with stuffed mushrooms." She opened her wall oven and pulled out a cookie sheet lined with the steaming hors d'oeuvres. A woody, herbal aroma filled the kitchen. "They're hot, so use the spatula," she said, balancing the cookie sheet on two stove burners.

Lily had never been more grateful for something to do. Lyle Lovett's tender voice floated into the kitchen from the speakers in the family room, and the friendly babble of voices drifted in through the screen door. Across the counter from where Lily was stationed with the mushrooms, Mitch Sterling and Erin's husband, Joe, were analyzing the current state of basketball at Riverbend High School. "You really think this year's team was better than us?'' Mitch asked.

"Either the kids are better or the coaching is better. What do you think?"

"It can't be the kids. They didn't have anyone half as good as Jacob Steele on their team this year. The only explanation for the season they had is—'' Mitch's eyes glinted with laughter ''—they played weaker opponents.''

Lily wanted to point out that Aaron was an outstanding coach, but of course she had no basis for such an assertion. She'd watched him for all of an hour, and he hadn't really been coaching. She'd intended to go back to the school to observe another session—having donated so much money to the program, she would certainly be within her rights—but she didn't want to turn his summer basketball program into an obsession.

Or, more accurately, turn the program's director into an obsession.

What would have happened if she'd phoned Aaron and invited him to accompany her to this party? He likely would have said no, thanks, or he'd have laughed uproariously and *then* said no, thanks. He'd never mixed with this crowd. How had he described his life in high school? *I didn't travel in any circle.*

It was true. He'd been a real loner, and Lily had marveled at his isolation. She'd always been with her friends, making group plans and organizing group outings, heading down to the river with the River Rats to sit on the riverbank and tease and flirt and argue about the meaning of life, or at least the meaning of Mr. O'Toole's trigonometry test. An only child, she'd seen the River Rats as her sisters and brothers. She'd felt more comfortable with them than by herself.

Ten years of marriage had taught her how to be by herself. She'd learned not to count on Tyler for companionship. Sometimes he'd been the greatest company in the world—funny, charming, attentive. But other times he'd been a surly, churlish boor. After a while, she'd been unable to trust him anymore. Being married to a man you couldn't trust was Lily's definition of solitude.

Standing in Grace's kitchen, with Grace, Mitch and Joe all within hugging distance, she still felt alone. A wall separated her from her friends, invisible but real. She knew what it was made of: her guilt, her responsibility, her unrelenting consciousness of the black mark on her soul.

"There," she said, sliding the last of the mushrooms onto the platter and forcing a smile. "Do you want me to take this outside?"

"Not yet." Mitch reached over the counter and snatched one of the mushrooms.

"They're hot. You're going to burn your tongue," Grace warned as she took the spatula and went to work on another cookie sheet from the oven, this one covered with what appeared to be tiny egg rolls.

"I'm tough. I can take it." He popped the mushroom into his mouth and grinned. "Mmm, delicious. Will you marry me?"

"You're just a few years too late, Mitch. Sure, Lily," she remembered to answer. "Take those outside, okay? Thanks."

Still wearing an artificial smile, Lily returned to

the deck with the plate. Everyone seemed so happy, so relaxed, so easy with who they were. But the wall between her and her friends, a solid, unbreakable pane of glass, enabled her to see them but not join them. She wondered if Aaron had felt like this in high school, aware of the warm friendships and social cliques he wasn't a part of.

Lily had always assumed he'd deliberately separated himself. He hadn't needed people like her and her friends. He could play basketball without becoming one of the school jocks. He could attend classes without becoming a true student. He'd always seemed out of place in Riverbend High, anyway. He'd seemed too old for school, somehow, not book-smart but street-smart, wise in a way that even the class valedictorian could never be. Wise enough to know he didn't belong. Wise enough to know he never would.

"Tell me about your house," Susie demanded, sidling up to Lily. "It's gorgeous from the outside. How have you fixed it up?"

Lily knew her manners. She set the heavy platter on the table and told Susie what she wanted to hear. She described the living room, explained that several of the bedrooms were serving more as storage areas than actual rooms, complained that the kitchen was too big. She mentioned her favorite corner bedroom, which she'd converted into a studio because it was filled with sunlight for half the day. Susie asked her about the floors—"Hardwood throughout? Wow, that's real quality!"—and the windows—"I just love that beveled glass, the way it turns the light into rainbows.'' Lily loved that about the leaded-glass windows, too.

But she didn't want to be here talking about her windows. She was experiencing a soul-deep sensation of emptiness, as if she'd been cut loose and was floating, disconnected. She wished she could leave without being noticed, but knew that was impossible. She would have to endure the party a little longer.

She did. She was amiable, she was pleasant, she asked questions about her friends' jobs and their children and silently thanked them all for being considerate enough not to ask her any questions about herself. She ate half a hamburger and several of the stuffed mushrooms, she sipped a soft drink, and by eight-thirty, with the sun low but glazing the sky in golden light, she apologetically said she had to go. She didn't want to have to lie to her friends about the reason for her early departure; to be sure, she wasn't exactly certain what the reason was, other than that having to remain amiable and pleasant was draining her of energy and giving her a headache.

Fortunately her friends didn't question her early departure. ''I understand,'' Grace murmured, walking Lily around to the front of the house. ''It's hard for you. I understand.''

They still thought she was grieving over Tyler. Fine. Let them.

She climbed into her car, waved to Grace and drove away. Turning the corner, she braked and let out a long breath. Deceiving her friends was just one more thing she hated about herself.

She wanted to cry, but tears seemed pointless.

What had happened had happened. It couldn't be changed. Her only option was to move forward.

Taking that concept literally, she shifted into gear and cruised down the street. If she went home, she would undoubtedly spend the rest of the evening roaming through the vast rooms of her ridiculous house and contemplating the debacle her life had become.

Instead, she kept driving, leaving the Penningtons' neatly settled neighborhood for the edge of town, passing a modest farm, an overgrown field, a copse of trees stretching its shadow across the road as the sun hovered on the horizon. By the time she reached River Road, there was more shadow than light, but she knew this area well. She'd practically lived on the river as a child, she and her friends. This had been their favorite hangout. Long before anyone had dubbed them the River Rats, they'd claimed the river as their own.

She drove slowly along the road that paralleled the river. After about a mile she came to the unpaved turnoff she was looking for. She bounced her car onto the rutted dirt road and braked. The trees canopied her car, their leaves mottling what little light remained in the sky.

Not much had changed here. If the trees were a little taller, so was she. If the ground had more undergrowth, more sticks and stones and mulch, well, she hadn't walked a smooth path in a long time. She got out of the car and picked her way carefully down to the water's edge.

The river hadn't changed at all. A wide silver

band, it glided serenely past the stones and reeds and low-growing shrubs that crowded the bank.

There was the tree limb, she thought with a sigh that was almost happy. How odd that the site of her fall imbued her with a sense of peace. Maybe because she'd survived that fall. Thanks to her friends, it hadn't been too bad. And it had changed her life for the better, at least in terms of a ten-year-old girl's desires.

They used to climb out onto the limb and jump from it into the river. All summer long they'd bike down here, drape their towels over tree branches, scramble out along the limb and jump. Jacob had been the first to try it, because he'd been the oldest and the biggest, and he'd felt it was his duty to test the situation before anyone took any chances on it. He'd climbed out carefully, clinging to the limb with his hands, as well as his feet, and dropped into the water. He went under, then surfaced. "It's deep enough," he'd reported.

After that, they'd all had to jump off the limb. Over and over, every hot sunny day that summer, they'd done so. The boys always had to show off, of course—they performed cannonballs, belly flops or somersaults off the limb. The girls weren't quite as flamboyant.

Lily still recalled the thrill of hurling herself off the limb. It hadn't been terribly dangerous, but it hadn't been exactly safe, either. She remembered the weird ecstasy of plunging through air that smelled of damp earth and foliage, and then suddenly she'd hit the water and sink through a swirl of bubbles and coldness. And then she'd swim back up and shake her head clear—and think only of climbing back onto the limb to jump again.

One day in August, while inching along the limb, she'd lost her balance. The boys might have liked to show off in their jumps, but the girls had liked to show off their grace while standing and walking on the limb. They never had to grip the limb with their hands. Their natural equilibrium kept them steady, as if the limb was a wide balance beam.

But one day, after a night of rain, the limb was wet and slick. As she started down its length, her foot slipped and she went over the side, very close to the water's edge. She angled her body to hit the water, and it did—except for her left foot, which slammed against a rock on the shore.

Standing just a bit downriver from the limb now, she scanned the shoreline in the dim light, wondering if the rock was still there. It had been practically a boulder, she recalled, a huge lump of unyielding granite. She remembered the sudden stabbing pain and the crazed yearning to keep her foot in the water, as if the sluggish current could wash the pain away. Her foot had throbbed horribly, and when Beth and Ed Pennington had hauled her out of the river, she'd seen that her instep was a purplish blue and beginning to swell.

Mitch and Jacob had immediately climbed onto their bikes and sped off, heading straight for Lily's father's office to get help, even though she'd insisted she was all right. Beth had refused to let her stand. "I read somewhere that if you have a broken bone you're not supposed to move it."

"I don't have a broken bone," Lily had argued,

although given the livid color of her ballooning foot, she'd had to conclude that the injury was more than a bruise.

Beth had slid a towel under her heel and wrapped the ends around her foot to keep it still and protected. Charlie had told her knock-knock jokes to distract her. Grace had offered her a cookie from the back-pack of snacks she'd brought, but the thought of eating had nearly made Lily throw up, which was more proof she hadn't just bruised her foot.

Her father had soon arrived, skidding to a pebble-spitting halt on the dirt road. He'd taken one look at her foot, bound it more tightly in the towel, then carried her to the car and raced back to his office, grilling her about what she'd been up to. "I just fell," she'd told him, satisfied it wasn't a lie. "I fell and hit my foot on a rock."

As it turned out, she'd broken two bones in her foot. Nothing life-threatening, nothing that wouldn't heal. She'd had to wear a cast, which meant she couldn't swim or ride her bike for the rest of the summer, although one of the boys was always will-ing to let her ride on his handlebars when the River Rats were going anywhere. And, best of all, she'd gotten to quit taking ballet lessons. She'd enjoyed ballet until that final year, when the teacher had made her start dancing *en pointe,* which she'd hated. It had hurt her ankles and toes and calves, and since she wasn't planning to become a ballerina, anyway, she didn't know why she'd had to study pointe.

Once she'd broken her foot, she didn't have to study it anymore.

Sometimes something positive came out of something painful. She'd be wise to remember that.

Now, twenty-three years after she'd tumbled off the limb, she inched along the shoreline toward it, wondering if she'd be able to find the rock that had liberated her from the agony of ballet lessons. She didn't see it at first, since it was covered in moss and dead leaves. But the shape was unmistakable, and the way it protruded into the river. This was definitely her rock.

She touched the furry moss on it and smiled. Perhaps if the rock had had so much moss on it twenty-three years ago, her foot wouldn't have broken. But if the rock didn't look and feel exactly as it used to, the atmosphere around it felt the same. The scent of the air was the same, the soothing whisper of the river, the sporadic *plunk* of some critter moving in and out of the water—a frog, most likely. She lowered herself to sit on the mossy cushion and gazed around her, feeling more content than she'd felt surrounded by friends at the Penningtons' house. She was surrounded by a friend here, too—the river.

In the distance she saw a light winking through the trees. She hadn't remembered a house so close to the river. The only buildings by the river back then had been shacks and fishing cabins.

Wasn't the Miller place just upriver from here? It had been a rustic cabin like the others, and the one time she and the River Rats had prowled around it, Old Man Miller had emerged and yelled at them to get away or he'd shoot them. Shrieking, they'd dived into the river and swum like fiends, certain their lives depended on their speed—until they'd reached the limb and started to giggle and argue about whether Old Man Miller would really have shot them. He was such a crabby old geezer, he'd probably derived more satisfaction from scaring them than he would have gotten from shooting them.

Aaron owned Old Man Miller's cabin now, she knew.

That light winking through the trees like a beacon, like a star, belonged to Aaron Mazerik.

GIVEN THE HEAT, the night wasn't too buggy. He had a couple of citronella candles burning, and he'd slapped on some insect repellent. The mosquitoes were steering clear of him.

One of these days he was going to have to consider investing in an air conditioner. Charlie Callahan had given him the name of an electrician, who had up-graded all the wiring in the three-room house to ac-commodate the electric range, the refrigerator and the hot-water heater. Aaron supposed one of those win-dow units wouldn't short-circuit the entire place, es-pecially since he couldn't imagine using it and the oven at the same time. If it was hot enough for air-conditioning, it was too hot to cook.

In the meantime the temperature was usually pretty comfortable on the deck off the back of the house. Once the sun dropped below the trees, a breeze would lift off the river and cool the deck down. A cold beer helped, too.

He was sprawled on his hammock in a pair of denim cutoffs, his shirt hanging open and his feet bare. He'd taken a few sips of beer and lost himself in the pages of a thriller. He'd had a long, tiring week, and he didn't want anything more than a quiet evening and a good book.

Well, of course, he wanted *her*. He always did. Which might have been why, when she suddenly appeared at the bottom of the steps that led down from the deck, he assumed he was hallucinating.

"I saw your light," she said.

He sat up slowly, the hammock swaying under him. The light above the back door spilled over her, giving her an almost ethereal appearance. She had on a long white dress with a white sweater over it, and her hair and face were pale. Behind her, the forest was dark.

Why had she come here? To torture him without even realizing she was torturing him? To tempt him with something he couldn't have?

"How could you see my light?" he asked. His house was barely visible from the road during the day. After sunset, no way could she have seen it. The deck faced the river, not the road.

"I was walking along the river," she explained. "I saw the light through the trees."

Walking along the river. At night. In a dress. Either she was insane or something serious was going on. He didn't think Lily Holden was insane.

"Come on up," he invited her, setting his book on the table next to his beer and pushing himself out of the hammock. She climbed the four steps to the deck and hit him with her shy smile, the one that pinched his nerve endings until they stung. "You want a drink?" he offered, gesturing toward his beer.

Her gaze ran the length of him. He knew he wasn't much to look at in his grungy after-hours attire, but if she could stomach him all sweaty and breathless in his gym clothes, she could handle this. It was too hot to put on trousers, although he supposed he could button his shirt. But to button it in front of her would suggest that he was embarrassed, which would likely embarrass her. He let it be.

"A glass of water would be nice," she said.

All right. Something serious *was* going on. She didn't look hurt or even upset. But her eyes were sad, her smile pensive. She'd taken a potentially dangerous walk along the river at night, and now she wanted a glass of water.

"Have a seat," he said, waving at the plastic sling chairs that occupied the part of the deck not consumed by his hammock. They weren't fancy like her wicker porch furniture, but they were a hell of a lot more comfortable. "I'll be right back."

He entered the house, grabbed a square of paper towel from the spool above the kitchen sink and ran it over his face, hoping he didn't smell too much like bug repellent. Then he filled a glass with water, added a couple of ice cubes and hesitated. If the bugs started biting, should he invite her inside? His house was really small—a kitchen, a main room and a tiny bedroom and bath. It was plenty big enough for him, and would be big enough for two as long as the second person wasn't Lily Holden.

God, she was beautiful. Or maybe she wasn't. Maybe he was the only person who was transfixed by her beauty. Maybe his attraction to her was perversely egotistical; maybe he saw something of himself in her.

In any case, he couldn't have her come inside. If

the mosquitoes started swarming, he'd let them suck their fill.

He carried the water out to her with a smile. "Thanks," she said before taking a delicate sip.

He lowered himself onto the hammock, sitting on the edge with his feet planted on the smooth boards. He'd reconstructed the deck with guidance from Charlie Callahan, and of all the improvements he'd made to the cabin, it was the one that made him the proudest. Insulating the attic, replacing the old windows with thermal windows, putting in an energy-efficient wood-burning stove had all been practical renovations, necessary if he was going to live full-time in the place. But the deck...well, it was his favorite part of the cabin, used more than any room. During the day he could see the river through the trees. At night, he could hear it.

"So, you were walking along the river," he said when she didn't speak. "You like taking nature hikes in the dark, wearing a dress?"

The candle nearest her flickered, the yellow flame making her cheeks glow like burnished gold. "I was at a party," she explained, glancing at her dress and picking at the twigs and bits of leaves that clung to the fabric. "I got...I don't know, sad. I just needed to leave." She turned her eyes to him and he swallowed, as if he could choke down the keen longing he felt when he gazed at her. "I came to the river because that was where I used to hang out when I was a kid," she continued. "I hadn't been back since..."

"Since your husband died," he said. Blunt, maybe cruel, but he wasn't going to sit quietly while she shadowboxed with herself, jabbing and parrying and dancing away from whatever was bothering her.

Unruffled, she stared at him. "Yes. Since my husband died."

He felt contrite. He shouldn't have pushed her—except that he wanted to push her *away,* to protect himself from his own inexcusable desire. But she was tough. He'd come at her aggressively, and she hadn't flinched.

"You used to hang out with all those other kids," he recalled. "The River Rats."

She nodded and grinned. "Yes, that was what we called ourselves. I don't even remember where the name came from, other than that we always spent our time together down by the river. This was Old Man Miller's fishing cabin. He used to yell at us when he saw us."

Aaron shrugged. He'd never met Old Man Miller. The guy was in a nursing home near his daughter in Terre Haute now. She'd sold him the cabin through a broker, dirt cheap and worth every penny. The place had been dilapidated, but the location was heavenly.

"You're right, though—it was foolish to go walking along the river dressed like this." She plucked another twig from the hem of her skirt, then touched her glass to her lips without drinking.

She had beautiful lips, at least as beautiful as her eyes. Her husband might have died young, but before he died he'd gotten to kiss those lips, and for that alone Aaron envied him.

"I guess you must miss him. Your husband, I mean," he clarified when she looked bewildered. Her smile vanished and he felt like a jerk for having mentioned her loss. "I mean, you said you were sad. I guess going to a party without him must be hard."

Her eyes filled with tears and she lowered her glass to the table with a trembling hand. He swore silently. Thinking of himself as tactless was too kind. He'd just skewered the poor woman.

A quiet sob escaped her and he launched himself to his feet. He had tissues in the house somewhere—in the bathroom, he was pretty sure. He raced through the house, found a box, tore off the cardboard seal and brought the tissues outside to her. A good thing, too. She was weeping as if her husband had just died yesterday, as if she would never recover from it.

"I'm sorry," he said lamely.

She shook her head, wiped her eyes, sniffled and wiped her eyes again. "No—*I'm* sorry."

"I shouldn't have mentioned—"

"No. I don't care. You should have." She pressed the tissue to her wet cheeks and let out another muted sob. "I don't miss him at all," she confessed, her voice so soft and shaky he wasn't sure he'd heard her right.

But then she looked at him with her watery eyes, and he saw the truth shining through her tears. She really *didn't* miss her husband.

He didn't know what to say. *I'm not sorry, then. I'm glad your husband died. Hey, let's break out the champagne!*

He'd already done enough damage for one night, so he kept his mouth shut. Sitting on the edge of the hammock, he hunched forward and rested his forearms on his knees while he watched her go through the methodical process of pulling herself together. She took a fresh tissue, dried the last of the moisture from her face, took another sip of water and placed the glass carefully on the table next to the box of tissues. She eyed him briefly, glanced away, then circled her gaze back to him. "I've never admitted that to anyone before," she whispered.

"I won't tell," he promised, then gave her a smile, hoping it would help her relax a little.

"He was an alcoholic. We had a terrible marriage. I know I should be missing him. Everyone thinks I'm in deep mourning over the loss of this wonderful man, this perfect marriage..." She sighed, a long shivery exhalation. "If people knew, they'd realize what a fraud I was."

"A fraud?" He frowned and shoved his hair back from his brow. "Just because your marriage wasn't perfect doesn't mean you're a fraud."

"I let everyone *think* my marriage was perfect. It's what everyone expects of me. They think I always do everything right, and I don't. I married the wrong man. I was miserable."

"So why didn't you leave him?"

"Then everyone would have known." She sighed again, less shakily. "Stupid, right? But people have these expectations and we're supposed to live up to them."

"Or down," he said lightly. "Maybe people thought you were perfect. They thought I was trash."

"No."

"Of course they did. Me and my mother. The

cheap waitress and her bastard son. Everyone expected the worst of me."

"No," she said again, although she didn't sound quite so vehement this time.

"I defied everyone's expectations, though. You can defy people's expectations, too."

"I think it's a little different when everyone expects the best from you, instead of the worst. For you, defying expectations means making a good life for yourself. For me, defying them means making a disastrous life."

"It means letting the world know you're human." He allowed himself a grim smile, remembering that he'd been just like everyone else, thinking Lily was a princess, an angel, pure and blessed. He never would have predicted that she'd marry an alcoholic and have a lousy marriage.

"I don't know why it's so easy for me to talk to you, Aaron," she said, lifting her glass once more and running a finger along the frosty surface, tracing a line through the dampness.

He could guess. "Maybe it's because we didn't really know each other back when everyone was busy expecting you to be perfect."

"Or maybe—" her gaze narrowed on him, as intense as a laser "—it's because we've both defied expectations. Or because we're both outsiders."

He laughed at that. "You're no outsider, Lily."

"I feel like one. If people knew the truth about me…"

"What? That your husband was a drunk? Big deal."

She shook her head. "I'm not the person they think I am. I'm not one of them. Not anymore."

He thought she was being awfully hard on herself, but he didn't argue. Someday when she was feeling better, he would set her straight about the fact that she was still a princess, kindhearted and virtuous. Of course, once she was feeling better, she would never indulge in such an intimate conversation with him.

"I'm sorry I barged in on you like this," she said abruptly, putting the glass on the table and rising from the chair. "You probably think I'm a pest."

"Not at all." He heaved himself to his feet, then slapped a mosquito that had landed on his forearm. "That's a pest," he said, flicking the dead bug over the deck railing. "You're…"

"A benefactor," she supplied with a wry smile. "I've given your program money, so now you feel obliged to humor me."

"If there's one thing you should know about me, it's that I don't humor anyone," he said.

Her smile lost its ironic edge. "I believe it. Maybe…" She looked oddly hopeful. "Maybe you could think of me as a friend?"

He swallowed again. A friend was probably one thing he could never think of her as, and yet, it seemed the only word that would work right now. "Sure," he agreed, aware that after his earlier bluntness, he owed her this gift. "A friend."

"I'll leave you alone now," she promised. "That's one thing friends should do for each other."

"You don't have to go," he argued, although he knew it would be best if she did. Friendship implied emotional involvement, and for damned sure, that was something he didn't want to have with her.

Fortunately she spared him from his own good manners. "No, I really must leave. It's late and I'm tired."

"How'd you get here?" he asked. "Did you walk from the party?" If she'd driven to his house, he would have heard the car. The world around his house was full of natural sounds—the chorus of crickets, the murmur of the river and the occasional crunch of a squirrel or raccoon moving through the underbrush. The sound of a car engine would have stood out.

"I parked down River Road a way," she said. Evidently sensing what he was about to offer, she added, "I can walk back. I'll take the road. It'll be safe."

"It's dark. I'll drive you." Without giving her a chance to argue, he ducked back into the house, grabbed his wallet and keys from the top of the microwave where he'd left them and reemerged onto the deck.

She conceded with a reluctant smile. He led her down the steps and around the side of the house to the open-front shed he'd built to house his car and the cords of wood he stored during the summer months. He held open the passenger door for her, refusing to feel inferior just because he drove a ten-year-old Pontiac and not a late-model BMW ragtop—he'd seen her car through the open doorway when she'd come to the gym last Monday. She was rich, and she drove a rich woman's car. He was just squeaking by, and he drove a car to match. No apologies required.

He backed up to the turnaround, then drove down the packed-dirt driveway to River Road. ''I'm parked this way,'' she said, pointing right. He made the turn.

The moon had risen above the road, slicing down through the trees in blades of silver. The night had grown cool, and he wondered whether her friends were still partying without her, talking about her, worrying. He wondered whether they would worry even more if they knew she was with him. Aaron Mazerik, the kid from whom everyone expected nothing.

He spotted her car tucked off the road in a turnoff, its glossy surfaces gleaming in the moonlight. He pulled off the road behind it.

''Thank you,'' Lily said.

''No problem.''

She shook her head. ''I wasn't thanking you for the ride,'' she said, as if that explained everything. Then, before he could stop her, she leaned across the seat and kissed him lightly on the mouth.

It lasted less than the time it took to blink. And then she was out of his car and gone from view.

But her kiss was still there, burning on his lips, burning into his soul.

CHAPTER SIX

SHE LAY AWAKE long into the night, thinking. About her friends, whom she couldn't confide in. About Aaron, whom she *could* confide in. About her marriage, about how the first thing Aaron had asked— "So why didn't you leave him?"—posed an idea Lily had never even considered. She'd married Tyler for better or worse, in sickness and in health, and she'd believed his drinking was a sickness. If she'd left her husband, she would have broken a vow. Instead, she'd stayed and come to hate him.

Aaron's way would have been better. But it would have taken more guts than she had. As a child she'd been brave enough to jump off a tree limb into the river. As an adult she'd been too cowardly to jump at all.

She thought about whether going to Aaron's house proved she was regaining a little of her childhood gutsiness. She thought about how incredibly easy it had been to talk to him, how incredibly comfortable she'd felt with him.

She thought about his chest.

Even if not out of modesty, he should have buttoned his shirt for the sake of her mental peace. But he hadn't. And while they'd talked, one small but stubborn sector of her brain had remained focused on the stretch of torso visible between the open cotton flaps. He'd been an athlete and still was; that he had an athlete's body was no surprise. His legs were a runner's legs, all muscle and sinew. His chest…she'd glimpsed it last Monday and now she'd had far more than a glimpse. It had looked smooth. Warm. Sleek and golden, tautly muscled. Nothing bulging, nothing overdone. Just a lean, tensile, very male chest.

She wanted to touch him. She wanted to press her lips to that smooth, warm skin. It had been so long, so very long since she'd felt such an urge. Since a man had aroused her.

And Aaron hadn't even done anything deliberate to arouse her. All he'd done was sit across the deck from her with his shirt hanging open.

She shouldn't have kissed him. It had been an impulsive act, a gesture of gratitude for his having tolerated her uninvited visit, for not laughing at her when she'd suggested they could be friends. But underlying the gratitude, churning it, roiling it like a quake on the ocean floor, a seismic event hardly visible at the surface, was desire.

Even as a teenager, she'd desired Aaron in some barely acknowledged way. He'd been like an exotic beast in their sleepy little town, dark and angry, a wounded creature desperate for a healing touch yet apt to sink its teeth deep into anyone who tried to touch him.

What if she had reached out to him back then? Would he have nuzzled her hand meekly, thankful that someone had tried to save him? Or would he have bitten her to the bone?

She had been afraid to find out.

Tonight *she'd* been the one in need of a healing touch. And Aaron had provided it. There'd been something in his manner she wasn't accustomed to, something that intrigued her and challenged her and made her actually look forward to the possibilities of her own life.

HE BRUSHED HIS TEETH for the third time, a man possessed. Then he rinsed his mouth and stared at himself in the mirror above the sink in his closet-size bathroom. And cursed, a low, agonized syllable echoing in his heart, in his mind.

How could she have kissed him?

She didn't know, obviously. If she'd known, she might have aimed for his cheek, or she might have been smart enough to leave things at a handshake.

Or she might have been *really* smart and not come to his house at all.

He gave up trying to scrub the sensation of her from his mouth. With one final uttered profanity, he turned off the light, trudged into his bedroom and sprawled on the narrow bed. His window fan could have cooled him down, but when he turned it on, the gentle hum of the motor sliced through his brain like a buzz saw. He needed silence. He needed to hear, see and feel nothing.

But that would never happen, not now that Lily Holden had kissed him.

His skin protested each wrinkle in the sheets, each degree of temperature in the air. His hair felt too heavy on his scalp. The scent of pine wafting through the open window irritated his nostrils.

God. She'd kissed him. He wanted her more than ever.

And she was his sister.

He ran it through his head one more time: the visits from her father; the way Dr. Bennett would talk to him, study him, seemingly memorize him; the cash he'd paid Aaron's mother at the end of each visit—child support in an unmarked envelope.

Aaron had given up asking his mother about his father years ago. It hurt too much to ask. She'd made a promise, she told him, and it was a sin to break a promise. One night, when Aaron was about fourteen, he'd retorted that it was a worse sin to keep your son from knowing who his father was.

"I promised your father," his mother had said. "I gave him my word. If anyone ever found out his identity, it would ruin him."

"He ruined you," Aaron had argued. "He got you pregnant. He stuck you with me."

"Yeah." His mother had sighed and lit a cigarette. "A son like you, in and out of trouble all the time—you're right. A kid like you can ruin a mother."

Aaron had wanted to smack her, his rage had been so great. Instead, he'd stalked out of the apartment, stormed down the stairs and taken a long walk. His own mother thought *he* had ruined her life. Not the bastard who'd knocked her up but the bastard who'd resulted from it.

The charade he and his mother were playing gnawed at him, chewed him up, mangled his soul. It was such a joke, pretending he didn't know who his father was. Dr. Bennett wouldn't have kept coming to the second-floor flat, checking up on him and paying Evie Mazerik guilt money, if he wasn't Aaron's father. He didn't give a good goddamn about saving Aaron's mother the cost of bringing her son in for checkups. If she'd been broke and her son had needed medical attention, either Dr. Bennett could have seen him for free or Evie could have applied for public assistance. Or she could have saved her tip money and paid the doctor.

Aaron knew why Dr. Bennett came every month, struggled through those awkward little chats with Aaron and paid Evie. He came because he wanted to see his son.

"It's Dr. Bennett," he'd accused his mother that night. "Just say it. It's Dr. Bennett."

"I'm not gonna tell you, Aaron, so stop asking."

"Damn it, I'm your son! I have a right to know who my father is!"

"No, you don't have a right. I made a promise. I loved that man, and I'm not going to betray him. Not even now."

She loved *that man* more than she loved her own son. The night he'd stormed out of the house to avoid hitting her, he'd forced himself to accept that cruel truth. He'd walked long into the night, smoking cigarettes from the pack he'd stolen from her purse, hiking as far as River Road, a mile west, and then down to the river's edge. He'd sat on a rock above the water, smoked cigarette after cigarette and cried like a baby. He'd been a man by then, already towering over his mother, his voice gravelly and his upper lip in need of daily razoring, but he'd wept because his mother had denied him his birthright.

Promise, *hell.* A mother had an implicit promise

to her son, too, a promise that ought to take precedence over any promise made to the bum who'd planted his seed and refused to do the right thing about it.

During that cold endless night, it hadn't mattered to him that he had long ago figured out who his father was. All that had mattered was his mother's rejection of him. He'd shivered in the cold, wrapped his arms around himself and smoked one more cigarette. When it had burned down to a butt, he'd tossed it in the river, watching the bright orange arc of the still-glowing tip. It had hit the water with a tiny hiss and vanished.

Aaron had felt a kinship with that cigarette. He'd once been burning with the need to know, the need to have his mother prove that he mattered to her—but that ember had been extinguished by the unfeeling river of his life.

That was a long time ago. He'd come to terms with it, developed some calluses, learned not to care anymore.

He would have been all right if only Lily hadn't kissed him.

But one light touch of her lips against his, and he wanted her more desperately than ever. He wanted her sweet innocence, her kindness, her loyalty. He wanted her blue eyes to fill with devotion to him, her soft mouth to open to him, the curves and hollows of her body to mold to him. He wanted her. As much as a man could want a woman. In his arms, in his bed. And she was his sister.

Another curse shaped his tongue, and he heaved himself to his feet. He was sick, perverted. What kind of a man had such cravings for his own flesh and blood?

He would have to avoid her. He couldn't let her near him, given the risk that she might kiss him again. If he had to return her generous donation to the basketball program, he'd do it—even though he'd already run an ad on the Internet and a print ad in the *Riverbend Courier*, looking for water-safety instructors who could fit a part-time position into their schedules. He'd already phoned a member of the high-school basketball team and attempted to lure him away from his summer job bagging groceries. "I can't pay what you're getting at the supermarket," he'd said, "but I can give you a chance to stay on top of your game and teach other kids at the same time. Great experience and lots of fun. Think about it."

He'd already budgeted Lily's money, damn it. He didn't want to have to return it.

But her donation hadn't bought her the right to make him crazy.

He stalked into the bathroom, rinsed his face with cold water and stared one more time at his reflection in the medicine-cabinet mirror. Yeah, he was crazy. His eyes blazed like a lunatic's. His lips were twisted in a grimace. His breath came short and shallow, pumping his chest like a broken bellows.

He wanted Lily. His half-sister. He could scarcely live with the understanding of who he was, what wanting her made him.

But he wanted her.

"HI, MOM, IS DAD HOME?" Lily asked.

Her mother laughed into the phone. "Lily, it's Saturday morning. Do you honestly think he'd be home?''

Lily smiled and sipped her coffee. ''He's golfing, right?''

''Things don't change much around here,'' her mother reminded her, amusement shimmering in her voice. ''Of course he's golfing. Is there something I can help you with?''

''Actually, I think I ought to talk to him. I want to discuss an investment I'm thinking about.'' Lily hated lying to her mother, but investments were a sure way to keep her mother from questioning her. Eleanor Bennett had absolutely no interest in or knowledge about investments. Financial planning was an area she ceded to her husband, along with schooling, career goals, home ownership and insurance, ambition and politics.

Lily didn't really want to discuss investments with her father, either. The only new investment she'd made recently had been in Aaron Mazerik's summer program, and that wasn't an investment she cared to consult her father about.

What she wanted to discuss with him was her mother's impending sixtieth birthday. It was still months away, but sixty was a big number, and if facing that landmark had to include anti-aging facial creams, it ought to include something celebratory, as well—a big party, a diamond solitaire, a cruise. It wasn't too soon to start considering the options.

She chatted with her mother for a few more minutes, long enough to drain her oversize mug of coffee, then hung up and stared out the back window.

Morning sun slanted into the backyard, casting a soft amber light over the east-facing wall of her detached garage and nudging awake the roses that grew there. Even though it was late June, dewdrops beaded the grass.

The house was too big, but she loved it. She couldn't imagine herself living in some old rehab-ed shack like Aaron's—except that his shack sat right by the river. She would rather have the river outside her back door than a porch overlooking a tidy lawn and a few rosebushes.

But then, she couldn't imagine Aaron Mazerik living in a house like hers, either. He'd probably consider it too Riverbend, too firmly planted in the heart of town. Although he was working at the high school and running a town program, Aaron didn't strike her as someone who wanted to live in such an established neighborhood, in a house whose foundation was sturdy, not just structurally but symbolically.

Lily had two reasons she wanted to confer with her father on her mother's upcoming birthday. The obvious one was that she loved her mother and wanted the birthday to be joyous. The other reason was that she wanted to focus on something other than Aaron. And here she was again, focusing on him.

She rinsed her mug, set it on the drying rack and grabbed her keys. Maybe when she was finished talking to her father about making plans for Eleanor's birthday, she could talk to him about what to do with her BMW. He loved talking while he golfed. When she was younger, she used to accompany him, not because she liked the sport but because while they golfed they would engage in great arguments about the president's latest foreign-policy initiative or whether Mr. O'Toole made trigonometry more difficult than it had to be, as Lily claimed. Hitting the little white ball was secondary to sharing their thoughts and ideas.

Leaving the house seemed easier to her today than just a week ago. She still felt racked with guilt about what had happened in her marriage, but she was tired of shutting herself up inside with nothing but her stormy memories for company. She would feel guilty whether or not she insulated herself from the world. And either way, her mother was going to turn sixty. Life went on and Lily was going to have to go on, too.

She crossed to the garage and slid open the door. As she backed the car down the driveway, she thought about how Tyler had never liked convertibles; in the summer he'd preferred air conditioning to Mother Nature's offerings. But Lily loved having the sky open to her, with only the shade of passing trees and the wind in her hair to keep her cool.

The golf course was located on the outskirts of town, surrounded by corn and soy fields and small copses of trees. At one time the golf club had been the exclusive domain of the town fathers; Abraham Steele and members of the town's elite golfed while their wives planned elaborate dances and parties in the clubhouse. But democracy had arrived in Riverbend long ago, and now the club was open to everyone. This didn't diminish Dr. Bennett's joy in it. He loved running into a cross-section of Riverbend on the links, catching up on local news between holes and in the clubhouse after his game.

Before she went off in search of him, she cruised

the parking lot, looking for his car. The large black Mercury with the MD license plate wasn't in the lot. She cruised it a second time, just to make sure she hadn't missed his car, then parked in front of the clubhouse and strolled inside. Perhaps her father had made a golfing date with a friend and they'd come in the friend's car… But he rarely did that; because he was a doctor, he liked to have his car with him, in case an emergency cropped up and he had to race to a patient's aid.

"Nope, haven't seen Dr. Bennett," the young man in charge of scheduling golf times told Lily. "I'd know if he was here. He isn't."

"Thanks." Lily walked out of the clubhouse, climbed back into her car and sat there, frowning. Why wasn't her father here? Where else would he be on a Saturday morning?

Maybe he'd already finished a round—although, at ten-thirty in the morning, he would have had to golf at the speed of light to accomplish that. Besides, the fellow at the clubhouse desk would have said he'd seen him.

Which meant he must have stopped somewhere on his way here. Maybe he'd had to run an errand. Or maybe there'd been an emergency and he'd been summoned. One of the things she admired about her father was his insistence on practicing medicine the way he'd always practiced it, even when that meant treating a patient on a weekend, or making a house call, or accepting payment in bushels of corn if the patient couldn't pay with money. Managed care and insurance might have forced him to alter the way he ran his business, but he refused to alter the way he practiced medicine.

She decided she would stop by his clinic on the chance that he or his office manager was there.

She drove back into town, top down and sunglasses perched on her nose. She could feel the stares of pedestrians as she cruised slowly down North Main Street and left onto Elm, but she convinced herself she didn't care. All she cared about was finding her father.

His clinic, which occupied a renovated house a couple of blocks from the Courthouse Square, appeared unoccupied, the windows dark. No sign of her father's car.

Where could he be? Why had he let her mother believe he'd gone golfing if he hadn't? Was he hiding something from her?

Maybe he was ten steps ahead of Lily, already planning some sort of surprise for her mother's birthday. Maybe although he'd told Eleanor he was golfing, he was, in fact, booking a restaurant for a gala surprise party or ordering a customized, engraved diamond bracelet for her.

Or maybe…he was doing something he didn't want anyone to know about. Lily had no personal experience when it came to cheating husbands—she was pretty sure Tyler had never cheated on her—but she'd seen movies and read books. Some men were the kind who told their wives they were going golfing when in reality they were doing something no decent, loving husband would do.

But Lily's father was decent and loving. If he'd lied to her mother about playing golf, he had a good reason.

She circled up to Hickory Street, slowing to the leisurely pace of the cars sharing the road with her, which gave her time to scout the vehicles parked along the curbs on either side. Spotting her father's car parked in the lot next to the Sunnyside Café, she released the breath she hadn't realized she was holding and smiled.

He'd met someone for breakfast. Maybe a friend or a golf buddy. Maybe they'd played a round so early the clerk at the golf club hadn't realized they'd been there, and now they were enjoying a leisurely brunch. Her mother would undoubtedly have been happy to serve a brunch at the house. But men were allowed their time alone, just like women. If her father wanted to eat at the Sunnyside with a friend, why not?

Lily parked and got out of the car. The morning hadn't grown too hot yet, and the breeze was pleasant on her bare legs and arms. Tyler used to hate it when she wore shorts in public. He believed shorts were lower class. At the house or on the tennis court, fine, but not out in public, in full view of neighbors and strangers. She used to ignore him and wear shorts, anyway. Could a woman drive her husband to drink by wearing shorts?

Out of respect, she wouldn't let herself be pleased that she no longer had a husband to criticize her wardrobe or blame her for his own shortcomings. She would accept what happened, accept her role in it, but refuse to take any more than that onto her shoulders.

As she neared the café, she spotted her father through the glass door. He was standing at the front counter, talking to Aaron's mother. In the relative dimness of the café, Evie Mazerik's hair didn't look quite as garish as Lily remembered. Her eyes were animated, nowhere near as beautiful as Aaron's, but sparkly and lively and quite pretty. She must have been a knockout in her youth, before unwed motherhood and hard work and health problems wore her down.

Julian Bennett leaned toward Evie, hands resting on the counter. His gaze was gentle, his mouth curved in a kind smile. Evie seemed to be doing most of the talking, but her father had always been a good listener. He nodded, said something, grinned at something Evie said. Straightening, he reached across the counter and gave her hand a squeeze. Then he turned toward the door.

Lily fell back a step. She didn't want her father to see her spying on him. Being solicitous with his neighbors and patients was simply part of who he was, a large part, but he'd probably be embarrassed if he knew she'd secretly caught him in the act of being compassionate.

He emerged into the sunlight and blinked. While he was still squinting to adjust his vision, Lily walked over to him. "Hey, Dad."

He spun toward her. His face broke into a smile. "Lily! What a surprise!" He opened his arms and she moved into them for a hug. Fifteen years ago she would rather have plunged headfirst into a compost heap than hug her father in public. One of the great gifts of maturity was that it allowed you to express affection for your parents openly.

"Were you having brunch?" she asked.

"Hmm?" He glanced back at the café. "No. I was taking care of some business. I just stopped in there to see how Evie Mazerik is doing. I don't know if you know her..."

"I do," Lily said, although that wasn't precisely true. She knew Evie's son, and wanted to know him better. "I understand she had a stroke."

Her father's lips thinned as he nodded. "She refuses to quit smoking. I swear, women can be so exasperating. Not all women, of course," he hastily added, beaming proudly at her. "You're not. You're perfect."

She felt a sharp twinge inside, a mix of guilt and self-loathing. She was not perfect. Not even close. She carried a big, dark stain on her heart, and nothing was ever going to wash it away.

Perhaps someday she would tell her father. He'd learn what his darling daughter, his could-do-no-wrong princess had done, and he'd never call her perfect again.

"Mom said you were golfing this morning," Lily told him.

His lips thinned again. "Your mother makes assumptions sometimes. She thinks if I'm going out on a Saturday morning, it can mean only one thing. If she'd opened her eyes, she might have noticed that I didn't take my clubs with me when I left."

The wry tone of his voice unnerved Lily, but she plowed ahead, anyway. "I wanted to talk to you about her. Do you have a minute?"

"To talk about your mother?" He frowned, then checked his watch. "Is something wrong?"

"Well, she's going to be turning sixty soon."

His expression relaxed. "Sixty isn't fatal. I'm a doctor. Trust me, there's no pathology in it."

She laughed at his joke. "You survived it fine," she agreed. "Mom threw a big party for you at the golf club." Lily had flown home for the festivities, happily leaving Tyler back in Cohasset and making excuses for him to her family. Too much work, she'd said. A big complicated merger he was involved in. He *had* been working on a merger; despite his weaknesses, he'd been an outstanding corporate attorney, sober until the moment he walked into their home each day at sunset. He'd been born into phenomenal wealth, but he'd added to it every day with his high-pressure, high-power work.

He could have taken the weekend off to attend her father's birthday party, though. Lily had talked him out of accompanying her. She'd been afraid he would start downing martinis, complaining all the while about the mediocre quality of the spirits and acting condescending toward her parents' friends, making snide remarks about his small-town wife, and her family would realize what a travesty her marriage was.

Shaking off the dismal recollection, Lily dragged her mind back into the present, the future. "I think we ought to start planning something for her birthday," she said. "Or at least we should be thinking about what we want to do for her."

Her father shifted his weight, sliding into the shadow cast by the building behind him. Even at sixty-two, he was extremely handsome, his complexion sun-bronzed, his eyes a silvery blue, his nose straight and his teeth even. He still had all his hair, graying only at the temples. He could have passed for a model or a movie star.

He considered Lily's suggestion thoughtfully. "What do you think she'd like? Not a party."

Probably not. Eleanor Bennett was nowhere near as gregarious as her husband.

"Jewelry?" he asked.

"Or maybe a trip. A cruise."

"A week at a golf resort."

"Dad." Lily laughed, and her father did, too. "This is for Mom, not for you." Despite her laughter, she was irked that her father didn't know what her mother might like. He'd lived with her for thirty-seven years. Surely he ought to have an inkling about whether or not she would appreciate a new piece of jewelry. "Maybe she'd like to spend a few days at a spa."

"A spa?" Her father looked perplexed. "Whatever for?"

Did he really not have a clue? Didn't he know his wife was buying anti-aging creams and reviving her hair with a new cut and a gray-concealing color? Wasn't he even remotely aware that she seemed to be approaching a significant birthday with less than wholehearted enthusiasm?

"I think she's worried about getting old," Lily said.

He frowned again. "That's silly. Getting old is better than *not* getting old."

His lack of sensitivity surprised Lily. He could be so considerate with his patients, yet he seemed to lack sympathy for the woman he was married to. "Aging isn't always easy for a woman," she said. "I may be wrong, but I think Mom is apprehensive about turning sixty."

"I haven't noticed," her father said.

She tamped down a surge of annoyance. He should have noticed. If he'd paid enough attention, he would have.

But she didn't want to be angry with her father.

Not this man whom she'd adored all her life. "I just think we ought to do something special for her birthday. Sixty is a milestone. Remember the party she hosted for you? She deserves something that big."

"I thought we already decided I shouldn't host a party. Have you changed your mind?"

His obtuseness annoyed her. Surely he knew Eleanor would feel uncomfortable being the center of attention at a fancy catered party. She loved arranging celebrations for others, but had never liked being feted herself.

"No," Lily said, joining her father in the shade so she could see him better. "I haven't changed my mind. Don't host a party. Mom wouldn't enjoy it."

"You really think she'd want to go to a spa?" He studied Lily, his brow furrowed. "You've been living a different sort of life from what we're used to in Riverbend, Lily. People around here don't go to spas."

It distressed her that she might have come across sounding like a snob. Even when she'd been attending fund-raisers and seeing her photo in the "Party Lines" column of the *Boston Globe,* she'd never fit in with the society of women who went to spas. She'd never gone to one; she couldn't picture herself with mud on her face and cucumber slices on her eyes, with strangers massaging every inch of her and dietitians prescribing microscopic portions of food—and charging her a fortune.

But that wasn't what she'd had in mind for her mother. She'd been thinking about a day of being pampered—a facial, a manicure to repair the nails she was forever chipping and breaking as she gardened, a pedicure just for the luxury of it and—why not?—a massage. Something that would make her mother feel beautiful and special. Something that would make her feel loved.

"All right," she said. "A cruise. Or fly to Hawaii. Just the two of you. Something romantic."

"Lily." Her father sighed, buried his hands in his trouser pockets and gave her a bewildered smile. "This is your mother and me you're talking about. We've been together forever. Running off to Hawaii…"

"Would be romantic."

"Would be terribly out of character for us. We're not like that."

Was he implying that he thought she *was*? Did her own father view her as a jet-setter? She had come back to Riverbend, hadn't she? She'd settled in, bought a house, reverted to the earnest, loyal town resident she'd always been.

No, not quite. She might have settled in and bought a house, but she'd also shared her secrets with Aaron Mazerik. And kissed him. Which was terribly out of character.

But people changed. Her father needed to give her mother a long, close look. Lily might be wrong, but surely she wasn't the only person transformed by time and circumstance. Maybe she wasn't the only one ready to abandon her watercolors and try to view the world through the vivid textured medium of acrylics.

Maybe her mother, like her, just needed a little goading to find the courage to stop playing it safe.

CHAPTER SEVEN

WALLY DRUMMER was already seated at a table when Aaron arrived at the Sunnyside Café at three-thirty Monday afternoon. Tall and tan, Wally looked better now than he had when he'd been coaching the high-school basketball team. Back then, of course, Aaron had viewed him through the eyes of an angry, alienated fifteen-year-old, a kid in far too much debt to the brusque burly coach who'd ventured into the police station one morning to shoot the breeze with his buddy Frank Garvey and noticed Aaron sitting in the holding cell.

"That's one of my kids," Wally had said, crossing to the cell.

Aaron remembered how he'd shrunk back on the bench, pressing his body against the cold cinder-block wall. In a lifetime of bad nights, the one he'd just spent had been the worst. His mother hadn't come for him. No one had come. He'd sat by himself all night, unable to sleep, unable to think about anything other than how alone he was. He'd refused the breakfast the clerk had given him, and he'd refused to speak when Frank Garvey had transferred him the two blocks to the courthouse to be arraigned. "I'll enter a plea of not guilty for you," the judge had said. "One hundred dollars' bond. Take him back to the station house, Officer. He's too young for my jail.''

Once he was back in the holding cell, the clerk had tried one more time to get him to eat. He couldn't. His stomach ached from rage, not hunger.

Through the bars he saw the phys-ed teacher from his high school, a man he didn't know too well because he'd spent more of his phys-ed classes cutting out to have a smoke than doing jumping jacks and situps in the gym. What he knew of Drummer he didn't like. The guy had a temper. He shouted a lot. He thought Aaron was a screw-up, which certainly didn't make the coach unique among the Riverbend High School faculty.

''What's he doing in here?'' Wally asked.

''I found him in an alley last night, drinking beer.''

Wally approached the holding cell, a tall looming figure through the bars. ''Drinking beer, huh?''

''It's not the first time I've caught him loitering late at night when he ought to be at home. Caught him drinking before, too. He's gotten more than his share of warnings. And he was working his way through a six-pack. He had an empty on the ground next to him and four more sitting unopened, nice and cold, waiting for him to work his way through them. I couldn't just give him a slap on the wrist and send him home.''

Sure, Aaron had thought. The cops in Riverbend had nothing better to do than to arrest a guy for chugging a couple of beers in an alley.

''You can't lock him up,'' Drummer argued.

"He's one of the stars on my team. How do I get him out of there?"

Aaron was certain he'd misheard Drummer. One of the stars on his team? Hardly. He was no athlete. If he'd pursued any sport, it would have been track— he was good at running away from people like Garvey. But sports meant going to school every day, and staying after school for the team practices. It meant hanging out with the jocks, the insiders, kids like the River Rats. Well-bred, studious, popular kids. Kids who knew who their fathers were. Kids who would never drink beer in an alley at midnight.

To say nothing of the fact that the only basketball Aaron ever played, outside of the few gym classes he didn't cut, was shooting hoops in the street outside the duplex where he lived, tossing the ball through the rusty ring the landlord had nailed to a tree.

But there was Drummer, writing a check for Aaron's bond and getting him released from the holding cell. Too dazed and exhausted from his sleepless night to question why the coach had lied and put out his own money to spring him, Aaron followed Drummer out of the police station and into the glaring morning sun. "You look like you could use some breakfast," Drummer observed.

"Not at the Sunnyside." Aaron's mother would be there—she generally worked from before breakfast to midafternoon—and he didn't want to see her, not after she'd made him spend the night in jail. At that point, he would have been happy never to see her again.

Drummer drove Aaron to the Burger Barn on the outskirts of town. He bought a jumbo coffee for himself and a fried-egg sandwich and a large milk for Aaron. They sat on one of the picnic tables beneath the awning out front, and Aaron wolfed down the food. Hot breakfasts were a rare treat for him.

Drummer still hadn't spoken by the time Aaron finished his sandwich. He'd studied the man across the table from him. Drummer had a stern face, with blunt features and iron-colored hair, but without a whistle on a cord around his neck he seemed a little less intimidating, a little less official.

"You're a good kid, Mazerik," Drummer said.

"Yeah, right." Aaron swigged some milk, admitting to himself that it tasted better than cheap beer.

"I know you've got it in your head that you aren't, and you're doing your damnedest to live up to your lousy self-image—or live down to it, I guess I should say."

Terrific. Drummer was going to psychoanalyze him. What a way to celebrate the end of his incarceration.

"The fact is, you *could* be a star on my team."

"Not in this life."

"Yes, in this life."

Aaron dissected Drummer's statement for any hint that he was joking, but found none. "I don't want to be on your team."

"You're wrong," Drummer argued. "You do."

Aaron risked a glance at him. The coach's eyes were the same color as his hair—dark gray. They were also cold. "I'm not into sports."

"You are now," Drummer said. "I just bought you. I own you. You're going to play for me."

"What is this? Slavery is illegal."

"Ah, so you've learned something in your history classes." Drummer stretched his long legs out under the table, kicking one of Aaron's boots with his sneaker. "You're tall, you're strong and you're fast. I need you on the team. And you need me in your life."

"I don't need anybody."

"You need someone who cares enough about you not to put up with your crap. And that's me, Mazerik. Get used to it. Be at practice Monday after school."

Aaron stared at him in disbelief.

"Oh, and no more beer. Or cigarettes. No smokers on my team. My boys take care of their bodies. It's a rule."

"Shove your rules," Aaron retorted, swinging his legs over the bench and rising to his feet. "Sorry you blew your money on me, Coach. But thanks for breakfast."

"You planning to walk home from here?"

Aaron halted in the dirt lot. At least two miles of hard hiking stretched between the Burger Barn and his house, but he'd hiked farther than that before, lots of times. Yet he didn't seem able to take the first step that morning. He wasn't able to walk away from the man whose will was as steely as his voice.

Everything Drummer had said was true—especially the part about him needing someone in his life who cared enough not to put up with his crap.

Without another word, the coach opened the passenger door of his car. Aaron climbed in. Drummer drove him home. And Aaron showed up for practice Monday afternoon.

Quitting cigarettes had taken a couple of difficult

months. Getting the other kids on the team to acknowledge him had taken a lot longer. If not for Jacob Steele, the team's captain and undisputed leader, they would never have accepted him. He'd been only a sophomore, the youngest player. Worse, he'd been who he was, a kid who'd spent a lot of his life in trouble, a kid who didn't fit in anywhere, a kid who played basketball not because he took pride in the school or wanted to be cool but because he was so damned pissed off at Drummer for having purchased him like a slave. He'd show Drummer. He'd play like a freaking fiend, just to show him.

Had he once hated Drummer that much? Had he once cringed when he heard the man's voice, when he saw the metallic glint in his eyes? Despite the fifteen years that had passed since Aaron had marched out of Riverbend High School with a diploma clenched in his fist, Drummer was still Coach. Even if Aaron now had the man's old job, Wally Drummer would always be Coach.

"You look beat," Drummer said as Aaron slid into the booth facing him. "Are the players running you ragged?"

"You should know," Aaron joked, shoving his hair out of his face and settling back against the stiff vinyl upholstery. This week's group of children participating in the basketball program were just as energetic as last week's—but this week's group also included Mitch Sterling's son, Sam. Aaron had his hands full, literally, trying to communicate with the boy. "I've got a player who can't hear," he told Drummer.

"Really? How are you managing that?"

Just then Lucy Garvey approached the table to take their orders. Drummer asked how she was doing and traded jokes with her about her late husband's uncle Frank. As soon as he and Aaron had both ordered iced tea, Aaron answered Drummer's question.

"The thing with Sam is, I've got to stay with him so I can tap him on the shoulder when I need to say something. If I get his attention, I can mouth the words and use my hands, and I think he gets what I'm telling him. But I can't blow my whistle and expect him to hear it."

"So he's making you run more than usual. Good for him. He'll keep you in shape."

"Hey, I'm in great shape," Aaron bragged, then laughed again. "The kid's got potential. He can't depend on his ears, so he depends on his eyes twice as much. He always knows where everyone on the court is."

The iced tea arrived and Aaron took a grateful swallow, savoring its coldness as it washed down his throat. Another gulp, and then he got around to adding some sugar.

"So, where did the money come from?" Drummer asked.

Aaron's head jerked up. "What money?"

"I hear you hired a lifeguard for the swimming pool."

"An hour a day. I think it'll work out."

"And you've lined up one of your high-school players to run the program with you, so you can expand it."

"How'd you find out about all this?"

Drummer chuckled. "We're in Riverbend, Maz. Everybody knows everything around here."

"I don't," Aaron complained, although he was grinning. "I'm not in the loop."

Drummer refused to let Aaron derail the conversation. "So, where did the money come from?"

"If you know everything, you should know that." In truth, Aaron didn't want to tell his old coach the source of the program's newfound riches. Partly, he wanted to protect Lily; if word got out that she'd given his program a donation, everyone would be pestering her for money. But more than that, Aaron didn't want to speak her name. He didn't even want to think about her. Every time he did—and it was far too often—his uneasiness returned, his self-loathing…and his inexcusable longing for her.

Fortunately he hadn't seen her since her mysterious visit to his house Friday night. A whole weekend and most of Monday he hadn't seen her anywhere except in his dreams—or maybe his nightmares.

"I received a donation," he finally said, because he knew the coach wasn't going to let up until he got an answer. "The donor wants anonymity."

"Really?" Drummer twirled his straw in his glass. "Why?"

"Like you said, it's a small town. If that's what the donor wants, that's what the donor gets."

"Well, it's a lucky break. I think your summer program is a great idea, Aaron. I should have thought of something like it myself when I was coaching the school team."

"You had a full plate at the time," Aaron reminded him. "You had all you could handle dealing with jackasses like me." He grinned.

"If there's anything I can do to help with the program…"

"No, it's going fine. As long as the school board doesn't charge me too much to use the pool, we're all set. The kids really need some time in the water. All that running around, they get so hot. They need the chance to cool off." He took a long sip of iced tea. He needed to cool off, too. "So how are you fighting the heat? Does that window unit do the job in your house?"

"Actually, we didn't need it this past week. We were visiting Megan." Drummer's daughter was some sort of high-tech genius in Seattle. She was a few years younger than Aaron; by the time she'd started high school he'd already left Riverbend. All he knew about her was what Drummer had told him: she was a computer whiz, she couldn't care less about sports and she was something of a loner, the way Aaron had been. Unlike Aaron, of course, she was a loner by inclination and choice.

Drummer used to talk to Aaron about his quiet, bookish daughter. He'd worried that she didn't socialize enough, didn't seem to have enough friends. He'd even to ask Aaron what he could do to help Megan.

Aaron had appreciated that his mentor actually trusted him enough to turn to him for advice. "With you as a father," Aaron used to assure him, "she's going to come through high school in a lot better shape than I did."

What an understatement that had been. She had

soared through high school and won a scholarship to Cal-Tech, and now she was doing something important in the computer industry, work so esoteric Drummer couldn't even describe it.

He told Aaron about the visit he and his wife had had with their daughter in the Northwest, where the sun shone only two days out of the six they'd been there and the temperature never climbed above seventy. Then the conversation wandered back to the high school, to Riverbend's prospects for the upcoming basketball season, to Aaron's mother, who apparently had made a fuss over Drummer when he'd entered the café today—Aaron was glad he'd arrived late enough to miss that—and from there to Abraham Steele's memorial service. "Any idea why Jacob didn't come back?" Drummer asked.

"You'd know better than me, Coach." Aaron sipped more iced tea. The second half of the glass was always more lemony than the first. The sour tang made his tongue curl.

"I haven't heard from him since just before he graduated from college," Drummer said. "He always used to drop by to see me while he was home from the university. All of a sudden I stopped hearing from him. Like he'd fallen off the face of the earth."

"Maybe he got sick of Riverbend," Aaron suggested wryly. "It's been known to happen."

"Don't give me that. You came back."

"I'm still wondering why."

They exchanged a smile. They both knew why he'd come back, and his mother's health had been only half of it. The other half had been Wally Drummer, telling him he could take over the basketball team if he was willing to remain in town, telling him he could demonstrate to Riverbend just how much a person could change. Aaron hated the thought of becoming a symbol or a role model, but the fact was, he'd been helping troubled kids in Indianapolis and he could help troubled kids here, too. He could prove to the town that had pretty much given up on him that *no* kid was ever worth giving up on.

If not for Drummer, Aaron would have stayed in town long enough to make sure his mother could cope on her own and then left. On the other hand, if not for Drummer, Aaron might well have been enjoying a prolonged stay in the state penitentiary by now. Drummer had saved his butt. If he wanted him to take over the high-school team, Aaron wasn't going to say no.

"My wife told me the ladies in her bridge club have all kinds of theories about Jacob," Drummer said. "One of them thinks he's living in Europe."

"Europe?" Aaron snorted.

"Another thinks he got married, and his wife hated Abraham so much she made Jacob sever all ties with his hometown."

"Don't those ladies have anything better to do than invent stories about Jacob? Maybe they should concentrate on their bridge."

"Bridge clubs have very little to do with playing bridge." Drummer grinned indulgently, then glanced at his watch. "I should be heading home. One thing about retirement, you eat dinner much earlier. Mary likes dinner on the table by five-thirty, and I can't very well tell her I'm going to be late because I'm running a team practice."

Aaron checked his watch, as well. Four-thirty. He drained his glass and stood up. He and Drummer both knew they'd be meeting again soon for an iced tea or a beer and maybe a game of pool. Aaron had no blood ties to the man, but Drummer was the closest thing to a father Aaron had ever had. In some ways, he was the closest thing to a mother, too.

Evie Mazerik smiled at both of them as they approached the front counter to pay. Her smile for Aaron was the usual—slightly astonished and abundantly proud that her son had turned out as well as he had—but for Drummer it seemed almost coquettish. "You still taking care of this boy?" she asked, her eyes sparkling with amusement.

"Actually, no, Evie. He's taking care of me," Drummer said as Aaron handed his mother a five-dollar bill. "I'm retired, you know. Fixed income and all that."

"I raised Aaron to be generous," she boasted, even though that wasn't even remotely true. "How is that daughter of yours doing, Wally? I hear you were out visiting her."

"She's great."

"This town needs some women in it. Younger women. Don't you think Aaron ought to think about settling down? Thirty-three years old. I think it's time. Don't you, Wally?"

"Aaron doesn't need any input from us, Evie," Wally said tactfully.

Aaron didn't need this entire conversation. His mother was in no position to counsel him about settling down. Besides, he couldn't think about women until he got over his despicable obsession with Lily Holden.

Drummer gave Evie a pat on the shoulder. "You take care, now, Evie."

Aaron pocketed his change, nodded a farewell to his mother and followed Drummer out of the café. "She ought to join your wife's bridge club," he muttered. "She's got more gossip inside her than all your wife's friends combined."

"Has she got a theory about Jacob Steele missing his father's funeral?"

"Let's see… He might be living on a beach estate in the Bahamas, or he might be dead."

"I like the first better than the second." Coach shrugged, then extended his hand to Aaron. "I'll give you a call. Let me know how the swimming pool works out. And for God's sake, if you've got the money, pay yourself a salary."

"If I can, I will," Aaron promised. "I have to see how fast I burn through the budget on other necessities for the program first." Something entered his vision peripherally, a flicker, a glint, a sharp sudden stab: Lily Holden just across the street, a few yards down, entering the bookstore.

He ordered himself to forget he'd seen her. But he couldn't forget. Knowing she was there had the effect of spilling ink over his brain. Every other thought was obliterated, submerged beneath the spreading black. All he could remember was the cause of the spill. Lily.

He gave a reflexive wave as Drummer headed down the sidewalk to his shiny new pickup truck. He stared without seeing as Drummer got in, revved the

engine and pulled into the flow of traffic. Then, un-
thinkingly, Aaron crossed the street to the bookstore.

She was somewhere inside, not visible from the
sidewalk, but he'd seen her enter, so he knew she
was there. And knowing that, he knew what he had
to do: make a U-turn and walk away, keep walking
until he'd reached his own car and then drive away,
and keep driving.

He went into the bookstore.

Lily wasn't in the front area of the store. He hadn't
seen her leave, but she might have wandered around
to the apartment where the Steele sisters lived, which
was connected to the store. Ruth and Rachel had
owned the store forever, but in the two years since
Aaron had moved back to town, Kate McCann
seemed to be handling most of the day-to-day oper-
ations. And after losing their brother so recently, the
sisters were probably even more dependent on Kate.

She was at the counter, chatting with a plump mid-
dle-aged woman who looked familiar to Aaron. But
then, everyone in town looked familiar to him, which
might just mean he'd been here in Riverbend too
long. When Kate caught his eye, he gave her a slight
nod, then moved past the carpeted front area, a
lounge where, he supposed, people could sit and
read, although he couldn't imagine pulling a brand-
new book from a shelf, reading it and then putting it
back on the shelf without paying for it.

He wandered through the lounge to the shelves
and pretended to browse. He was close to finishing
the Grisham he'd bought a couple of weeks ago. But
he had a new legal thriller, one recommended by
Kate, sitting on his dresser, so he didn't really want

to buy anything. What he wanted was what he shouldn't want: to see Lily, to talk to her. To torture himself by standing close to her and gazing into her magnificent eyes—and feeling like some kind of depraved creep for desiring her.

He spotted her in the art section, leafing through a coffee-table book. Her back was to him, which gave him the opportunity to study her undetected. She had her hair pulled into a ponytail, held with a silver clip, and she wore neat khaki shorts and a white T-shirt made out of some kind of fancy fabric that created intriguing shadows as it draped from her shoulders to her narrow waist. Her bottom was small and round, and her legs were slim. He'd never seen them before; she'd always been wearing either jeans or a long skirt. Her thighs and calves were tan and taut, as if she worked out or played tennis. Her ankles were absurdly slender.

He swallowed. Gorgeous legs, gorgeous figure and gorgeous golden hair. The urges she aroused in him were exactly the sort that would prompt a decent brother to slug any man who experienced them. Maybe he should slug himself.

No. He should turn around and leave. That was what he should do.

But she pivoted, and her smile at seeing him was so spontaneous, so obviously pleased, he couldn't move. "Aaron!"

"Hi." He swallowed again, took a deep breath and moved toward her, as if he hadn't been swamped with X-rated thoughts, as if she wasn't his half sister, as if there was nothing wrong with their smiling at the sight of each other.

"I decided I needed a new book of art prints. I'm looking for inspiration," she told him. "I'm trying not to be safe."

He wasn't sure what she was talking about, although he guessed it had something to do with her painting. "You don't need a book for inspiration," he said.

"Not inspiration," she conceded. "Courage." She extended the book she'd been thumbing through. He took it, balanced its heavy weight in his palms and checked out the cover: *Renaissance Masters*. Then he opened it to the page she'd been admiring and scrutinized the print. The painting featured a pale naked woman with a pot belly and pudgy thighs, her hair fluttering in ribbons about her face and plump little angels flying bare-ass around her head.

That would teach him to open his mouth. He'd made one comment about her watercolor rendering of a jug and pear, and now she was sharing great art with him as if she thought he was an expert. What the hell kind of painting was this? The woman was fat. The angels were fat. They'd all look a lot better with some clothing on them.

They were the opposite of Lily.

And that was an unforgivable thought.

"Um…what is this?" he asked cautiously.

"It's a Titian. Have you ever heard of him?"

"He was a Renaissance master," Aaron guessed, flipping to the cover of the book.

She took it back from him. "You need an education," she said, grinning. "Maybe I ought to buy this for you."

"Don't do me any favors."

"Then I'll buy it for me. I haven't bought an art book in years." She flipped a page, sighed with apparent delight at another painting of a fat naked woman and closed the book with a thud. "Maybe I ought to audit an art course at the college this fall. What do you think?"

He didn't know what he thought, other than that her asking him his opinion about what she should do struck him as uncomfortably intimate. Of course she should audit an art course if it would make her happy. Then again, she might find an art course boring. She'd finished her education more than a decade ago. She could probably *teach* an art course at the local college as easily as take one.

His silence tweaked her. "You think I'm a pest, that's what you think."

"No." He thought she was beautiful and elegant and her shirt looked like silk, and he'd bet all the money she donated to the summer program that her skin felt silkier than the shirt. He thought she was the worst temptation he'd ever faced. He thought talking with her on his deck last Friday night was one of the highlights of his life, even though she'd been in tears for most of the conversation.

He thought he was in big trouble.

"Are you free tomorrow night?" she asked.

Oh, God. *Very* big trouble. "I don't know," he answered, a flat-out lie. He knew damned well he was free tomorrow, and he knew damned well he should tell her he wasn't. But he was hedging, hoping, playing with fire.

"I was thinking about having some friends over

to celebrate the Fourth of July, after the parade. Nothing fancy.''

She wanted him to come to her house to celebrate the Fourth of July? With a bunch of her River Rat buddies? *What's wrong with this picture?* he thought, suppressing a wry smile.

''I don't think so,'' he started to say, but when she touched his forearm and gazed into his eyes, the words got stuck in his throat. He felt something akin to an electric shock searing through him, jolting his entire nervous system with sizzling heat.

''I haven't had any of my friends over to the house since I bought it,'' she admitted, her eyes still locked with his. ''I don't even know if they'll come.''

''Of course they'll come,'' he said, his voice sounding tight to him. ''Why wouldn't they?''

''Because... Just because.'' Apparently that was all the explanation she could manage. She sighed, then tried again. ''Because they don't know about me.''

And Aaron did. Aaron knew about her because she'd told him, and what he knew didn't seem particularly troublesome. She'd had a bad marriage. Her husband was dead. Now she was back in town. End of story.

''There's no reason for your friends to stop being your friends, Lily,'' he assured her. ''Even if they knew, they'd still be your friends.''

She didn't appear entirely convinced, but she gave him a brave smile. ''So I can count on you to be there?''

Damn. No. She couldn't count on him.

''I'd like to think of you as my friend, Aaron,''

she murmured so earnestly the current buzzing through his body jumped a few volts. "I know we weren't friends when we were younger, but we're friends now, aren't we?"

They were more than friends. And less. But like a man under a spell he nodded. "Sure."

"Then I'll see you tomorrow night," she said, releasing his arm and sending him such a sunny smile he couldn't seem to muster a protest.

Later he would regret this, he thought as she waltzed toward the counter to pay for *Renaissance Masters*. Later he would call himself seven kinds of a fool for agreeing to go to her house—if he'd actually agreed to go. He wasn't sure he had.

But he hadn't said no. He hadn't *wanted* to say no. Damn it, he wanted to be her friend.

CHAPTER EIGHT

WHATEVER HAD POSSESSED HER to tell Aaron she was inviting friends over to her house after the Fourth of July parade?

Aaron had possessed her. She'd seen him and felt brave, the way she always seemed to feel brave when he was near. The art book might give her courage, but true courage—like Aaron's, the courage to stand tall despite one's background, one's mistakes and transgressions, one's insecurities and fears—didn't come from a book. It came from character.

So she would make a few calls and see who was available after the parade. She would have her friends over to her house—*all* her friends, not just the old ones but the new one, the special one. Aaron.

She didn't have a barbecue grill, but that was all right. Back in Cohasset, it would have been considered déclassé to host a barbecue on July Fourth. The parties she and Tyler used to attend at the club had been studiedly casual, with towers of shrimp and cold cracked crab, squab instead of chicken, polenta instead of corn on the cob, and exquisite blueberry-and-strawberry tarts with whipped cream—red, white and blue. Microbrewery beers rather than the usual brands—although, of course, Tyler had skipped those for more potent spirits. She'd always driven home after those parties. She'd insisted on that, despite Tyler's voluble protests that he was perfectly capable of taking the wheel.

Merely thinking about his protests made her shudder.

All right. Tomorrow was a day to honor the courage of the nation's founders. If they could declare their independence from England, surely she could find the nerve to declare her independence from the ghosts of her past, the sins of her marriage. Surely she could find comfort with her friends.

RIVERBEND'S FOURTH OF JULY parade hadn't changed much since Aaron's childhood. As it had then, it still started with a caravan of fire engines, all blaring their sirens and deafening the throngs lining the sidewalks along the Courthouse Square. After the fire engines came the kids on bicycles, their handlebars draped with red, white and blue crepe-paper streamers. Then a fellow on stilts, dressed as Uncle Sam. A few clowns. Mayor Baden and her husband, waving to the crowds as they cruised along in a Chevy convertible. A Conestoga wagon. Floats, some advertising the downtown stores, others highlighting various civic organizations. The garden club's float was covered with flowers. Killian's float featured high schoolers posing like models on its flatbed. The local grange float held bales of hay with kids in overalls and straw hats perched on them, waving.

Aaron could have sworn this year's bales of hay were identical to the bales on the grange floats of his youth. He could have sworn the same guy was teetering on those stilts, portraying Uncle Sam. The only change between then and now, as far as he could tell, was that Abraham Steele wasn't in this year's parade, seated with the mayor in the convertible and waving to the onlookers.

The only other change was inside himself. As a child, he'd always felt as if he hadn't belonged at the parade. His classmates used to stand along the curb, waving small flags and diving for the hard candies that people tossed at them from the floats. Sometimes they'd climb onto the mailboxes and fire hydrants, or sometimes they'd swerve their own bicycles into the street and ride along with their friends on the decorated bikes. They'd watch in groups, in gangs, munching on cotton candy and hot dogs, laughing and jostling each other. They'd never asked Aaron to join them, and he never had.

Sometimes he'd watch the parade with the other outsiders—the farm kids who'd traveled into town just for the parade, the kids who journeyed to school on long bus rides on the county roads. They were isolated the way he was, removed from the social world of Riverbend. They never objected if he wanted to stand with them as the parade passed by.

Today, however, the moment he reached the square after parking his car on East Chestnut Street and walking the few blocks to the parade route, Mitch Sterling waved him over. He had Sam with him, and Sam gave him a shiny grin as he approached. The boy clutched a flag and wore a cap with the Indiana Pacers logo above the visor.

"Hot, isn't it?" Mitch observed, adjusting his own hat, which featured the logo of a tractor brand on it.

"Sure is," Aaron agreed. The sun beat down on his head, making him wish he'd worn a hat, too. Around him children pressed close, smelling like bubble gum and popcorn and fruit-flavored ices. Half a block down, across the street, he saw his mother seated on a lawn chair next to her landlord and his wife. She'd phoned Aaron that morning and told him she wouldn't need a ride to the parade, which had been a relief because until he'd left his house he hadn't been sure he would even come.

He'd come not because he wanted to remember those long-ago parades when he'd woven among the crowds, feeling cold stares on his back, feeling the absence of a group to hang out with, but because he figured everyone at Lily's house would be talking about the parade and he'd feel pretty stupid if he had nothing to contribute to the discussion. Attending Riverbend's July Fourth parade was practically a civic obligation. Aaron wouldn't have minded skipping that obligation, but he'd mind people knowing he'd skipped it.

So he was here.

Sam Sterling tugged his arm and pointed at the vendor across the street, his cart straining beneath a colorful load of flags, megaphones, bicycle horns, balloons, whistles and other generally useless trinkets. "Don't buy him anything," Mitch warned. "He doesn't realize how obnoxious most of those noise-makers are."

Aaron smiled. He wondered whether Mitch was going to be at Lily's house later. Then again, he still hadn't decided whether *he* would be there.

Yes, he had. She'd said she would see him tonight,

and he hadn't disagreed. So he would go. Even if seeing her made him crazy. Even if he'd be much better off staying as far away from her as he could.

A chorus of wails tore through the afternoon heat, the fire-engine caravan wending its way toward the Courthouse Square to launch the parade. Children squealed and scampered, their energy revved up by the noise. Parents leaned out over the curbs, as if they couldn't wait to see the lead engine. As Aaron felt the summer sun bake him on the outside, a different kind of warmth filled him from inside, an unwelcome warmth, the warmth Lily had been stoking in him since the day she'd stepped out of the art classroom and into his consciousness so many years ago.

He really shouldn't go to her house that evening. But he knew he would.

CHARLIE CALLAHAN was out on the back porch, seated in one of the wicker chairs with his feet propped on the railing, when Lily emerged from the kitchen with a chilled bottle of beer for him. "That was Grace on the phone," she reported. "Her daughter ate too much junk food at the parade and has a tummy ache. So they're not coming."

Charlie accepted the beer with a sigh. "Kids can really spoil plans," he said. "So is it just you and me tonight?"

"No," she answered, although her gathering had shrunk drastically between conception and execution. Mitch had been unable to attend, since he'd already agreed to go with Sam to a barbecue at the home of one of Sam's friends. Erin and Joe Wilson had other plans for the holiday. Lily shouldn't have waited until the last minute to ask people over.

But she couldn't force herself to be disappointed that her Fourth-of-July gathering was going to consist of only three people—assuming Aaron didn't also back out at the last minute. Two guests—one of her oldest friends, and her newest—were plenty for her first attempt at entertaining.

"Who else is coming?"

"Aaron Mazerik."

Charlie's gaze swung to her and his brows shot skyward. "Aaron Mazerik?"

"We've talked a few times. We've gotten friendly." *I can confide in him,* she almost said. *I trust him as much as I trust you. Maybe even more.*

"Really."

"He's changed since high school. Of course, we all have." She had, probably more than anyone else. "I like him," she added. "He seems like a good man." She smiled, aware that Charlie was gaping at her as if she'd just announced she was planning to tattoo a bloody dagger onto her forehead. "You two must know each other pretty well. You helped him rebuild Old Man Miller's cabin when he bought it, didn't you?"

"Yeah, we get along," Charlie confirmed. "But...*Aaron Mazerik?* How in the world did you get together with him?"

Lily pursed her lips and stared out at the yellow roses climbing the trellis frame abutting her garage. She hadn't "gotten together" with Aaron, but she contemplated getting together with him shamefully often. She spent too many idle hours picturing his eyes, his mouth and the rippling surface of his chest and abdomen. She dreamed about things she shouldn't, things good girls didn't think about, things a grieving widow shouldn't want.

That wasn't why she'd invited him over, however. If she'd wanted to seduce him, she wouldn't have asked Charlie to join them, or the Penningtons, or Mitch, or Erin and Joe. And she *didn't* want to seduce Aaron. She was a long way from being that brave. When she thought about Aaron's eyes and mouth and body, she was only indulging in a little harmless fantasizing, something she hadn't done since she'd met Tyler. She was only exercising her imagination to make sure it still worked.

The evening was hot but not humid. Charlie appeared comfortable in a pair of khaki shorts and a plaid shirt. Lily was wearing one of her thousand-dollar summer dresses and hoping it didn't look as expensive as it was. She went back into the kitchen to get the bowl of mixed nuts and the platter of vegetables and dip she'd fixed. Before she could lift them, she heard the doorbell chime.

A dark tingle fluttered through her. She braced herself for the sight of him and strolled through the kitchen, down the hall to the front door.

He stood on the porch, clad in a pair of faded jeans, a navy blue shirt and sandals. Seeing him sent another dark tingle through her. Aaron Mazerik had a stunning physique. As an artist, as a woman, Lily was aware of such things. All too aware.

She smiled, and her smile relaxed her as much as she hoped it would relax him. ''Thanks for coming,'' she said, beckoning him inside. "Charlie Callahan's on the back porch with a beer. Would you like one?"

Aaron entered the foyer without speaking. His gaze wandered across her face and down her body, making her feel a little less relaxed. She kept her smile in place, though, a defensive shield against his attractiveness.

"I'd love a beer," he finally said, his voice surprisingly quiet.

All right, maybe she'd made a big mistake inviting him over. Maybe she wasn't ready to accept the temptation Aaron offered. Maybe she ought to go back to being a hermit, trusting no one, keeping to herself. Maybe she ought to discard the acrylic paints she'd just purchased and the canvases she'd spent the past few days framing and stretching, and resume painting her timid little watercolors.

But it was too late to change anything now. Aaron was in her house and he wanted a beer. She'd hosted plenty of difficult parties during her marriage. Surely she could manage a gathering that consisted of two friends.

She summoned her good-hostess manners as she led him down the hall to the kitchen. "Mitch Sterling and the Wilsons couldn't make it tonight. And the Penningtons were going to join us, but they have a sick child," she informed him. "Do you know them? Ed and Grace." She glanced over her shoulder in time to see him frown slightly. She didn't know whether that meant he didn't know the Penningtons, or he knew them and didn't like them.

It didn't matter, she reminded herself. They weren't coming. And this wasn't a dinner party. And she ought to stop analyzing everything and fretting about nonsense.

He surveyed her spacious kitchen, then accepted the bottle of beer she handed him from the refrigerator. "Would you like a glass?" she asked.

"No, thanks."

The room felt smaller when he was in it. The walls seemed to lean in, compressing the air, compelling her to move closer to him to prevent being crushed. Resisting the urge, she poured a glass of iced tea for herself and gestured toward the back door. He opened it for her, and she passed in front of him. He smelled of pine and mint.

"Hey," Charlie greeted them as they stepped out onto the porch. He hoisted his beer in a silent toast to Aaron, who nodded and lifted his bottle back at Charlie. "Happy Independence Day, Maz."

"Happy Fourth." Aaron crossed to the railing and leaned his backside against it.

"What did you think of the parade?" Charlie asked.

"Noisy. Corny." Aaron grinned.

"There wasn't enough free candy," Charlie complained, then returned Aaron's grin. "So, how's your deck holding up?"

"It's great. You did a good job on it."

"All I did was tell you what to do. You did the actual work."

Lily let herself relax again. Charlie and Aaron were getting along wonderfully. Fifteen years ago they might not have had much to say to each other, but fifteen years…fifteen years was a lifetime.

She left them to return to the kitchen for the nuts

and vegetables. Spying on them through the window, she saw that Charlie was still seated, Aaron still leaning against the railing, and the two of them were talking like old pals. She smiled. At her fancy dinner parties in Cohasset, one of her primary functions as hostess had been to make sure her guests got along, mixed and mingled, made friends with one another. She felt like a good hostess tonight, witnessing two people she adored as they became friends.

No, she didn't adore Aaron. She didn't know him well enough. She just…felt something. Something deep and resonant. Something that could blossom, with enough water and sunshine.

Their voices drifted in through the screen. "Just as well the Penningtons aren't coming," Charlie was saying. "We get along fine, but I'm always afraid that won't last. Ed's sister is my ex-wife."

"Oh?"

"Beth Pennington. Remember her from school?"

Aaron ruminated, then shook his head.

"Yeah, well. One of those small-town things." Charlie lifted his bottle to his lips and drank. So did Aaron.

Lily didn't know if Charlie intended to get maudlin—he'd certainly never indicated any lingering scars from his brief marriage to Beth—but she thought it best to get back outside, just in case the conversation started to deteriorate. She carried the snacks to the table by the wicker chairs, and Charlie immediately dug into the bowl of nuts, helping himself to a fistful.

Aaron turned his gaze to her. His eyes were uncannily focused, eerily beautiful. The multitude of colors in them unsettled her almost as much as the potency of his stare. What did he see when he looked at her like that? A friend? A wealthy pushover with a checkbook? A woman?

A woman who saw an incredibly tantalizing, almost frighteningly sexy man when she looked at him?

Charlie's attention shuttled back and forth between the two of them, and Lily forced herself to stop thinking about Aaron before Charlie read her mind.

"So," she said brightly, "how are things going with the basketball program?"

"Better," Aaron said, his steady gaze implying that she was the reason it was going better. More accurately, her money was the reason. She realized she didn't want Charlie to know about her impulsive donation, though she was gratified it was making a difference in Aaron's work.

She scrambled for another subject. Fortunately Charlie came to her rescue. "How about you, Lily? You feeling better these days? You're sure *looking* better."

"Thank you."

"I think it was a great idea for you to invite us over tonight. Don't you agree?" he asked Aaron.

"She's going to feed us. Of course it's a great idea."

Charlie laughed. Lily hastened to set them straight. "You're not getting any kind of elaborate dinner. I've got fresh rolls and a loaf of rye bread, cold cuts, cheese, lettuce and tomatoes at the grocery store. It's do-it-yourself sandwiches."

"My favorite!" Charlie declared cheerfully. "You

sure learned about sophisticated entertaining in Boston, didn't you?''

Ordinarily Lily wouldn't mind Charlie's teasing. But she still felt too fragile about her years in Boston.

It was Aaron's turn to rescue her. ''Did you go to the parade with anyone?'' he asked.

''My father.'' She sighed, recalling her futile attempts to get her father to take her mother's upcoming birthday seriously. She'd attempted to raise the subject with him again during the parade, but he'd remained just as dense. Abruptly she had an idea. An odd one, perhaps, but she was with two friends, each with his own unique viewpoint. ''You know, I could use your help.''

''Uh-oh.'' Charlie sent Aaron a grim smile. ''See? There's no such thing as a free do-it-yourself sandwich.''

Lily poked him in the arm to silence him. ''It's my father. My mother, actually. She's turning sixty soon, and I want to do something wonderful to celebrate her birthday. My father seems completely uninterested. But turning sixty is a big event.''

Neither man spoke. Charlie's expression went blank. Aaron's gaze didn't waver.

''I'm really stumped. I just don't know what would be appropriate. Maybe you guys can help.''

''How can we possibly help?'' Charlie asked.

''You know my parents. And, Aaron—'' she turned to him ''—you can help because you obviously have a special relationship with your mother.''

Aaron's gaze grew chilly. He finally smiled, but it was a tight, bitter smile. ''Oh, yeah,'' he muttered. ''Our relationship is special, all right.''

Lily shrank inwardly. She'd made a serious miscalculation, although she wasn't sure exactly what the damage was, or how bad. "I thought, since you came back to Riverbend because your mother had fallen ill…"

He drank some beer, then addressed the bottle. "My mother and I have worked out a truce. I can't say it's solid, but we've gotten this far, which is something of a miracle. If that means our relationship is special, all right. It's special."

"Did you do anything for her sixtieth birthday?" Lily asked him.

"She's fifty-three." His tone of voice led Lily to suspect he would not be planning anything big seven years down the road.

Okay. She'd botched things in assuming Aaron and Evie Mazerik were close. If Aaron hated her for it, he could leave.

She looked at Charlie, once again hoping for rescue. He didn't seem all that eager to bail her out. Indeed, he looked rather intrigued by the tension churning in the air between her and Aaron.

"I'm going to get the sandwich fixings together," she said. "If you get any brainstorms, let me know." She escaped to the kitchen.

She didn't expect them to come up with brainstorms. She hoped they would talk about anything other than her mother and her own ineptitude. They could congratulate each other some more over Aaron's deck, or discuss the parade, or their cars or sports, or whatever guys talked about while drinking beer on a back porch. She'd been an idiot to think she was ready to have a couple of friends over for a casual get-together. But if she left them alone, they might distract each other from that fact.

In the last couple of years of her marriage, she recalled as she pulled the cold-cuts platter out of the refrigerator, Tyler used to criticize her even when her dinner parties were perfect. He used to complain that she'd been stingy with the cocktails—and she supposed she had been, whispering to the bartender she'd hired to mix Tyler's drinks weak. Tyler would complain that she kept glaring at him, although she glared only when he was on his fourth martini and the effect of all that liquor was starting to show. She could never enjoy her parties, because she spent so much energy worrying about how drunk he was going to get. He refused to believe her when she told him she was thinking only of him, wanting to prevent him from making a fool of himself in front of his guests. Maybe he'd been right not to believe her. She'd been thinking of herself, too, thinking about how unpleasant things might become after everyone went home and she was left with an inebriated husband to put to bed.

She wasn't going to have to deal with an inebriated husband tonight, thank God. Even if she'd inadvertently touched a sore spot with Aaron when she'd mentioned his mother, this party was going to be okay.

Once the rolls were in a straw basket lined with a linen napkin, the bread arranged on a silver bread plate and the meat, cheese and garnishes out on the table, she called the men inside. They were engaged in a cheerful argument about whether Larry Bird was truly the greatest basketball player who had ever laced on a pair of sneakers. "He's from Indiana," Charlie asserted. "That says it all."

"He played his best games for Boston," Aaron shot back. "He had to leave Indiana in order to reach his peak."

"But he came back to Indiana," Charlie said. "He learned what he needed to know while playing for Boston, but then he brought all that wisdom back home. Just like Lily, right?"

She hadn't peaked in Boston, but she'd certainly brought some wisdom home with her, even if she'd earned her wisdom the hard way.

Aaron and Charlie seemed thrilled by the array of food, which made her smile. Heaven only knew what bachelors in their thirties ate for dinner most nights. They all sat around the kitchen table—much cozier than her high-ceilinged dining room with its chair rails and moldings and elaborate brass chandelier— and constructed overstuffed sandwiches for themselves.

Once they had exhausted the subject of Larry Bird and tucked into their food, Lily attempted to return to the problem of her mother's birthday. She could pick their brains without mentioning Evie. "Okay, guys," she said. "It's your wisdom I need right now. How can I convince my father that my mother's sixtieth is important? You're men. Tell me how to get through to him."

"Just explain to him that it's important," Charlie suggested. "Men can be thick, but if you explain it enough times, he'll eventually catch on. What do you think, Aaron? You know Dr. Bennett, don't you?"

"Yes," Aaron said, then took a bite of his sandwich.

"Do you think Lily should bludgeon him until he's prepared to do the right thing for his wife?"

"Dr. Bennett always does the right thing," Aaron said, an ironic undertone to his words.

"What do you mean?" Lily asked, curious about how her friends saw her father.

"I mean, if it's the right thing to do, he'll do it. Pay house calls, make sick children smile, stay on top of the latest treatments..." Aaron studied his sandwich, as if the layers of turkey and ham and cheese truly fascinated him. "Meet his obligations, whatever they are."

"Do you think he views celebrating my mother's birthday as an obligation?"

"It shouldn't be an obligation," Charlie said. "He should be happy to help you plan something because he loves your mom." He took a bite of his sandwich and chewed, thoughtfully. "Tell him to buy her diamonds."

"Diamonds are on the list," Lily agreed with a smile.

"Tell him he has to devote the rest of his life to satisfying her every need. She'll love that."

"She will," Lily agreed again. "She's devoted her whole life to fulfilling *his* needs. Why shouldn't he devote his life to fulfilling hers? What do you think, Aaron?"

"It's the least she deserves," he said coolly.

Something about him had changed. He seemed more reserved, as if protecting his words. He no longer looked directly at her, but instead concentrated on his food.

He clearly didn't want to talk about Eleanor Bennett's birthday. "Diamonds sound like a good solution," Lily concluded, accepting that it was time to let the subject drop.

Aaron came back to life as they veered to other topics. He contributed a few opinions about the summer's crop of movies, argued about whether the mosquito population was on the increase and debated theories about why Jacob Steele hadn't come home for his father's memorial service. Charlie and Lily did more talking than Aaron, but he let his guard drop a little.

She wished she could ask him about his relationship with his mother. Truce or no truce, his bond with Evie Mazerik was clearly not a simple thing. Perhaps he'd come back to Riverbend not because he loved his mother, but because he'd been honoring his obligations. Perhaps he was like her father that way.

She wished she could ask him about himself, about the undercurrents pulsing beneath his quiet surface. About how he'd transformed himself from a kid who had trouble obeying the rules in school to an adult who was now in a position to make and enforce the school rules himself. About why he'd agreed to come to her house tonight, why he looked at her the way he did, whether she was totally insane to think they were friends.

She had ice cream for dessert, but none of the three flavors she'd bought enticed Charlie. He really had to be leaving, he insisted. He had "stuff" awaiting his attention at home. Thanking Lily for the meal, he promised that if he came up with some other ideas for her mother's birthday, he'd give her a call. Then he kissed her cheek and headed out the front door.

Lily closed it behind him, sighed and turned to find Aaron looming at the other end of the entry hall, filling the kitchen doorway. She'd known Charlie long enough and well enough to comprehend that having stuff awaiting his attention at home wasn't why he'd left. He'd sensed something between her and Aaron. And yes, he would be calling her, possibly with ideas for her mother's birthday, but more likely to ask her what exactly that something was.

If he asked her now, she wouldn't be able to answer. All she knew was that just as the kitchen had seemed smaller when she'd stood in there with Aaron, so her entire house felt smaller when he lurked at the other end of the hallway, as if unseen forces were drawing them closer.

They stared at each other long enough for her to feel the strange dark tingle again, sliding down her spine and settling in her hips. So much had changed in the past fifteen years, but not the shiver of desire she'd always felt when she'd seen Aaron, even when they'd been teenagers and she'd been too innocent to know what she was feeling or what to do about it.

"I should be leaving, too," he said.

"No." The word came out so automatically she knew it was the truth. She didn't want him to leave yet. She'd failed him by asking him about his mother, and she had to make things right before he disappeared, or whatever kind of friendship they had would be ruined. "I want to show you something," she said.

He eyed her warily. It occurred to her that he might be desperate to leave, that without Charlie there, he didn't want to be with her. But stronger than her attraction to him was a need to count him as a friend. Aaron was the only person she knew in Riverbend who might understand what she'd done. He'd done bad things, too, and he had redeemed himself. When she looked at him, she saw the chance for her own redemption.

So he couldn't leave, not until she was sure things were okay between them.

She started toward the stairs. His mouth tightened and his gaze hardened, but he fell into step behind her. Like a condemned man marching to his doom, he climbed the long stairway without saying a word.

What did he think would happen to him on the second floor? she wondered. Was he aware of her attraction to him? Did he fear she was going to drag him into her bedroom and have her way with him? She barely had the courage for what she was about to show him. She certainly didn't have the courage for anything more.

She didn't bother with the hallway lights, since early-summer sunlight spilled through the open windows of the rooms flanking the hall. Not looking behind her—for fear that Aaron might have stopped following her—she headed down the hall to the bedroom at the end that she'd converted into a studio. It was the brightest bedroom in the house, a corner room with windows on two walls. Once she entered, she stepped out of the way of the door and turned to him.

He followed her in and stared. The room's only furnishings were a few lamps, an easel, a long work-table and a comfortable stool. Along one wall she'd propped her newly stretched canvases. One canvas stood on the easel, with a faint charcoal sketch across its taut white surface. The table held her new acrylic paints, neatly sorted, a few old plates for mixing colors, jars, brushes, palette knives and a can of solvent.

Aaron gazed around the room. "This is your studio," he said, stating the obvious.

"I've put the watercolors away. I'm going to start working in acrylics," she told him.

He surveyed the tubes of paint.

"Acrylics have texture and vivid colors, like oils," she explained. "It's a much stronger medium." She smiled. "Riskier."

He crossed to the easel and studied the sketch. From the few vague lines she'd drawn, he probably couldn't tell that the painting was going to be a cornfield. By the time she was done with it, it might not look like a cornfield, either. In her conception, the cornstalks would be slashes of green and brown and black, the sky burning down to night, the horizon as flat as Riverbend's own. It would be impressionistic, almost abstract. Only by standing back and taking in the entire context would a viewer recognize that it was a cornfield.

"It's not a still life," she told him.

"Good." He assessed the tentative sketch. "What is it?"

"You'll have to wait until I paint it."

"Okay." He didn't smile, didn't look pleased. The studio, which was flooded with natural light through most of the day, was fading into dimness as the sun angled toward the opposite side of the house. Lily could have turned on the floor lamp near the easel, offering strong artificial light, but she didn't. She liked the play of shadows across Aaron's face, the way they emphasized the sharp lines of his nose and chin, the intensity of his brow.

He scrutinized the blank canvases along the walls, the tubes of paint on the table and the canvas on the easel. Then he turned to her. "I'm glad you're painting with these acrylics," he said. "But I had no right to say what I did that day. I don't know squat about art."

"You said what I needed to hear."

"I was out of line."

"Sometimes it's good to be out of line." A year ago, or ten or fifteen, she would never have believed such a thing. But she'd crossed the line herself, and Aaron's willingness to cross it was one of the things she admired most about him.

"So, this painting—" he waved toward the easel "—is going to be out of line?"

"I don't know. I haven't painted it yet." She let him look around for a minute more, then moved toward the door. As they went back down the hall to the stairs, he seemed much more relaxed.

"How about some of that ice cream?" she asked as they reached the first-floor hall. "Or would you like another beer?"

"A beer sounds good," he said.

She smiled inwardly. He was going to stay long

enough to drink another beer. Even without Charlie to buffer them, he was willing to stay.

They entered the kitchen, and she pulled a bottle out of the refrigerator for him. She refilled her glass with iced tea and led him out onto the back porch. The air had cooled a good ten degrees since midday, and the sky was glazed with pink light. She settled into one of the wicker chairs, and Aaron took the other.

"I'm sorry if I jumped to the wrong conclusions earlier," she said.

He quirked his eyebrows questioningly, but said nothing.

"About your mother," she clarified.

"Oh." He shrugged. "Forget it."

"It's just…" She sipped her tea. "I came home for myself, for my own selfish reasons. You came home for your mother."

He remained silent.

"I'm sure it was a big adjustment for you to come home. You must have had a life somewhere else, a job."

He shrugged again. "It was a good job, but not as good as what I've got at Riverbend High."

"Coaching the old team. And you're a guidance counselor, too, right?"

"I work with high-risk kids," he said. "I was doing that in Indianapolis before I came back here. I was working at a youth center, coaching basketball and trying to keep kids out of trouble." He cracked a smile. "I was the hick there, the token white guy from the sticks. It was kind of fun. I think I opened some eyes during my time there."

"I'm sure you did." She tried to picture him as the "token white guy" among a group of inner-city kids. Surely his adolescence had been just as tough as theirs, his resilience and survival instincts just as strong as theirs. "Did you like the city?" she asked.

"I don't know." He sipped some beer, then propped the bottle on his knee and gazed out into her backyard. "Yeah. I liked it. It wasn't River-bend." His quick grin stole the bitterness from his words.

"You probably had an exciting social life in the city," she said, then bit her lip at her tactlessness.

He gave her a sidelong glance. "I was pretty serious with a woman there," he admitted. "But when I decided to move here, she refused to come. She didn't want to leave the city."

"And you came, anyway?" That surprised Lily. "You broke up a relationship to take care of your mother?"

He shook his head. "I came back to make sure my mother was taken care of. But it was Coach Drummer who got me to stay. Not my mother. I did it for the coach."

"You wanted to run the high-school team that badly?"

"Drummer is a good man," Aaron said, his voice hushed but fervent. "He saved my life. I'd take a bullet for that guy. Fortunately he didn't want me to take a bullet. He only wanted me to take over the high-school team. I didn't have to think twice about it."

The sun dropped below the trees, stealing most of the light. Crickets launched into their sweet summer chorus, and fireflies glittered along the hedges bordering her property. She remembered how much she used to love summer nights in Riverbend when she was a child, how soothing the air could be, how tranquil the breeze. She hadn't needed anyone like Coach Drummer to persuade her to move back home. She belonged here, despite the fact that she was no longer the person she'd been when she left.

"I'm glad Coach Drummer convinced you to stay." She was glad for herself as much as for him. Her fantasies about him notwithstanding, she was thrilled to have someone nearby with whom she could feel this comfortable, someone with whom she could sit on her back porch, talking and sipping a cool evening drink. "If it weren't for you, Aaron, I'd still be hiding from the world."

"You've got no reason to hide," he argued, his tone gentle. "You told me your deep dark secret, and it's nothing, Lily. It's a zero."

"You don't know all my secrets," she warned.

He shifted in his seat so he could look at her. Even in the fading light she felt the power of his gaze. She felt his presence, his strength, the sheer masculinity of him. His hands seemed too big for the bottle they held. His hair seemed too long, his chin too sharp, his smile too tender for a man who'd known so little tenderness in his life.

No matter how much trouble he'd seen in his youth, he'd never done anything as bad as what she'd done. Lily Bennett Holden, the good girl, the perfect young lady, was far more evil than Aaron could ever imagine.

"Your husband was a drunk. You told me," he reminded her. "It's not a crime to admit you aren't exactly sorry he died."

"I killed him," she said.

CHAPTER NINE

FOR A LONG MINUTE all Aaron heard was the crickets. And Lily's voice, reverberating inside his skull: *I killed him.*

She'd killed her drunken lout of a husband? Good for her.

That was a terrible thought, one that shook him up a little. He and Lily shared genes, after all. And while he'd never murdered anyone, he'd been in trouble more than a few times. Maybe the genes they'd both inherited from good old Dr. Bennett were evil ones.

"You didn't really kill him," he said. No matter how evil her genetic makeup was, in his heart, deep inside where it counted, he knew she wasn't capable of murder.

"I did," she said, her voice cracking with emotion. "Really."

He wondered if she was going to cry the way she had at his house a few nights ago. He wondered if she had invited him to her house tonight not to celebrate the holiday or test her entertaining skills but to unburden herself. For some reason she seemed to view him as her confessor. She could have talked about this with Reverend Kendall, or some other minister in town. But she'd chosen him.

"All right. You killed your husband," he echoed, measuring the words to see if they felt true.

She nodded, her eyes downcast, her fingers fidgeting with her glass.

"Do the Boston police know about this?"

"He didn't die in Boston," she said, her voice still wavering, still raw. "He died in Cohasset—it's a shoreline town south of Boston. But no, the police didn't know it was my fault. No one knows."

"You've just told me." He was surprised at how calm he felt, and then not so surprised. This wasn't real. Lily couldn't kill anyone.

"You're it. The only one who knows." She sighed and lifted her eyes to him. They were glassy with tears. "Do you hate me?"

"Actually," he admitted, "I don't believe you."

"He was drunk," she said, her words sounding choked. "I knew he was drunk that night, drunker than usual. He came into the bedroom and I kicked him out. I couldn't…" She issued a shaky sigh. "I couldn't let him touch me. Not when he was like that. I told him to get the hell away from me."

Understandable. Aaron nodded.

"I heard him go downstairs. I thought maybe he was going to watch some TV or take a walk to clear his head or… I didn't know. To tell you the truth, I didn't care. All I cared about was that he wasn't going to get in bed with me when he was drunk." Another sigh escaped her. "By the time I realized he was in the garage, it was too late to stop him. I heard him gun the engine of his car. He was bombed, stinking drunk, and I heard him drive away. If I hadn't kicked him out of bed, he wouldn't have gotten behind the wheel that night.''

Aaron could see where she'd feel some responsibility for what had happened—but it wasn't her fault. She'd been within her rights to refuse to sleep with him when he was stewed. ''You didn't know he was going to get behind the wheel. He did the drinking and he did the driving, Lily.''

''What if he'd hit someone? What if, instead of slamming into a tree, he'd slammed into another car? Or run someone over? Given his condition, a bartender would have been legally required to take his keys away.'' She sounded too weary to cry, too sad. Too lost. ''I could have stopped him, Aaron. I could have gotten his keys and hidden them. And I didn't.''

Aaron took another sip of beer. He didn't swallow it right away but held it on his tongue, felt the bubbles pop, absorbed the bitter flavor. He absorbed her words, as well, and conceded that there was something in what she was saying.

He wasn't an amateur, when it came either to taking responsibility for one's own choices or to helping a troubled soul work out a personal crisis. He had a degree in psychology and a master's in counseling. He knew this stuff.

''When someone drinks the way your husband drank,'' he said carefully, hoping he wasn't coming across like a pompous know-it-all, ''he's got a self-destructive streak. Okay? Alcoholism is a disease, but drinking is a behavior. Do you know the difference?''

She eyed him quizzically. Obviously she hadn't

been expecting an expert lecture, but she seemed receptive.

"Alcoholism has to do with brain and body chemistry. Lots of alcoholics never drink, and they function well. Lots of people who aren't alcoholics drink too much and don't function well. I don't know if your husband was technically an alcoholic or not. But he drank too much. That was the behavior he chose."

She listened intently, leaning toward him, her eyes glowing with a light that looked a lot like hope. Did she think he would absolve her? At least make it possible for her to forgive herself? He would do his damnedest.

"Your husband was miserable and depressed," he continued, "and he engaged in self-destructive behavior. I know an awful lot about self-destructive behavior, Lily. I tried my hand at it as a kid."

"You never—"

"I did," he assured her. "But we're not talking about me. We're talking about your husband."

"I thought he drank as a way to hurt me."

Aaron suppressed a reflexive surge of anger. Who would ever do anything to hurt Lily? She was such a good person. "There's no question his drinking hurt you, but if all he wanted was to hurt you, he would have found a way to do it that wouldn't damage himself so much. Your being hurt by his drinking was only a by-product. He was out to destroy himself."

"Do you think so?"

Aaron nodded. "And his decision to drive into a tree—"

"It wasn't a decision. He was too drunk to decide anything like that. It was an accident."

He gave her a long hard look.

A transparent look, given how easily she read his thoughts. "You think it *wasn't* an accident?"

"I think he was hell-bent on self-destruction. I think if he was all alone and drove into a tree... No, it wasn't an accident. He had other options. He made a choice."

She contemplated his words. Her head was slightly ducked, her hair pale and lustrous in the dwindling light, her knees pressed together primly, her eyes closed. If he could convince her to stop blaming herself for her husband's self-annihilation, he would feel as if moving back to Riverbend had been worthwhile. Even more than living up to Drummer's expectations, salvaging Lily's life would validate his return.

He wasn't sure how he'd gone from despising her to wanting to be her savior. Well, he'd never actually despised her, except in the most irrational way. He'd despised her for being Julian Bennett's daughter, not for anything she'd done. But he would no more blame her for her father's decisions—and they were every bit as deliberate as her husband's had been—than he would blame her for having blond hair and delicate lips.

She stirred, emerging from her meditation. Her eyes fluttered open and she smiled, the saddest smile he'd ever seen. "We were really in love when we started out," she told him.

"I figured." At her quizzical look, he explained, "You wouldn't have cared so much if there hadn't been something good there. You would have left him.''

''Maybe. I don't know.'' She let out a breath. ''He was so smart. So generous. And he used to tell me he loved me because I was sweeter than any woman he'd ever met before.''

''He got that much right.''

Her smile grew slightly, tinged with amazement. ''Why are you so kind to me, Aaron?'' she asked.

''Kind?'' He snorted.

''Is it because I gave your program money?''

He almost dropped his beer. ''No,'' he said, wondering if she could hear the irritation in his voice. ''I'm not for sale.''

''I didn't mean it that way. I meant…'' She closed her eyes and shook her head. ''Let's not count the ways I've offended you tonight. It's a miracle you're still sitting here.''

''You haven't offended me.''

''All that stuff I implied about your relationship with your mother—I had no right to assume anything. I always come up with the best possible interpretation of things. I heard you came to Riverbend to take care of your mother, and I assumed you did it out of love.''

''Maybe I did,'' he muttered. ''Who knows?''

''You love your mother?'' she asked.

''Damn it, yeah.'' It was his turn to sigh, his turn to let her peel away a layer of him. ''She pisses the hell out of me, but she's the only family I've got.''

''I'll bet she's proud of you.''

He nodded, looking away. His mother was proud of him. She probably even loved him, in her way.

But like Lily's late husband and her father, Evie Mazerik had made her own choices, and she'd made them without regard for how they would affect anyone else.

She had chosen never to tell Aaron the truth about who he was. She had raised him with no father. She had chosen to deny her son the one thing he needed to know. That choice of hers still hurt him. Even if he loved his mother, he could hate her for that.

He drained his bottle, set it on the table with a quiet thump and stood up. His mood was going south, fast. He'd made Lily feel better about herself; he'd better leave before things deteriorated. "I've got to go," he said.

She sprang to her feet and put her glass down next to his bottle. "I'm sorry." She gave him a sheepish smile. "I must be the worst hostess you've ever had."

"I don't deal with hostesses on a regular basis," he said, then smiled. "You're fine, Lily. Why do you keep apologizing?"

Her smile expanded. "I'm a long way from fine. And you're very tolerant to put up with me."

"Tolerance has nothing to do with it." He put up with her—God, no, he didn't do that. He enjoyed being with her, enjoyed talking to her, enjoyed looking at her far too much—because she was Lily. Because she was lovely. Because in spite of everything she'd been through, she had a core of innocence and generosity. Because even being caught in a nightmare marriage for ten years couldn't make her cynical. Because, like her husband, he believed she was the sweetest woman he'd ever met.

She peered up at him, and he realized she was standing too close to him. "Why do you put up with me, then?" she asked.

Because when you look at me, I can't look away, he almost said. *Because you're everything I want and can't have.*

And then, before he could stop her, she rose on tiptoe and touched his lips with hers.

No, he thought, but the word wouldn't emerge. His throat slammed shut against it, barring it from escape.

His lungs filled with her scent, faintly flowery but subtle, and his eyes filled with the sight of her, so near, so womanly. His hands curled into fists at his sides, aching from the amount of energy it took to keep them away from her. He wanted to touch her hair, to feel its feathery softness. He wanted to touch her shoulders, her back, to pull her against him and kiss her the way a man kissed a woman.

No.

She stretched to kiss him again, perching her hands on his shoulders for balance. Her mouth moved beneath his, so soft. Whisper soft and so, so sweet.

The only way he could keep from responding would be if he died right that instant. But he was alive; every damned cell in his body was bristling with life. He couldn't stop all that life from surging through him, clamoring for Lily, hungering for her.

He lost the battle with his hands. They lifted to her cheeks, cupped them, tipped her head back.

And he kissed her. The way he'd wanted to the first time he'd ever seen her. The way he'd wanted

to every day since that first time. The way he'd
wanted to in his car the other night. The way he'd
sworn to himself he never would, never could.

His mouth opened over hers. She parted her lips
and lured his tongue in. A low moan broke free from
him, desolate, desperate. If only he could have kissed
her and felt nothing, his obsession with her would
wither and he'd get on with his life. But this...

It was too good. Too deep. Too wrenchingly
erotic. She nestled into him, her slender body tight
against him, her breasts flattened against his chest.
Her breath mingled with his, her sighs, her fingers
twining through the hair at the nape of his neck until
they could lace together there. Arousal shot through
him, hot and fierce and painful, making him shudder
inside.

Lily, he thought. Lily. The woman of his dreams.
The girl of his fantasies.

His sister.

"God," he groaned, pulling back, twisting away
from her. "Stop."

He was talking to himself, not her, but she obviously didn't understand that. She released him, her
hands flying from him as if burned. Her cheeks were
flushed, whether from passion or embarrassment he
didn't know. It didn't matter. He couldn't bear to
look at her long enough to figure out what she was
feeling.

He staggered to the porch railing, gripped it,
leaned over and let the cool night air wash over him.
His stomach roiled; he hoped he wouldn't throw up.
He was still aroused, and that alone nauseated him.

His sister. God help him, his sister.

A stark silence lengthened between them. He listened to that silence until his breathing grew steadier, until his pulse ceased drumming in his ears. Until his body subsided and his hands no longer trembled and the crickets filled the emptiness with their chirping.

"I suppose you'll be saying I shouldn't apologize for that, either," Lily murmured.

She sounded wretched. Distressed but resigned, as if she considered his rejection of her natural and inevitable, as if she counted herself the biggest loser in the world.

"Don't apologize," he said, his voice rusty and ragged. "It's not your fault."

"Whose fault is it?"

He wished he had the guts to face her, but he knew if he turned around, he would see sorrow in her eyes, disappointment—and that disappointment would be directed at herself. "Mine," he said, staring out at the roses. They looked platinum in the night. "It's my fault."

"Why is it your fault? You can't help it if you don't want me."

He swore, a quiet, ugly word. "I want you," he said, the most painful three words he had ever spoken. "I want you, Lily. I just…can't."

"Can't want me? Or can't act on it?" She sounded bewildered. "Why not?"

He couldn't tell her she was his sister. Not now. Not after they'd already told each other too many things. Not when his only proof of their relationship lay in the beating of his heart.

"I can't. That's all." Before he could say another word, before he could destroy her world any more, he turned and stalked down the porch, around her house to the front and into his car. Gravel flew as he drove into the night.

TRYING TO FALL asleep would have been futile, so she didn't bother. After cleaning the kitchen, she changed out of her dress and into an old shirt and jeans, then slammed a Don Henley CD on her stereo, a collection of songs about lovers screwing up, wounding each other, leaving each other in forlorn solitude and staggering alone through the landscape of love. Then she attacked her canvas.

The halogen lamp blazed in her studio, filling it with a light brighter than the sun at noon. The paints lent their pungent scent to the air. She mixed them on a plate, slapping browns and greens together, stabbing the dollops with her palette knife and slashing the resulting colors onto the canvas.

She was painting corn. Indiana. The open endless fields of her home, the bleakness of her world. Dying corn, broken stalks beneath a lemon-hued sky.

She wouldn't cry. Not over the mess she'd made of her life. Not over the travesty of her marriage, the decade she'd spent trying to prevent her world from crashing and burning, and not over the ultimate crash, the ultimate burn. She wouldn't cry over her inability to reach out to her old friends or her inability to connect with a new friend.

She wouldn't cry over Aaron. She wouldn't shed a single tear over how she'd taken the biggest risk of her life by kissing him, and he'd pushed her away.

How many failures could the golden girl of Riverbend High rack up? How many imperfections could Miss Perfect carry inside her? How many times could a woman crash and burn before all that was left were ashes?

He'd said he wanted her, she recalled, studying the Dijon-mustard blob of paint on the plate and adding more green to it. She blended the paints until the blob was the shade of a drying husk, then daubed it onto the canvas with a half-inch brush.

Aaron had said he wanted her, and he hadn't had to say it. When he'd kissed her, those few blissful moments when he'd let go, given in, taken the same chance she'd taken, he hadn't had to say what had been so obvious. She'd felt it in his kiss, in his ragged breath, in his hands stroking her cheeks, in the pressure of his arousal.

Her own husband hadn't responded to her like that, not at the end. The last few years of her marriage had been as bleak, as dry and broken as the cornfield she was painting. Half the time Tyler had been too drunk to function—and she'd been relieved. The other half, she'd given in to him to avoid a fight. Until that last night, when she'd had enough and thrown him out of their bed.

Aaron hadn't completely convinced her she wasn't responsible for Tyler's death. But he'd made her feel a little better, a little less guilty. Before tonight she'd found him irresistibly attractive. After he'd said what he had, she'd gone beyond simple attraction. Any man who could offer such healing words to a woman like her...

She could fall in love with him.

But he wouldn't let her. What felt so right had suddenly turned wrong. Aaron had seemed sickened by her, and he'd run away. The man who had goaded her to stop playing it safe had fled like a coward at the first sign of danger.

She stepped back to study her canvas. She'd been at it for hours. The CD was finished; the house was silent. Someone who didn't know what the painting was supposed to be might not guess by looking at it. The canvas was covered with angles and points, stalks bent and broken as if they'd just been pummeled by a midsummer hail storm. The sky had an eerie post-storm glow.

It was a sad picture, she realized. A mournful picture. An angry picture.

It was the most honest picture she'd ever painted.

"HI, MOM," LILY SAID.

It was eight-thirty in the morning, and she was running on fumes. She'd dozed off on the floor of the studio for a few hours and been awakened by the warmth of the sun spilling in through the windows. As her eyes had adjusted, she'd kneaded the stiffness out of her neck and studied the painting on the easel. It was still angry, still mournful, still an honest depiction of her life—only, she noticed something else: some of the stalks were still green and standing.

If the painting was a reflection of her, she wasn't dead yet.

She'd taken a long hot shower, loosening her cramped muscles a bit more, then consumed a cup of coffee. She'd felt odd, as if she had one foot in Riverbend and the other in a dream somewhere, a dream brimming with possibilities. If she could survive one risk, she could survive others. Her life might be a disaster, but at least it would be an interesting, daring disaster.

She'd decided to pay a call on her mother, another golden girl of Riverbend, someone who had always lived up to everyone's expectations. Maybe Lily and her mother hadn't been close when Lily had been younger. But that was no reason for them not to become close now. Eleanor might have knowledge she could teach Lily. Lily wanted to learn.

She found her mother still in her bathrobe, her breezy blond hair unbrushed and her face untouched by makeup. Eight-thirty was perhaps a half hour before civilized people dropped in on each other. But Lily was family. Her mother didn't have to groom herself for a visit from her daughter.

"Lily! Hello!" Her mother's smile was warm enough to assure Lily she was welcome. "Dad isn't home. He's already left for the clinic."

Lily suffered a pang at the realization that her mother thought she would stop by only to see her father. "That's fine," she said softly. "You're the one I want to talk to."

A fleeting look of bewilderment crossed her mother's face, and then her smile widened, its courtesy failing to mask her curiosity. "Come on in," she said, holding the door wider so Lily could enter. "You must think I'm a lazybones, not even dressed at this hour…"

"I think lounging around in your pajamas is a blessed luxury." Lily said. "No need to explain." She followed her mother into the sun-filled kitchen.

The room hadn't changed much since Lily had left home. It was still cheery, the knotty-pine cabinets golden in the morning light, the tile floor spotless. Lily's mother could afford to pay someone to wash and wax her floors, but she didn't. Her career was keeping her husband's life tidy and comfortable, and she wasn't ready to retire.

"Coffee?" she asked.

"Yes, thanks." Even though Lily's mind was alert, her body was sore and sluggish from having slept on the floor—and slept too little. Another cup of coffee would give her nervous system a much-needed jolt.

Her mother fixed two cups, adding skim milk to Lily's as well as her own. They sat facing each other at the round pine table by the window.

"How are you?" Eleanor asked.

Could she tell Lily was teetering on a fine edge? Was she asking a question she already knew the answer to—that Lily was a wreck? Or was she just being polite?

"I don't know," Lily replied, determined to remain as honest with her mother as she'd been with her painting last night, and with Aaron before that.

Her mother's gaze softened with concern. "Ah, sweetie. You've been through so much these past few months. Losing Tyler so horribly, selling your house, moving back to Riverbend—"

"Tell me about love," Lily said. Her voice sounded young to her, a child begging for a lesson.

Her mother's eyes widened. She sat back in her chair, and Lily almost laughed at the puzzlement in her mother's expression. Her eyebrows quirked up, her mouth pursed; even her hair looked more mussed, stray tufts standing on end. "Love?"

"I've been married, I've been widowed, and I still don't get it."

Her mother regarded her thoughtfully. The puzzlement seemed to fade from her eyes as she took a sip of her coffee. "Didn't you love Tyler?" she asked.

"Of course I did," Lily said. She *had* loved Tyler—very much at the beginning and intermittently even at the end. He'd swept her off her feet, but even swept, she wouldn't have married him if she hadn't loved him. She wouldn't have tried so hard to keep the marriage alive if she hadn't cared. "But…there were bad times in the marriage, too, Mom."

"There are always bad times in a marriage."

"Not yours," Lily argued. Her parents were perfect together. Yet her mother abruptly looked away, staring out the window into the morning sun. Lily leaned forward and covered her mother's hand with her own. "Mom?"

"Even the best marriages have bad times in them," her mother murmured.

"But you and Dad love each other so much. I know you do."

"I love him more than I can say," her mother confessed, her voice barely more than a whisper.

"And he loves you."

Her mother snapped her head around to Lily, and she saw the pain, a damp shimmer in her mother's eyes. "I don't think so."

Lily's heart thumped against her ribs. Her own woes and frustrations went forgotten as she absorbed her mother's words and joined them to her own recent observations: her mother's investing in anti-wrinkle cream and perking up her hair, her father's seeming indifference to her mother's upcoming birthday. "What are you talking about?" she asked, trying to tamp down her suspicions.

"Oh, it's nothing," her mother said hastily, blinking away her tears and shaping a poignant smile. "I don't know why I said such a thing."

"You said it because you believe it."

"No. It's just the silly insecurities of an old lady."

"You're not old, and your insecurities aren't silly. Talk to me, Mom. We need to talk to each other about these things." She tightened her hold on her mother's hand, as if she could pass trust from her fingertips through her mother's skin and into her heart.

"It's really nothing." Her mother used her free hand to dig a tissue from the pocket of her bathrobe. She dabbed at her cheeks, blew her nose and attempted another feeble smile. "Your father and I have been together forever, Lily. You know that. Maybe the fire is just burning itself out a little, that's all."

"Dad is devoted to you," Lily insisted, wanting desperately to believe it.

"Dad has his life. He has his job, his golf, his friends. He has glory in this town. Everyone knows and loves him. I—" she sighed deeply and gave up trying to smile "—don't fit in anymore. I think he's...bored with me."

"You aren't boring!"

"He's been staring at the same face across this table for thirty-seven years, Lily. That's an awfully long time. He's tired of me."

"But you're not tired of him."

"I'm different from him. It takes much less to make me happy." Eleanor sighed again. "I used to think all I needed to be happy was to know that I was making *him* happy. And you. When my loved ones were happy, I was content. It was all I needed."

"You need much more than that, Mom. Everyone does." Lily stroked her mother's hand gently, feeling the bones beneath the skin. "Has Dad said he wants to leave you?"

"No, but—"

"Is he cheating on you?" It hurt her to speak the words, but she forced herself to get them out into the air.

"I don't know."

Lily's heart slammed against her ribs again. "Do you have any evidence?"

Her mother sipped her coffee. She seemed stronger, not quite as shaky or close to tears. "He's inattentive. He sometimes seems to forget I'm here. He drifts off when I'm talking to him. I wonder if he's thinking about someone else."

"Just because he drifts off—"

"And he doesn't tell me where he's going. He leaves and goes off and I have no idea where he is."

Lily recalled that past Saturday, when she'd gone to the golf course to find her father and he hadn't been there. Where had he been while her mother had thought he was golfing? Lily had finally found him at the Sunnyside Café, chatting with Aaron's mother, of all people, but where had he been before that? What had he been doing Saturday morning?

"All these things add up to circumstantial evidence," Lily said, resorting to the legalisms she'd learned in her decade as a lawyer's wife. "They don't prove a case. Maybe Dad assumes you know where he is. Or he thinks it's not that important that you know. Maybe he leaves intending to go one place, but he gets sidetracked and winds up somewhere else. Without more concrete evidence, you can't say he's having an affair."

"What should I be looking for? Lipstick on his collar?" Her mother smiled sadly. "I'm a fifty-nine-year-old woman. Your father is a handsome man. I can't compete with the young women out there. They flirt with him and he loves it."

"Of course he loves it. What man doesn't love to flirt with young women?" Lily drank some coffee, her eyes never leaving her mother. "Maybe you ought to flirt with him."

"Me?"

"If you think he's bored, why not put the spark back in the marriage? Flirt with him. Seduce him."

"You've been reading too many of those women's magazines," her mother scolded.

Lily had certainly read her share of them during her years in Massachusetts, searching for ways to repair her relationship with Tyler. But her marriage had been in critical shape. Her mother's marriage— God, she hoped she was right about this—seemed only to be in the doldrums. "You said you loved Dad," she reminded her mother.

"Of course I love him."

"Then do what it takes to get your marriage back on track. Fight for it if you have to. When you love someone, sometimes you have to fight for him." She'd fought for Tyler when she'd hoped there was still a chance of salvaging their marriage. She'd talked to his parents, to doctors, to experts at lectures and participants at Al-Anon meetings. She'd talked to the minister of the Congregational church she used to attend with him—and, more often, without him. She'd bought books, read articles, fought with him about the martinis, thrown away unopen bottles before he could open them. She had tried and tried, until it gradually became clear she couldn't win the battle.

Had her mother tried? Anti-aging cream was a start, but if her father was bored, the condition of his wife's skin wasn't going to make a difference. "If Dad means enough to you, you've got to fight," she repeated, no longer thinking of Tyler. Not thinking only of her parents.

She was thinking of Aaron.

She tried to convince herself she didn't love him. He'd rejected her last night, after all. How could she love a man who had pushed her away so emphatically?

But he meant so much to her. He meant enough that she was willing to fight. Before he'd said no, his mouth and hands and body had said yes.

She wasn't willing to give up on him. Not yet.

CHAPTER TEN

"So, Sam's doing okay?" Mitch asked.

Aaron stood in the open gym doorway overlooking the parking lot. The other kids had already left, and Jeff was collecting the balls and pinnies in the gym. Jeff was a guard on the high-school team, the kid Aaron had convinced to quit his summer job at the grocery store so he could work in the basketball program. Especially this session, with Sam Sterling participating, Aaron needed an assistant. He was grateful to have Jeff, grateful for the money that had enabled Aaron to hire him.

Grateful. That was the only positive sentiment he'd let himself feel for Lily. Grateful and nothing more.

It took all his willpower to shove her out of his mind and focus fully on Mitch. Sam stood beside his father's car, waiting for Mitch and Aaron to finish talking. The rest of the kids had left already.

"He's doing great," Aaron said.

"I know it's a challenge working with him—"

"Hey, no. We're doing fine. He's having lots of fun." Then, because Mitch seemed to need more assurance, Aaron added, "The other kids aren't having any problems, either. They're all getting along, making themselves understood. Really, Mitch. Relax. Sam's great.''

Mitch smiled, obviously relieved. "He likes you, Aaron. He was excited that you watched the parade with him yesterday.''

Aaron didn't want to remember anything about yesterday, but he gamely returned Mitch's smile and signaled Sam with a wave. As for the parade, well, it had been kind of fun to watch it with someone who'd actually wanted to be with him.

He heard the drone of a car cruising around the side of the building—maybe Jeff was expecting a ride home. He turned back toward the open gym door. "Guess I'd better help Jeff get everything put away. See you tomorrow.''

"See you,'' Mitch said. "Thanks.''

Aaron abandoned the muggy heat of the parking lot for the cooler indoor air. In the past few hours the sky had changed from summer blue to heavy gray. The air felt oppressive—thick and sticky. Any minute now the clouds would open up and douse the earth. The sooner the better, Aaron thought. The humid warmth was so dense he was practically choking on it.

From behind him he heard the click of a car door being opened and then Mitch's voice: "Lily! Hi!'' Aaron's step faltered, as if someone had just delivered a hard blow between his shoulder blades.

Damn it. Damn *her*. Why was she here? Certainly not to offer Jeff a ride home. Aaron wished he could believe she'd come looking for Mitch. He was her friend, one of her River Rat buddies.

But Aaron knew she'd come for him. She wanted

him to be her friend, too. And he would gladly have been her friend, if it was at all possible.

After last night, he knew it wasn't.

He sucked in a breath and continued farther into the gym, scooping up a stray basketball and carrying it toward the mesh sack Jeff was filling with balls. Jeff grinned at him, then glanced past him toward the door. "Hey, Coach Maz, would you mind if I left now? I gotta bike home, and it looks like it's gonna rain."

"Go ahead."

"Thanks!" The boy passed him the sack and headed for the door in a loose, long-limbed jog. Aaron kept his back to the door, as if by not seeing Lily he could pretend she wasn't there.

"Aaron."

So much for pretending. Her voice traveled through the vaulted room, echoing off the metal rafters of the high ceiling, the cinder-block walls, the folded wooden bleachers. Even without turning he could see her, slim and blond and trusting. Across the vastness of the gym, he felt her presence. Through the protective layers he'd tried to wrap around himself since he'd left her house last night, he responded to her. His throat tightened, his head throbbed. Electricity crackled through him, as threatening as the lightning he knew would soon shear through the late-afternoon heat outside.

He gathered the last basketball, shoved it into the sack and tugged the drawstring. If he kept his back to her, would she walk away?

No. He could hear her footsteps, a light tapping sound on the painted hardwood, approaching him. He swallowed, but his throat was definitely tensing shut. If he didn't choke on the weather, he'd choke on the dread of knowing Lily was only a few yards from him, closing in, demanding a confrontation.

You don't want this, he almost shouted at her. *You don't want to come any closer.*

But she came closer, too close. He felt her hand on his shoulder and labored not to flinch. "Aaron, we have to talk."

"No." *You don't want to hear what I have to say.*

"Please."

Oh, God. With one word she could melt a polar ice cap and raise the ocean high enough to turn Pittsburgh into prime oceanfront real estate. One simple syllable. *Please.*

He turned around.

He saw no supplication in her gaze. Her eyes were clear and steady, her chin raised in determination, her shoulders squared. He hadn't noticed the breadth of her shoulders before. He should have; last night he'd run his hands over them. They were strong and stubborn, like her.

He wanted to kiss her. The way he had last night. Deeper. He wanted to kiss her shoulders, shove down the narrow sleeves of the sundress she wore and kiss her bare skin, her collarbones, her breasts. His throat slammed completely shut and he closed his eyes. He was a sick son of a bitch, and if she insisted on talking to him, she was going to hear about just how sick the whole thing was.

"Please, Aaron," she said, the firmness of her tone at odds with the gentleness of her request.

"All right." If talking to her would keep her away

from him, he'd do it. She'd be horrified by the truth.
Her life might crumble just as she'd begun rebuilding
it, the foundations turning to rubble beneath her. But
at least she would understand why he'd run from her
last night, and why he would keep running until the
day he died.

He heaved the ball sack over his shoulder and motioned with his head toward his office. He wasn't
going to have this conversation in the middle of the
gym.

She followed him to the far end of the room,
waited while he deposited the balls in an equipment
closet, and then entered his office ahead of him. He
gestured toward a chair and she sat, her eyes wide
and wary, her lips pursed. He closed the door, then
sank into his own chair, wishing the desk between
them were about two miles wider.

She drew in a deep breath, and he realized she was
not quite as calm as she was trying to project. Her
fingers fluttered against her knees and she clasped
her hands to still them. Her chin quivered slightly
and she lifted it again, as if seeking confidence in
the pose. "Something's going on between us," she
said, "and I don't understand it."

"Lily—"

"We're both adults." He heard a tremor in her
voice, so faint no one else would have detected it.
But he was acutely aware of everything about her.
The strand of hair that had wandered to the wrong
side of her part. The beauty mark on her neck below
her right ear. The braidlike pattern in the gold band
of the watch circling her wrist. The ovals of her
knees beneath the loose beige linen of her dress. The

movement of her throat as she swallowed. "We're attracted to each other. When we kissed yesterday—"

"Lily." He heard dread in his voice.

"I'm not very experienced, Aaron, but I was married for ten years. I know when a man is turned on."

He closed his eyes, as if it would help not to have to view her and remember just how turned on he'd been.

"Until last night," she went on, "I felt I could trust you. I also felt I could trust my own instincts. Now…I'm completely lost. Explain it to me, Aaron, okay? Tell me where I misread the signs. I know you want me to leave you alone, and I promise I will, if you'll just set me straight."

"You don't want to know," he warned.

"If I didn't want to know, I wouldn't have asked."

"I'm your brother."

Silence billowed around them, filling the room like toxic fumes. He opened his eyes to see her staring at him, eyes round, mouth agape, cheeks ashen as the blood drained from her face. After a long moment she shut her mouth. Her eyes remained wide with shock.

When he couldn't bear the silence anymore, he said, "Your father is my father."

"No." The word had as much impact as her first "please" had had, only in reverse. Her "no" could freeze the planet, the entire galaxy. Her voice plummeted to absolute zero.

But she had asked him to talk, and now that he'd started, he wasn't going to stop. "Your father used to visit my mother and me every month when I was a kid. He'd come to our apartment and spend a half hour or so. He'd ask me how I was doing and he'd give my mother money. Child support.''

"No." Her voice was a bare whisper now.

"He'd ask what I was learning in school and whether I was reading any good books. Then he'd ask my mother about my health and my diet. He'd hand her an envelope of cash and say, 'Make sure he takes a multivitamin every day,' or 'I think he needs new sneakers.' Every month without fail.''

Lily shook her head. Her eyes remained on him, glittering with something that looked like fear. ''My father wouldn't do that.''

"Do you think I'm making this up?" His quiet tone undercut the accusation in his question. He could tell her heart was splintering, and his anger and resentment vanished, replaced by sympathy. ''Lily, you're right, I'm attracted to you. It kills me to admit it, but I am. If I could do anything about it, I would.''

"Do anything?"

"Act on that attraction. Or stop being attracted. God knows, I've tried to stop wanting you.''

She shook her head again, her gaze on her hands in her lap. They were clenched so hard he could see the contours of her bones and veins through the skin. ''My father wouldn't have an affair. I know he wouldn't.''

"My mother was gorgeous when she was young. She could take a man's breath away.''

"I don't doubt that, but—"

"And there she was every day at the Sunnyside, flirting with all the men who came in. What makes you think your father was immune? Lots of men in this town weren't. She had plenty of boyfriends, even after I was born. But only one of them came to our home every month to give her money and ask me about my schoolwork.''

''He wouldn't have done it. He wouldn't have fathered a child that way.''

''Being a medical man and all, he probably would have asked her to get an abortion. But my mother would never have agreed to that.''

''Has she…'' Lily flicked her tongue over her lips, as if moisture would help the words slide out more easily. ''Has your mother told you this? About my father?''

He felt another sharp pain, his own pain at his mother's refusal to grant him the truth. ''No. She won't tell me who my father is. She never will. She'll protect him to the grave, and beyond. I think she's still in love with him.''

Lily winced. A shiver racked her, as if something clammy had brushed against the back of her neck. ''I saw them talking the other day,'' she whispered, looking stricken. ''Their heads were bowed close together, so intimately, and—'' She broke off, tears shimmering in her eyes.

He searched his office with his gaze, seeking a box of tissues. He saw the file cabinets, the clipboards, the schedules and the photos, team after team after team, three of them featuring a young, defiant Aaron, a kid with a chip on his shoulder and a rage burning inside him—and one of them, last year's photo, featuring an older, supposedly wiser Aaron, Coach Maz, a man who had come home changed, a man who cared more about other people's pain than his own.

Lily's pain was so great now it beat like a second pulse inside him. If she hadn't forced this conversation, he never would have told her. He would have kept his knowledge to himself, just to spare her the agony of it.

"I'm sorry," he said. A couple of clean towels sat on a shelf, and he got up and pulled one down for her. Only a few tears had filtered past her lashes to streak down her cheeks, but the towel was all he had to give her.

She looked at it, bewildered, and placed it in her lap. Then she reached into her purse, pulled out a tissue and dabbed her eyes. "We spend too much time apologizing, Aaron," she murmured.

"I'm not apologizing. I'm sorry I can't—" He cut himself off.

"Can't what?"

"Can't love you." His stomach clutched, that now familiar queasiness momentarily overtaking him. He stared past her at the photo on the wall behind her, his first year on the team. So much of the anger in him then had been based on his life, his circumstances, his status or lack of it, but some of it had arisen from his desire for a magnificent blond classmate, a golden girl who had cast an unbreakable spell on him. "I wanted you in high school," he confessed, studying his younger self, the cocky angle of his head, the resentment burning in his eyes. "I was crazy about you. And when I found out you were Dr. Bennett's daughter, it destroyed me."

"You wanted me in high school?"

"Like a junkie wants his drug." He let out a long

sigh. "I couldn't—I can't—ever let myself want you, Lily. You understand, don't you?"

"I understand," she said, her words softer than a sigh. She lifted the towel from her knees, set it on his desk and stood up. "I understand." She walked out of his office, her head once again high, her shoulders thrown back, her bearing regal. He watched through the open door as she crossed the gym in slow, measured steps.

He would never forget the pride in her, the strength, the grace. He would never forget how much he wanted her, even now. He was still a junkie craving her. Like a junkie he would stay clean because to survive he had to.

But he knew the craving would never go away.

IT WAS RAINING when she stepped outside. She'd left the top of her car down, and the seats were wet.

As if she cared.

She slumped against the damp leather, turned on the engine and raised the convertible roof. Then she sat, listening to the rain pelt the canvas above her head as shudders ripped through her. She heard a low keening sound and realized it was her own voice, seeping out of her like blood, as if she'd been sliced open, right through her gut, through her soul.

Last night she'd suspected she was falling in love with Aaron Mazerik. This morning, after his rejection—and after talking to her mother—she'd more than suspected it. The worst part was that now, when she knew loving him was forbidden, she loved him even more. For his honesty, for his valiant attempts to protect her from the appalling truth, for his own obvious anguish... God help her, she loved him.

He was her half brother.

She grieved over the loss of what had never been, what she could never have: his passion, the fierce physical connection she'd known for a few moments last night, when she'd kissed him. That grief mixed with an equally wrenching grief: her father's infidelity. Had he had an affair with Evie Mazerik? Was he still having an affair with her? Had there been others? Was her mother right in believing he no longer loved her?

Outrage began to churn in Lily, flooding her with adrenaline that made her heart pound and her thoughts grow excruciatingly clear. She flicked on the windshield wipers, shifted the car into reverse and backed out of her parking space.

The drive into town took only a few minutes. She steered up the driveway that bordered the neat shingled building where her father had located his practice twenty years ago, when it became clear that even a small-town doctor needed partners, as well as an office staff to navigate his patients through the paperwork.

Lily parked behind the building, then got out of her car and darted through the rain into the building. A couple of people sat in the front room, thumbing through magazines as they waited for their appointments. If she'd bothered to look at them, she probably would have recognized them. But she was in no condition to exchange pleasantries with anyone, so she kept her gaze straight ahead as she marched to the office manager's desk. "Janet, I need to see my father."

Janet looked up from her computer monitor with a smile, which faded rapidly when she read Lily's expression. "He's with a patient right now, Lily."

"I have to see him."

Apparently Janet recognized the unarguable truth in Lily's claim. "Why don't you go wait in his office?" she suggested gently. "When he's done with his patient, I'll send him in."

Lily nodded and hurried through the doorway into the back hall that connected the waiting area with the examination rooms and offices. She raced down the hall to her father's office and slipped inside.

She had always felt at home in this room. He'd decorated it to his taste, with warm paneling on the walls and built-in shelves on which he displayed family photos, including one dating back to her childhood and a formal portrait of her in her bridal gown, bowing her head to smell her bouquet.

She sat in one of the two upholstered armchairs that faced her father's polished mahogany desk. Then, too edgy to sit, she sprang to her feet. She paced around the small room, blind to the array of medical texts and pharmaceutical reference books on the shelves, blind to the diplomas hanging in frames on one wall, blind to the diminishing rain on the other side of the window, which overlooked the parking lot. She sat again, rose, paced, sat—and stood when her father entered the office.

He closed the door behind him, his face creased with concern. "Lily, what's wrong? Janet said you were upset."

Upset? Lily almost laughed at the understatement. "Dad..." Her voice wobbled as a sob threatened. But she was too enraged to succumb to tears. If what Aaron had told her was true, she had no interest in weeping. Once this was done, once she'd heard the truth from her father's mouth, she could fall apart. But not now. Not yet.

She trusted her anger to carry her through the next few minutes. "Are you Aaron Mazerik's father?" she asked.

He looked startled. "No. Of course not." Frowning, he maintained a safe distance from her, his hands tucked in the pockets of his white coat. "Why would you even ask me such a thing?"

"Aaron thinks you're his father."

He shook his head. "Is he...are you and he friends?"

"Dad." She didn't want to discuss her relationship with Aaron. The only reason it would even matter to her father was if she and Aaron were half siblings. "He says you're his father. He says that when he was a child, you visited him and his mother all the time. You brought them money."

Her father's frown relaxed slightly. He nodded, moved around her to his desk and stood leaning against it. "That much is true," he said. "I did visit and bring his mother money."

"Child-support money."

"Yes." He pulled his hands from his pockets as if he wanted to reach for her. "I did it for a friend."

"A friend." Did he actually expect her to believe that?

"Aaron's father was someone who trusted me, and

I did it for him. He didn't want his identity revealed. There were valid reasons, and while I can't say I agreed with the decision he made, I accepted it. He wanted to make sure Aaron was being properly cared for as a child, so he asked me to bring money to Evie Mazerik and to make sure Aaron was healthy and well cared for.''

"So you were…what? This guy's bag man?''

Her father grimaced. "As I said, I didn't agree with his decision, Lily. I thought he should visit the boy himself and acknowledge him, and I told him so. But he made his choice. He trusted no one else to get money to Evie and to make sure Aaron was growing up all right.''

"Aaron *wasn't* growing up all right,'' Lily said. "He was growing up to become a juvenile delinquent.''

"I know that.'' Julian Bennett sighed. "I shared my concerns with Aaron's father. Evie Mazerik was ill prepared to raise a child by herself. I'd talk to her about nutrition, about disciplining her son, structuring his time, reading to him. I honestly think he raised himself. It's amazing that he's turned out to be such a good man.''

"You're proud of him,'' she said, testing her father, still not persuaded.

"If he were my son, I'd be proud to say so, yes.'' He raked a hand through his hair, evidently frustrated that he hadn't yet convinced Lily. "If he were my son, I would have said so from the start. Even if it had cost me the love of your mother. It would have been the right thing to do.'' He laughed and shook his head. "Of course, I can't imagine ever doing anything that might cost me the love of your mother. The thought of even being with another woman..."

"You love Mom?"

He seemed taken aback. "Do you have to ask?"

Lily didn't want to get sidetracked by a debate about the tenuous state of her parents' marriage. But it was all related—Aaron's claim and the insecurities her mother had confided to her that very morning. "She thinks you're bored with her. She thinks you've grown tired of her."

"Your mother said this?"

"Yes."

"How could she think such a thing?" He looked appalled.

That, more than anything, swayed her. That her father could be more disturbed by his wife's doubts than by the allegation that he was Aaron's father proved to Lily that his marriage was essential to him. If Lily's mother wasn't the center of his life, he'd still be talking about Aaron, defending himself, denying everything.

He didn't even seem to care about Aaron. Only his wife mattered. "She thinks I'm bored with her? My God! My definition of hell would be to have to face a single day without her. She's everything to me! She's like the air I breathe."

"Which you probably don't pay much attention to, either," Lily said.

He seemed on the verge of arguing, then relented with a deep sigh. "Damn," he murmured. "You're right."

"Do something about it," Lily ordered him.

"Don't wait for her sixtieth birthday. Do something now. Pay attention to her."

"I will." He shoved a hand through his hair again, and she saw a sheen of tears in his eyes, just as her own eyes dried. She was feeling better. More certain. More hopeful.

"If you're not Aaron's father," she asked, "who is?"

"I can't tell you that."

"Why not?"

"I was sworn to secrecy," he explained. "I gave my word."

"But—" frustration welled up inside her "—Aaron's own mother won't even tell him who his father is. Every child has a right to know his father. Why can't someone tell him?"

"I wish I could. But I made a promise. I imagine Evie did, too. Beyond that, she understood that if she revealed Aaron's father's identity, she would no longer get any money from him. She needed that money. So I don't suppose she would have risked it by telling anyone, even Aaron, who his father was."

"He thinks she won't tell because she's still in love with the man."

"It wouldn't surprise me." Her father smiled wearily. He seemed battered, just as Lily had felt only minutes ago. "I can't speak for Evie. I can't begin to figure out what's going on inside her head. I wish I could help Aaron out, but I won't go back on my word. It's really up to Evie to tell him."

"Or his father," Lily said wryly.

"His father should have stepped forward right from the start. It would have been the right thing.

Lily…" He sighed. "God knows, I may be an idiot, but I'm not a sinner. And I love your mother more than I can say."

She felt all the tension drain from her. Her father loved her mother. Aaron wasn't her half brother.

Which meant that all the years he'd wanted her, all the years he'd tormented himself over her, all the times he'd told himself he could never act on his attraction to her…it hadn't had to be that way. Maybe he'd been a punk, maybe she'd been a River Rat, maybe they'd been far too different to connect. But he'd torn himself up inside over something that had never been true.

Turning toward the window, she noticed that the rain had stopped. A hint of late-day sunshine was fighting through the clouds, glazing the damp earth.

She remembered yesterday evening on her back porch. Before Aaron had pulled away, before he'd rebuffed her, before he'd said, "I can't," he had responded to her. Eagerly. Wildly. As overwhelmingly as she'd responded to him.

He might not love her. It didn't matter. For now, what mattered was that they could take a chance on it. They could reach for each other without fear or shame.

They could try.

"I love you, Dad," she murmured, giving his cheek a kiss.

"I love you, too, Lily. And I'm in your debt. I'm so glad your mother told you how she was feeling and that you told me. I only wish *she'd* told me." His eyes still shimmered. "I'll make sure she knows

I adore her. I'll make sure she never spends a moment wondering how much.''

"Tell her you like her new hairdo."

"Her new hairdo? Does she have…?" Realizing what he'd been about to say, he shook his head in disgust. "She has a new hairdo, huh?"

"Since last week. Pay attention, Dad."

"I will. I swear."

"I've got to go see Aaron," she said, starting toward the door. "Thank you for telling me as much as you could."

"Is there something going on between Aaron and you?" he asked as she turned the knob.

She thought about evading the question or blowing it off with a joke. But Aaron had inspired her to stop playing it safe, and so she had grown daring. Daring enough to have gone to see him that afternoon, in spite of his rejection of her. Daring enough to have confronted her father. Daring enough to speak the truth.

"Yes," she said. "There's something going on between Aaron and me."

CHAPTER ELEVEN

AN EERIE TRANQUILLITY had settled along the river. The rain had blown through quickly and now the air was warm and dry, sucking the moisture out of the evening, leaving everything clean and still.

Aaron felt cleansed, too. He'd told Lily. She knew. Just like the air in Riverbend, the air between them had been cleared.

He couldn't exactly say he felt good. He'd inflicted pain on the one person in the world he had never wanted to hurt. It wasn't his fault; all he'd done was speak the truth. But knowing how much that truth had wounded her tied his soul in knots.

He sat on his hammock, elbows resting on his knees, an unopened bottle of beer propped on the floorboards between his feet. He'd rummaged through the contents of his refrigerator and nothing had enticed him. He had no appetite.

He stared out through the trees at the river, smooth and silver in the calm after the storm. Sometimes, he thought, working with a client in counseling went like this. Sometimes he had to tear away a scab to treat the festering sore underneath. He hated doing it, but if it was the only way to heal a person, he did it.

He told himself Lily would feel better eventually.

He told himself he'd saved them both from disaster. He told himself that maybe in time they *would* be able to become friends, now that no more secrets stood between them.

Yet telling himself those things didn't revive his appetite. He couldn't even bring himself to drink his beer. The bottle was inches from his hand, the brown glass sweating, the cap sealing the liquid inside. Aaron's throat was still tight. His stomach still clenched. Merely thinking about consuming anything made him queasy.

A crow cawed. He saw it break free from a tree limb and soar above the river, a slash of black in the sky. It sailed east and away.

Footsteps thumped on the stairs leading up to the deck. He spun around in the hammock so fast he almost capsized it. He wasn't entirely surprised to see Lily standing on the top step.

Her dress was wrinkled, her hair mussed, her eyes unnervingly bright. "Maybe I should have called first," she said, "but I don't have your phone number."

His pulse revved up, even though he knew nothing was going to happen between them, nothing more than talk. She wouldn't tempt him now, wouldn't press her lips to his the way she had last night. She wouldn't dare. He was perfectly safe.

So why was his heart pounding in double time? Why were his muscles tensing, his blood heating?

Seeing her now was more difficult than before. He still responded to her, in spite of everything. Her cornsilk hair and dazzling smile and slim curves were so patently off-limits he shouldn't have felt a thing when he gazed at her. But the desire hung on like a lingering cough after the flu, a symptom he couldn't seem to shake.

"I talked to my father," she announced. "He said no."

"He said no," Aaron echoed, his voice flat.

"He's not your father. He said he would have acknowledged you if he was. He would have done the honorable thing. He said he delivered the money to your mother from your father as a favor for a friend, and he was sworn to secrecy about who your father was, and—"

"Lily." Aaron didn't want to sit in the hammock on his deck, observing the sheer relief that animated her face while she repeated her father's lies. "Of course he said he's not my father. What else could he say? 'Gosh darn it, you found me out'? 'I was the one noodling around with old Evie Mazerik all those years ago'?"

"I believe him," she insisted, crossing the deck to stand before Aaron, forcing him to crane his neck to look at her. "If he'd been your father and hadn't wanted you to know about it, why would he have visited your home every month?"

"He wanted to see me."

"If he was your father and trying to hide it, visiting you would have been just the sort of thing to arouse your suspicions. Think about it, Aaron. If he was your father and wanted you to know, he would have told you. If he was your father and didn't want you to know, he wouldn't have visited you all the time. He would have done what your father did—

find someone else to check up on you and get money to your mother.''

There was something to what Lily was saying. He wasn't convinced, but…

She hunkered down in front of him, gazing directly into his face. ''Three people know who your father is,'' she said. ''My father, your mother and your father. My father can't tell you who your father is because he made a promise. Your father isn't going to tell you, because if he were, he would have done it by now. Your mother is the only person who can tell you.''

''She won't,'' he said, wishing Lily's eyes weren't so luminous, her smile so beautiful, wishing she didn't believe so strongly in what she was saying. He still refused to believe it, because if he let himself believe it, he would kiss her. He'd hold her and touch her and make love to her, the way he'd wanted to right from the start. And then, if it turned out she was wrong about Dr. Bennett, he'd be doomed. He would never be able to live with himself after that.

''He's your father,'' he said. ''You want to think the best of him, Lily. I don't blame you for believing what he told you.''

''Your mother could confirm it.'' She rested her hands on the edge of the hammock near his legs and scrutinized him. She was so earnest, so ingenuous. ''I know she's refused to tell you who your father is, but she could tell you it's not Julian Bennett.''

No doubt Lily wanted to hear his mother exonerate her father. The trouble was, his mother might say what Lily *didn't* want to hear. Lily was prepared for only one answer. She could handle a no, but not a yes.

Not that she would ever need to handle anything. "My mother won't tell," Aaron said.

"Let's go ask her."

Aaron sighed. He didn't want to ask his mother. If she'd cared enough to make his life even the slightest bit easier for him, she would have told him the truth a long time ago. She hadn't. She wouldn't.

Lily had already straightened, captured his hands and hauled him out of the hammock. "Come on, Aaron. Let's go and ask your mother. What do we have to lose?"

"Plenty," he warned. "If she says your father is my father…"

"Then I'll be back where I was this afternoon. It can't get any worse than that. Nothing your mother says could shock me more than what I've been through today." Still holding his hands, she urged him toward the stairs.

He halted, freed his hands from hers and turned around to lift his beer from the floorboards. He wasn't going to let her drag him off—at least not until he'd grabbed his keys and put the beer back in the refrigerator. He might need it when he got home, and he'd want it cold.

He was worried about Lily, but he was more worried about himself. He'd endured nasty, futile, frustrating conversations with his mother many times before. Every time he'd attempted to open the door and peek inside, she'd slammed it in his face. He'd heard the key click, shooting the bolt into place, locking him out. His mother had made it quite clear that she would never let him in.

But Lily hadn't gone through what Aaron had with his mother. She was pushing for it. Fine. Let her have her way. His mother would say nothing, and Lily would be able to spend the rest of her life believing her father was innocent. And Aaron would be stuck where he'd always been—locked out.

As long as there was plenty of cold beer waiting for him when it was done, he supposed he could endure it one more time. For Lily.

THE DUPLEX ON THIRD STREET off West Hickory was pathetic. Lily wished she could think of a kinder word, but Evie Mazerik's home had a mean look about it. The shingles were cracked and crooked, the paint peeling, the concrete front steps crumbling. An old car scabbed with rust sat in the driveway. Tufts of uncut grass sprouted through crevices in the front walk.

This was where Aaron had grown up, Lily realized. Not just on the "poor" side of town, but in a drab dreary house with filthy windows, a broken couch on the sagging porch and a netless basketball hoop nailed to a tree in front. She bit her lip to keep from blurting out how bleak the house seemed, how sorry she was that he'd had to grow up there. Aaron was strung so taut the merest hint of pity might be enough to make him snap.

"I don't even know if she's home," he muttered, although lights shone through several of the windows, both upstairs and down. He climbed the porch steps, pressed the doorbell beside one of the two doors, then stood back and watched one of the up-stairs windows.

After a minute Evie Mazerik appeared at the win-dow. "Who's there?" she shouted through the screen.

"It's Aaron. I've got my key."

"All right. Come on up."

He crossed the porch to the door. "It's hard for her to get up and down the stairs," he explained to Lily as he unlocked the door and held it open for her.

She entered a narrow hallway that led directly to a steep, dark staircase. Aaron flicked a switch near the door, turning on a ceiling fixture at the top of the stairs that spilled an uneven light on them. The air smelled musty.

Climbing the stairs, Lily wondered whether she'd made a mistake in forcing Aaron to confront his mother the way she'd confronted her father. But she wanted him to take a chance. Thanks to him, she'd been taking chances ever since his first visit to her house, and taking those chances had opened up new worlds to her. She'd stopped feeling paralyzed by guilt, blaming herself for everything that had gone wrong in her marriage. She'd discovered a perilous flaw in her parents' relationship and forced them to attempt to repair it. She'd found the courage to invite a few friends to her house—even though most of them hadn't been able to come—and to think big with her painting. She'd broken through, broken out. Come alive.

She'd opened her heart to the possibility of love. Love for the man who had brought her back to life.

Now she had to do this for him. Even if the possibility of love was never realized, she had to give Aaron something as valuable as what he'd given her. Not money for his summer program but something far more essential: himself.

By the time they reached the top of the stairs, Evie Mazerik had opened the door to her flat. She seemed surprised to see Lily, but her fleeting scowl gave way to a gracious smile. "Hello," she said, peering past Lily at Aaron. "You didn't tell me you had someone with you."

"I have someone with me," he said belatedly, flicking a humorless smile at Lily. "Can we come in?"

"Of course. I only meant, if I'd known you were bringing a friend, I would've straightened the place up a bit." She led them into the cramped living room of her apartment. Lily took in the yellowed walls, the faded curtains at the open windows, the brown carpet's pile flattened in places, bald in others. Metal wall brackets held adjustable shelves filled with clutter—vases, figurines, magazines, souvenir ashtrays. A small TV on a stand in a corner broadcast the fabricated frenzy of a game show, cheers and whoops and flashing dollar signs on the screen. The stale scent of cigarettes hovered in the air.

"You're Lily Bennett," Evie said when Aaron failed to introduce them. "I guess I know just about everyone in this town. You work at the Sunnyside Café long enough, you get to know everyone." Clad in a plain T-shirt and slacks, her reddish hair slightly disheveled, gaudy paste-and-glass earrings adorning her ears and traces of pink lipstick trapped in the tiny creases in her lips, she had the same slightly faded, slightly cluttered look as her living room.

"Thanks for letting us stop by, Mrs. Mazerik," Lily said, then realized "Mrs." wasn't right.

"Would you like a cold drink? I'm sure I've got lemonade or iced tea or something." She made her way to the kitchen. Aaron followed her, and Lily followed him.

This room was smaller and smokier, thanks to the cigarette still burning in a glass ashtray on the circular table near the window. Used dishes were stacked in the sink, but the countertops were clean. The appliances were almost old enough to be vintage, except for a relatively new microwave oven. Despite the open window, the air in the room was stagnant, tinged blue from the smoke.

Evie inspected the contents of her refrigerator, then closed the door and spun around, a smile stretching her mouth. "I could fix some lemonade, no problem. Or would you like me to make some coffee? I know it's hot, but—"

"No, really, that's all right," Lily said. Coming here had seemed like a terrific idea when she'd been at Aaron's house. But now, trapped in the stuffy kitchen with his mother, Lily was having second thoughts.

Evie was trying so hard to be a generous hostess, offering things Lily and Aaron didn't want. What they wanted she wouldn't easily give. Lily might have made as big a mistake tonight as she'd made yesterday, when she'd assumed Evie and Aaron had a loving relationship.

He crossed to the table and stubbed out his

mother's cigarette, smashing it until smoke stopped curling from the ashtray. Lily chose to view that as a loving act, or at least a caring one.

"I've got some cookies," Evie continued, moving in a lopsided gait to one of the cabinets and swinging the door open.

"We didn't come here for food," Aaron said, placing a hand on her shoulder and drawing her away from the cabinet. "We came because Lily wants to ask you about my father."

Evie's smile vanished. Her eyes narrowed and her brows angled into a frown as she glared at Lily.

"Sit down, Mom." His hand still on her shoulder, Aaron guided her to one of the chairs by the kitchen table and gently pushed her into it. She reached past the napkin holder, a plastic wedge shaped like a butterfly, for the pack of cigarettes lying there. Her hand shook slightly as she lit a cigarette, but that could have been a result of her stroke rather than anger or apprehension.

She inhaled, then blew out a stream of smoke. "I'm not going to talk about that, Aaron," she announced.

Aaron shot Lily an I-told-you-so look.

Refusing to be discouraged, Lily pulled up another chair and sat, resting her hands on the table and smiling, as if she could will Evie back to her former cheeriness. "You probably think this is none of my business, Ms. Mazerik, but Aaron believes his father is my father. So, you see, it is my business."

"I'm not going to talk about it," Evie said, her voice coarse from the smoke.

"I appreciate that it's your own private life—"

"It's not just her life, Lily," Aaron broke in. He leaned against the counter, his arms folded across his chest and his expression grim. He'd been through this before, and he clearly wasn't in the mood to cheer his mother up. "It's my life. But she doesn't care about that."

"Don't start, Aaron," his mother warned. "I'm tired of having this argument with you."

"We haven't had this argument in years. And the reason we haven't is that I know Dr. Bennett is my father. So there's no point in discussing it anymore."

"I know Dr. Bennett *isn't* your father," Lily stated, then turned back to Evie. "He won't take my word for it, or my father's. You're the only one he'll listen to."

Evie's expression was completely shuttered now. "Julian Bennett is a gentleman, and that's all I'm going to say about him."

"You've got to say more than that!" Lily experienced a wave of empathy for Aaron, even though his mother's intransigence amused her in a strange way. She admired stubborn women. She'd recently discovered a wide streak of stubbornness in herself, and she liked it. "*I* know my father's a gentleman, Ms. Mazerik. Aaron thinks he's the kind of man who would father a son and pretend that son wasn't his."

"You're implying that's what Aaron's father did?"

"It *is* what my father did," Aaron remarked dryly, still leaning against the counter, refusing to join the women at the table. "Here I am. Where is he? When is he going to throw an arm around my shoulder and say, 'Hello, son'?"

"I won't have you speaking ill of your father," Evie declared. "I mean it. Your father…" Her voice shook the way her hand had before. She steadied herself by taking another drag of her cigarette. "All I'll say, Aaron, is he's a better breed than I am. Everything that's good inside you, you have him to thank for it."

"Wonderful. I'd like to thank him in person. Could you tell me who he is?"

"No! You know I can't!" She was openly irate now, her cheeks flushed, her hazel eyes glinting with resentment.

"Why can't you?" Lily asked quietly.

"I gave my word. He begged me, and I promised. I would never do anything to ruin his reputation."

"He didn't have any compunctions about ruining yours," Aaron retorted.

"For crissake, I had no reputation to protect. I was just a farm girl come into town because my folks had too many mouths to feed. I was what I was—and that's what I am. Him? He was so much better than me, Aaron. I couldn't believe he'd even look at me, let alone love me."

"He didn't love you. He got you in trouble and walked away."

"He never walked away. He did what he had to do." She pressed her lips together and glared at Lily. "We all do what we have to do. That's the best you can say for any of us."

Lily longed to reach across the table and take Evie's hand, tell her that she wasn't under attack, that she didn't have to defend herself. "So much time has gone by, Ms. Mazerik. The past isn't going to change. How can anyone's reputation be ruined at this point? All Aaron wants is a name.''

"And what do you want?" Evie accused.

Lily smiled hesitantly. "A name that isn't Julian Bennett.''

"I start talking about who it isn't, it's almost the same as talking about who it is. And I gave my word, Lily. *He* knows that." She jabbed an accusing finger in Aaron's direction, then took a final puff of her cigarette and smashed it out in the ashtray. "Respect and honor come from keeping your word. You can give birth to a bastard child and still have your respect and honor in this world. But only if you live by your word, if you don't break your promises. And I won't break mine.''

Lily glanced over her shoulder. Aaron no longer wore an I-told-you-so expression. He looked both exasperated and deeply hurt, and she didn't blame him.

She pivoted back to Evie. The woman wasn't going to grant her son his only wish, the one bit of information any son deserved. Out of respect and honor—or out of sublime selfishness—she wasn't going to do it for him. Lily's only hope was that Evie would do it for her.

"I'm falling in love with your son, Ms. Mazerik," she said quietly but fervently. She wouldn't look at Aaron now. She didn't want to see his reaction to her words. It might make her falter, regretting that she'd verbalized her feelings when they were still so new. "If he and I share a father... You see the problem? I love him.''

Evie seemed stunned. "You just lost your husband," she reminded Lily.

"Seven months ago," Lily told her. "And it was…complicated. My marriage and my mourning aren't important right now. What matters is Aaron and me, and finding out if my father is his father. Our future is riding on it, Ms. Mazerik. We need to know."

Evie's gaze traveled back and forth between Lily and Aaron. Lily still refused to look his way. If Aaron was staring at her with contempt or disbelief, she didn't want to know.

"No," Evie blurted, then turned to gaze out the window. "It wasn't Julian. And I won't say another word about it. I'm done."

Lily let out a breath she hadn't realized she was holding. Her spine went limp; sweat slicked her palms. She felt wrung out.

But *it wasn't her father.* Aaron wasn't her brother. And through her exhaustion crackled a spark of energy: she and Aaron were liberated. They could be anything they wanted to each other, anything at all, because they weren't brother and sister.

She heard footsteps behind her. Turning, she saw him exiting the room without a word. She hastily stood and covered Evie's hand with hers, just as she'd wanted to before. "Thank you," she whispered before darting out of the room after Aaron.

He was already halfway down the stairs when she closed the apartment door behind her, already at her car by the time she reached the front steps. He waited stoically while she hurried across the scruffy grass to the street. As soon as she unlocked the car doors, he flung himself into the passenger seat, slammed his door and stared straight ahead. His face might as well have been a stone sculpture for all the life in it.

She took her place behind the wheel, ignited the engine and drove away from his mother's house. Sending him a sidelong glance as she steered around the corner, she saw that he was still rigid, his eyes cold, his mouth set. "This is good news," she ventured gently.

"Sure." The single word was like a chip from a sculpture, a sharp, cold piece of stone falling from his mouth.

"We aren't related."

He said nothing.

"Aaron, it's a start. She's revealed this much. Maybe in time she'll tell you more."

"Sure."

He was as stubborn as his mother was, refusing to acknowledge that he'd gotten more from his mother tonight than he'd gotten in his entire life. He sat beside Lily, obviously seething, denying himself even a tiny smile of triumph. It seemed he would rather dwell on what he hadn't gotten, instead of what he had.

She tried not to be annoyed with him. She was so happy—for her parents and especially for Aaron and herself. He wouldn't have to hold back any longer. They could explore the attraction that had been simmering between them for so long, and it wouldn't be wrong.

Aaron had desired her since high school, and in the past two weeks he had awakened her to her own strength and courage. He'd opened her eyes to everything an honest relationship between a man and a woman could be. Surely this was a moment to celebrate.

She concentrated on her driving, figuring she'd goad him back into a conversation when they reached his cabin on River Road. The few times she glimpsed him—when they passed beneath a street lamp, when the headlights of a passing car flashed across his face—he appeared forbidding. But even the glowering lines of his face, the implacable furrows of his brow and the austere angle of his jaw couldn't squelch her joy.

She and Aaron shared no blood. They could be lovers. Now, or tomorrow, or someday. The path lay before them, and they were free to take it if they chose.

She pulled up the dirt driveway to his cabin and set the parking brake. Before she could speak, he had yanked open his door and leapt out.

''Aaron!'' She raced after him, up the path to his front door. He stomped inside but didn't slam the door shut behind himself, so she followed him in.

His home was nothing like his mother's. The walls of the main room were paneled in raw pine. Solid comfortable-looking furniture was arranged around a wood-burning stove. The shelves in his house were filled, not with knickknacks, but with books and a compact stereo system. A counter separated the living area from the kitchen, which was clean and brightly lit.

Aaron marched around the counter, through the kitchen and out the back door to the deck. Lily marched out after him.

He stood by the railing, his fingers curled around

the wood, his gaze fixed on the river, which was barely visible through the trees as the last pink of dusk gave way to night. She studied the unyielding lines of his back, the tension in his shoulders.

She wanted to close the space between them, to wrap her arms around him. She'd do it—if she wasn't afraid he'd toss her over the railing.

She remained near the door, leaving him some space. "Why are you angry with me?" she asked.

"I'm not angry with you."

With his mother, then. Lily didn't need to ask him the reason for that anger. "Despite everything, Aaron, something good came out of this."

"For you, sure."

"For *us*." She hoped she wasn't presuming too much.

"Lily." He rotated slowly until he was facing her. She saw cracks in his stony facade, fissures through which heat seemed to leak, red-hot with rage and pain. "She won't tell me. She'll never tell me. It's like getting stabbed through the heart again and again. You wanted to ask her, so we asked her. Don't expect me to be thrilled that I got stabbed through the heart one more time."

"She told you my father—"

"Swell. Great news about your father. He's off the hook."

"I thought you'd be pleased."

"You can be pleased for me, Lily." He gazed skyward, as if searching for the right words in the fading light. "Of course you should be pleased. She gave you your father, She didn't give me my father, and she never will."

"Yes, but…" It hit Lily then, a jab to her solar plexus so fierce she almost couldn't breathe. Her relationship with Aaron was irrelevant at the moment. He was hurting so badly, nothing else mattered—certainly not her, her love for him, his longing for her.

She wanted to weep, to take Aaron's suffering onto herself. She wanted to heal him the way he'd healed her, and she had no idea how to begin.

He seemed to recognize the change in her. "Go home, Lily," he said, the harshness gone from his voice. "I'm not fit to be around right now."

"That's a good reason not to leave you."

"I'm cut up inside, okay? I'm bleeding." He turned back to the river. Anguish underlined his voice, shaped his posture, shimmered in the air. "I don't want you to see me like this."

She had already seen him. And it only made her love him more.

Her love gave her the strength to cross the deck, to circle her arms around him from behind. She pressed her cheek to his back and linked her hands around his waist.

She felt a shudder tear through him, more of the stone cracking, shattering, falling away. She hugged him more tightly, feeling herself shatter inside, too. Never had she realized how lucky she was, how blessed to have her family, her friends, her solid connection to this town, to her home. Aaron had never had what she had. He had always been alone—until now.

"I won't go," she whispered, so softly she could scarcely hear herself.

But he heard her. When he turned in her embrace and gazed down at her, she knew he'd heard. When he bowed his head to hers, when he pressed his mouth to hers, when he circled his trembling arms around her and clung to her as if she was his only hope, she knew.

His kiss was hard, urgent, needy. She wanted to assure him that she'd meant what she said, that she wasn't going to leave him, that even wounded and dangerous, he couldn't frighten her away. She wanted to tell him that his life was a miracle, that he'd grown up stronger than any other man she'd ever known, including those with two parents and all the security in the world. She wanted to tell him that it was his own fault she was here, kissing him. He'd been the one to make her brave.

But she couldn't talk when he was kissing her, so she only kissed him back, hoping her kiss would tell him everything he needed to know.

He slid his hands up her arms. His fingers were warm and leather-smooth against her bare skin. She wasn't sure if he was still trembling or if the trembling came from inside her, in her racing heart, her bristling nerves, the dark tug of sensation in her womb. His hands rose to her neck and then higher, to her cheeks. He ran his thumbs along her jaw and up to the corners of her lips, which parted as if he'd found latches there and flicked them open.

His tongue conquered her mouth. He was aggressive, almost rough, but she didn't mind. His kiss was like the painting she'd created the other night, fueled by rage but ultimately beautiful and redemptive. His kiss was the storm in her painting, but she tasted life in it, hope, resurrection.

She wouldn't leave him. She couldn't. Not now.

Through his shirt she felt the flexing of the muscles of his back, the warmth of his skin, the ragged pumping of his lungs. He hauled her tight to himself, so tight she could feel his heartbeat against her breast, his erection pressing her belly through his jeans. He curled his fingers around the sleeveless strips of fabric at her shoulders and pushed them down her arms, exposing her collarbones and upper back. The zipper gave way between her shoulder blades, and her dress went slack. Aaron's body was the only thing holding it up.

He was still kissing her, his tongue claiming her again and again as he shoved the dress down between them, to her waist, past her hips. His hands roamed her back and sides, the calluses on his fingertips scraping her skin. He wedged his hands between them, then tore his mouth from hers and leaned back. His eyes seemed to burn as he gazed down at her, his breath uneven as he watched himself caress her.

She watched, too. His hands were large, dwarfing her breasts, covering them, kneading the flesh and chafing her nipples until she shivered. She felt her knees weaken, felt her hips grow heavy with heat. He backed up and sat on the hammock, pulling her between his legs so he could kiss her breasts.

She choked back a moan. The only sounds were her gasps and his and the shrill chirp of crickets. As he took one breast and then the other in his mouth, he shoved down her panties, then cupped his hands around her bottom, spanned her hips, slid one hand between her thighs.

Her legs gave way as the heat sank deeper into her, molten and pulsing. A small cry escaped her, so soft she heard it only in her heart. He swung her around until she was lying on the hammock, then stood and tore off his clothes, his big, beautiful hands deft and purposeful even as his eyes continued to blaze. She had less than an instant to view his naked body, so tall, so lean and limber, so visibly aroused. All from his touching her. She'd hardly touched him at all.

She wanted to. She wanted to explore his magnificent body, every rippling muscle and sinew, ever supple contour. She wanted to slide her hands down his chest, dance her fingers over his skin, kiss the dark nubs of his nipples, make him feel what he'd made her feel. She wanted to trace his ribs, his collarbones, his shoulder blades, the ridge of his hipbones. She wanted to fill her hands with him, to treasure this strong, healthy, potent man who had done so much for her, who meant so much to her.

But he gave her less than a moment to appreciate his body. He joined her on the hammock, stretching above her, kissing her again and again, his hand between her legs, rubbing her, parting her, and she had only a chance to ring his waist with her arms as he plunged into her. His body stroked hers, hard and fast and deep, striking sparks inside her with the friction of his thrusts. She went with him, closing her eyes and letting the fire blaze through her, swift and wild. She climaxed in the heat, a piercing, almost painful convulsion that left her weak and weary and helpless.

It was too intense. Too fierce. She felt branded inside, scorched, stripped as naked emotionally as she was physically.

This hadn't been the sweet generous lovemaking she'd fantasized about when she'd dreamed of Aaron. This had been cataclysmic, an explosion of fury and desperation.

But it had let her see Aaron's soul. It had stripped his emotions naked, too, exposed him, revealed the pain and yearning that lived in his heart.

He couldn't scare her away. Not with his words and not with this. She loved him, and she was going to stay.

CHAPTER TWELVE

HE CURSED.

His body was drained, utterly spent. The hammock had some give to it, and her hands were drifting vaguely on his back, so he knew he hadn't crushed her to death. But he had to get off her.

In a minute. As soon as he found the strength.

As soon as he stopped hating himself.

She lay beneath him, so slender, so delicate. Her skin reminded him of pearls, smooth, with a mysterious luster. Her hair was softer than he'd imagined it, her mouth more lush, her body…

He felt an unexpected lurch in his groin. He was still inside her—empty, but the tight heat of her kept him hard. He could try moving a little for her, slowly, gently—and he'd be lucky if she didn't smack him or scream in pain.

He despised himself for what he'd just done. Lily, the golden girl, the woman he'd been dreaming of most of his life, the glorious creature he didn't deserve… He'd gone at her like an animal, unable to think, unable to slow down, unable to do anything but lose himself in her and pretend, for a few frenzied moments, that he wasn't drowning in bitterness.

‘‘Aaron?’’

Her voice was muted, cool and soothing against

his raw nerves. He lifted himself off her and stared out at the river, afraid to meet her gaze.

"Aaron, are you okay?"

Was *he* okay? He shifted, trying to keep the hammock from wobbling too much as he pulled back. She tucked her hand under his chin and steered his face around so he was forced to look at her.

Her beauty sucked the breath from him. He didn't need her body; he could lose himself in her eyes. "I'm sorry," he murmured, his voice a hoarse rumble. "If I hurt you…"

"Hurt me?" She smiled faintly and shook her head.

"I was…" He closed his eyes. He'd been too fast, too rough. Maybe he'd managed to avoid hurting her, but it couldn't have been good for her. "I'm usually better at this," he finally admitted, aching with embarrassment.

"Better at sex?"

He nodded.

"I guess you'll just have to show me how good you usually are."

He opened his eyes and peered into her face, searching for a sign that she was joking. After such an abysmal performance, she couldn't possibly want him again.

Another curse escaped him, partly from disbelief and partly from concern. "I didn't use anything," he murmured, a fresh pang of remorse seizing him. "Protection, I mean."

"I'm on the Pill," she told him.

Right. She'd been married. And given what a jerk

her husband had been, she probably hadn't wanted a baby with him.

Even so, Aaron was ashamed of himself for not exercising care. He wanted to protect Lily from everything: the heartache of her marriage, the trauma of thinking her father might have cheated on her mother, the difficulties of returning to town so different from the person she'd been when she left. And him. He wanted to protect her from him.

"Aaron," she murmured, her hand still on his chin, her thumb moving gently over the day-old stubble of beard. "You're reminding me of me, taking the blame for things that aren't your fault."

"This wasn't my fault?" Her touch thawed him, consoled him, made his heart squeeze. He brushed a stray blond lock back from her cheek and was amazed all over again by how silky her hair was.

"We made love. It was something we both wanted." She seemed to search his face. Even in the night's descending shadows, he could see the tiny frown lines creasing her forehead. "We did both want it, didn't we?"

"I've wanted to make love to you from the first instant I saw you," he said. "But that's not what happened here."

"What *did* happen?"

I was hurting. I was angry. I was hostile and resentful, and you wouldn't leave when I told you to go. "I don't know," he confessed in a broken whisper.

She took a minute to digest his answer. She had every right to be insulted, yet apparently she wasn't. Her frown faded and her eyes sparkled, lit from within. "At your mother's house," she said in her sweet, healing tone, "I said I was falling in love with you."

"To get her to tell you about your father."

"No. I said it because it's true." She raised herself to kiss him, a tender kiss that told him she didn't need to hear him say he loved her, didn't need him to pay lip service to meaningless sentiments, didn't need him to apologize or rationalize or explain.

She loved him.

He had never been in love before, not with Cynthia, not with any of the other women he'd known over the years. He'd never seen love up close. He wasn't sure how it worked. He didn't believe he carried the gene for it. Some people seemed to understand it, but he'd never experienced it, never witnessed it in his own home, never felt the staggering force of it.

Yet now, as Lily gazed up at him, her eyes steady and her mouth curved in a confident smile, he felt its force. More than the sex, this frightened him. It overpowered him. Something was breaking apart inside him, something that hurt and felt good and scared the hell out of him.

"I love you, Lily," he heard himself say.

THE MOSQUITOES drove them indoors. He gathered up their clothes and ushered her into the cabin, letting the screen door clap shut behind them. She squinted in the glaring light of the kitchen, but when she would have taken her dress from him, he instead clasped her hand and led her down a short hall to his bedroom. It was tiny, barely big enough to accom-.

modate its furnishings: a narrow bed, a tall bureau and a chair. He dumped their clothing on the chair, then pulled open a drawer and removed a T-shirt for her.

Better than her dress, she thought with a smile as she shook out the folds. The shirt was white, with "Riverbend Hot Shots" across the front in bright red. She pulled the shirt over her head; the soft cotton fell to her knees.

He donned a pair of gray gym shorts. "I'm starving," he said. "Are you hungry?"

"Yes."

He seemed almost bashful, spinning away from her and retreating to the kitchen. Whenever his gaze met hers, she felt a connection between them, something humming with energy, like an electrical circuit. But then he would turn from her, as if the current burned him.

Maybe it did. Maybe she ought to be careful around it, too. She'd never felt it with Tyler. He'd been romantic and glamorous and pretty much irresistible to a twenty-one-year-old small-town girl from Indiana. But she'd never felt so bound to a man, not the way she felt with Aaron.

She drew in a deep breath before joining him in the kitchen. He was hunched in front of the open refrigerator door, and when he straightened he was holding a bowl of grapes and an apple. He set the grapes on the table, then carried the apple to the counter, where he proceeded to slice and core it.

"Can I help?" she asked.

"There are glasses in the cabinet to the left of the

sink," he told her. "I don't know what you want to drink."

"Water would be fine." She couldn't handle anything stronger.

He nodded and continued slicing the apple.

A minute later the plate of apple wedges joined the grapes, a jar of peanut butter and a knife, a box of crackers and two tumblers full of water on the table. It was an odd sort of meal, but it was perfect.

He gestured her toward a chair, then sat facing her. She watched him lift an apple wedge, spread a thick layer of peanut butter on it and hand it to her. "Thanks," she said. She hadn't eaten apples and peanut butter since she was a child. She'd forgotten how delicious the combination was, the clash of tart, juicy fruit and salty, gooey peanut butter.

He fixed a wedge for himself, leaned back in his chair and bit into it. Her view of his chest was tastier than the apple she was munching on. She remembered the first time she'd glimpsed his torso, when he'd lifted his shirt to wipe the sweat from his face. She still wanted to touch him, slowly and thoroughly. She wanted to run her fingertips along the ridges of muscle and bone. She wanted to press her lips to his skin, rest her cheek against him and listen to his heartbeat.

She hoped he would show her how good a lover he could be.

She hoped he'd meant it when he said he loved her.

He had to have meant it. Why else would he seem so ill at ease, avoiding her gaze, concentrating on the crackers he was shaking from the box, saying nothing? Some men used the word love so cheaply it was meaningless. Aaron wasn't that kind of man.

Still, the silence between them felt awkward. She scrambled for a subject they could talk about. Basketball? His summer program? The weather? After the day they'd both lived, everything seemed trivial.

Everything but what they'd experienced in the past hour. Everything but the love and fear and doubt spinning in the air around them.

"Whose name is on your birth certificate?" she asked.

His eyes flashed at her, the silver in them like mercury, fluid but opaque. "Unknown."

"Unknown?"

"It says, 'Father: Unknown.'"

She plucked a grape from the bunch and bit into it. Its sweet tang bathed her tongue. Across the table Aaron continued to watch her. At last he was no longer refusing to look at her. "Have you ever thought about hiring a detective?" she asked.

He laughed. "Right. That would go over really well in Riverbend."

"Your father could be someone from outside town," she suggested. "Then no one in town would be offended if you used a detective to track him down."

"It's someone from town." He devoured a cracker. "Someone your father knew, since he was the guy's agent, running money to my mother."

She sighed, hoping Aaron wouldn't hate her for what she was about to say. "I can almost sympathize with your mother. I can understand why keeping her

word is so important to her. She has so little in her
life. Her word is one of the few things she has.''

"She has a son.''

"A son is a person, not a possession. She doesn't
have you. You're not something she can keep, the
way she can keep her word.''

"Yeah, well, she's managed to hang on to me
pretty well. Here I am.''

"Because you love her. You told me that, in spite
of everything, you came home to help her because
you love her.''

He smeared another apple wedge with peanut butter and took a bite. He chewed slowly, his gaze still
on Lily. "If I hadn't come back, the town would
have had to take care of her. As it was, her insurance
didn't cover everything. The Community Church
held a pancake breakfast to raise money. They helped
pay for her physical therapy.''

"That's what community is all about,'' Lily said,
proud of her neighbors for rallying around Evie Mazerik when she'd needed their assistance. "It must
have made it easier for you to come home to a town
that would do that for your mother.''

He nodded. "There are good people in Riverbend.
There always were, even when I was a kid.'' He
gazed into the distance for a moment, remembering.
"Some folks treated my mother and me nicely. Most
of them saw us as the town trash.''

"No one ever—''

"Don't kid yourself, Lily. Lots of people talked
about us. But some people didn't.'' He reflected for
a moment. "The Steele sisters, for instance. Ruth and
Rachel always treated me with dignity.''

"They're wonderful," Lily agreed.

"And Coach Drummer. I told you—I wound up staying in Riverbend as much for him as for my mother. He's always been like a—" Aaron stopped abruptly and glanced away.

Lily had been about to pop another grape into her mouth. But she realized what he'd been on the verge of saying, and its obvious logic stunned her. Coach Drummer had been instrumental in getting Aaron to settle in Riverbend after his mother's stroke. He'd lined up his old job for Aaron. Eighteen years ago Coach Drummer had brought Aaron onto the varsity basketball team as a sophomore when other equally talented sophomores had been relegated to the junior-varsity team. It had been so sudden. Here was a team with standouts like Jacob Steele and Mitch Sterling, big, older boys who'd always been committed to the school and the team, and abruptly Aaron Mazerik, the town troublemaker, a kid who'd spent time behind bars, had been added to the roster.

Coach Drummer had been like a father to Aaron.

"Aaron?"

"No," he said sharply.

"Isn't it just possible—?"

"No."

"How can you be sure?"

"Coach would never do that. He loves his wife."

"My father loves his wife, and you thought *he* had done it."

"No," Aaron said, his tone vehement. "It's not Coach."

Maybe that was why Aaron hadn't hired a detective—he didn't want to know. He could have accepted the truth if it had led to Lily's father, because he hadn't revered Lily's father. He revered his high-school coach, and he refused to think anything ill of him. If Wally Drummer turned out to be the man whose name belonged on Aaron's birth certificate, Aaron would never forgive him. He would never be able to admire him again.

But as Lily had told Aaron's mother, it had all happened way in the past. Wouldn't Aaron be able to forgive a man's long-ago mistake? Wouldn't he accept the truth and move on?

He reached across the table and covered her hand with his. His palm was broad, his fingers warm as they closed around hers. That he would touch her when she was assailing him with such troubling possibilities pleased her.

She raised her eyes from their clasped hands to his face. "I'm not an easy man," he murmured, the words so simple, so blunt. "You might want to re-think this whole thing."

"I don't want to rethink it," she said with absolute certainty. She'd been through a difficult relationship, much more difficult than anything Aaron might bring. No matter what he'd endured, he wasn't self-destructive like Tyler. He would never cause her that kind of heartache.

His hand tightened on her, and his gaze seemed to tighten its hold on her, as well. Without releasing her, he shoved back his chair and stood up, then pulled her out of her chair. His arms went around her, safe yet demanding, gentle yet covetous. His mouth descended on hers, strong and warm and confident.

She scarcely remembered walking down the hall

to the bedroom. She scarcely remembered his sliding the T-shirt he'd lent her over her head, shucking his shorts, easing her down onto his bed and stretching out beside her. It was too narrow for two people, but she didn't care. She wanted him as close as he could be.

What happened outside wouldn't happen here. Aaron had been possessed then, desperate to find in her a way to make his pain disappear. Now she sensed no desperation in him, only love.

He lay on his side, his head propped in one hand, the other tracing her body. His fingertips glided over her cheeks, down her nose, along the curve of her lip and lower. When he touched her throat she sighed, and he let his hand linger there to feel the beat of her pulse. When he touched her breasts she moaned. A thick lush pressure gathered in her belly as he circled her flesh, stroked her nipples, teased them into taut points.

She lifted her hand to his chest, mimicking his exploration, drawing delicate lines across his skin with her fingertips. His nipples grew taut, too. His breath caught. When she skimmed down to his abdomen, his muscles flexed and he groaned.

It was sweet, this slow, patient loving. Sweet and frustrating, a clash of delicious sensations. She wanted Aaron to go faster, but she wanted to make every moment last. She wanted him to bring his hand down between her legs, where tension was building, her body straining—but she didn't want him to stop stroking her skin, toying with her breasts, roaming as high as her shoulder and down again. She wanted everything now—but not yet.

He shifted, sliding lower on the bed so he could kiss her breasts. His tongue was rough, his lips soothing. Her hips lifted as need and pleasure pooled deep inside her.

He moved lower, kissing a path downward, spreading her legs and pressing his mouth to her. She cried out, a keen spasm tearing through her.

She forgot how to breathe. She forgot how to think. She knew only how to feel, how to love the man who could elicit such searing sensations in her. Her body arched against him, but still he kept kissing her, using his tongue and his lips on her, stroking her thighs with his hands until she could do nothing but surrender. As her climax pounded through her, she heard a strange sound, her own choked voice repeating his name over and over, as if it was the only word she knew. Right then, it was. He slid back up her body until his face was even with hers, and the beauty of it, the passion and longing in his eyes, replaced his name as the sum of her knowledge.

He bowed to kiss her, his hands framing her face, his body heavy on hers. She felt him between her thighs, hot and seeking. She groped for him, guided him to her, opened herself to him, welcomed him.

He moved slowly inside her, almost cautiously, as if afraid of hurting her. She clamped her hands to his hips and urged him deeper. She didn't want his caution now, after what he'd already done. She wanted only him, all of him, as merciless with his body as he'd been with his mouth.

"Please," she whispered, "don't hold back."

He groaned and kissed her again.

She tightened her grip on him, wrapped her legs around him. She hadn't thought she could feel more than she had just moments ago, but she could. She did. Her soul was no longer alone. It was mating with Aaron's, merging with it, in a reaction as volatile as nuclear fusion. The explosion roared through her, through him, and in that flash of ecstasy the boundaries between them disappeared. They were one entity, one being, held together by nothing but love.

HE DIDN'T KNOW how he was going to get through the day. He and Lily hadn't slept much. How could they, cramped together in his skinny bed? Every time Lily had moved, every time she'd breathed, he'd felt her against him and gotten hard.

She would tilt her head and her hair would splash against his shoulder. Or her hand would alight on his rib cage. Or she'd roll over and her bottom would curve into him, soft and round and inviting, and every ounce of blood in his body would speed straight to his groin.

He'd tried not to wake her. But hell, it wasn't *his* fault. Even before her eyes opened, she would rub up against him or drape her arm around him, and then they'd be kissing again, weaving their legs together, finding each other in the dark, in the night. All night long.

Okay. So now it was the morning after, and he was exhausted. That was the least of his concerns.

He felt inexplicably shy, gazing at her in the early sunlight that filtered through the bedroom window. People made love at night because it was easier, he realized. It had been easier to expose himself when he was blanketed in darkness, when what he was showing wasn't actually visible. Easier to kiss Lily when he wasn't confronted with the shocking beauty of her face, a face he'd spent his whole damned life dreaming about, a face that shook loose so many conflicting emotions inside him.

Standing in his bedroom doorway after a shower, he observed her relaxing in his bed, smiling sheepishly, her hair tousled and one breast visible above the edge of the sheet he'd spread over her. In the morning light she was no longer just the magnificent woman he'd spent the night with. She was Lily Holden, the young widow. Lily Bennett the popular student. Lily, the woman who'd wrestled more information from Evie Mazerik in one evening than Aaron had gotten out of her in thirty-three years.

She was Lily, a woman people respected and liked simply for who she was. And he was Aaron Mazerik, with all that implied.

"What time is it?" she asked, her voice a sleepy purr.

He rubbed a towel through his wet hair. He'd thrown on a fresh pair of shorts; he wanted to wear the T-shirt he'd lent her last night, but if he did, he'd be distracted by thoughts of her all day. Entering the room, he pulled open a dresser drawer and found a clean shirt, one that didn't carry her scent. "Time for me to eat breakfast and get to the high school. I have to be there before the kids arrive."

She stretched and the sheet slid down to her waist. Her beauty rocked him. Her grace, the perfect proportions of her body, the pure femininity of her...

He turned away, aware that if he continued to stare at her he wouldn't be able to resist her.

"Breakfast," she murmured, then yawned.

"I'm making eggs. You want some?"

"Mmm. Thanks."

Even with his back to her he was turned on. Her voice was as sexy as her body. The sleepy thickness of it, the languor in her movements… He swallowed and bolted from the room, wishing he had time for another shower. A cold one.

By the time she joined him in the kitchen, she was wearing her dress and he was under control. He spooned the scrambled eggs onto two plates, stacked the toast on a third plate, poured the coffee. "This is about twice as much as I usually eat," she told him. "I guess, being an athlete, you need a substantial breakfast."

Also being a man who'd indulged in sexual acrobatics for half the night after consuming only a light snack for supper. His body craved protein and carbs almost as much as it craved Lily. And sleep. And a chance to figure out what the hell had happened yesterday.

He knew what had happened. He'd told Lily he loved her. He'd spoken from his heart. His brain was having trouble working through it, though.

"I'd like to see you after work," he said, then forced out the rest. "I don't think I should."

Her eyes flashed at him, filled with surprise and bemusement. "Why not?"

It was too late for anything but honesty between them. "I need time to think."

She eyed him curiously, then scooped a chunk of

egg onto her fork. "You don't like company when you think?"

At least she hadn't asked him what he needed to think about. She could probably guess. She seemed able to read him well. "I think better alone," he told her.

"All right." Her tentative smile reassured him. "I'll spend the evening painting."

"I'll call you tonight," he promised. Hearing her voice while remaining apart from her would be torture, but he could handle a little torture.

"All right."

"And I'll see you tomorrow."

"Aaron, it's all right." Her smile grew. "You want to think. I'll stay out of your way."

He smiled, too. He couldn't help himself. If she could be so understanding, so sympathetic…she really must love him.

"I love you," he said, only the second time in his life he'd ever uttered those words. He still wasn't sure he could live up to the promise in them, the commitment, the terrifying power of them. But he didn't regret saying them.

He loved Lily. Just one more truth he was going to have to get used to.

CHAPTER THIRTEEN

"AARON!" WALLY DRUMMER'S WIFE beamed at him through the screened back door. She quickly pushed it open and waved him into the kitchen. "What a nice surprise! How are you?"

"I'm fine." He gazed about the square, sun-filled room, taking in the wall calendar, the refrigerator magnets shaped like little copper-hued pots and pans, and the potatoes and vegetable brush sitting at the edge of the porcelain sink. He looked everywhere to avoid looking at Mary Drummer. "Is your husband around?"

"He's downstairs in the basement, fixing my wall clock. Why don't you go on down, Wally?" she hollered as she opened the door to the basement. "Aaron Mazerik is here! Go on down," she murmured to Aaron. "He'll be glad of the company."

Aaron forced himself to give Mary Drummer a quick smile. She was a compact woman, short and beginning to thicken in the middle, her brown curls framing the sort of face a person might expect to see on a box of cake mix. For as long as Aaron had known her, she'd been the consummate homemaker, always holding open the back door to welcome "Wally's Boys," organizing bake sales to raise money for the school's sports programs, sending homemade snacks on the bus with the basketball team when they had ''away'' games. When Aaron had first joined the team, he'd hated her. She had been everything a mother should be—stable, predictable, dependable and always armed with a plate of cookies fresh from the oven—and she'd reminded him of what he lacked in his own life.

His mother was prettier. But Mary Drummer was warmer. Would the coach have cheated on her?

Aaron didn't want to think about it. But he couldn't stop himself.

All day at the high school he'd been distracted, bombarded by a hail of thoughts that had nothing to do with teaching basketball to ten-year-old's. Not just thoughts of Coach Drummer, but thoughts of Lily, memories of the night he'd spent with her, twinges and twangs so physical it was if he was still in bed with her, feeling her breath on his shoulder, her hair spilling over his skin. At one point he'd been running a drill, jogging pace for pace with Sam Sterling while Jeff shouted guidance to the rest of the kids as they passed balls back and forth…and suddenly he was haunted by the sound Lily made, low and throaty, when she came. And the ball bounced right past him.

Later the kids had been practicing layups, aiming the ball at the X's he'd marked on one of the backboards with strips of red tape, and he'd been elbowed by a recollection of his morning conversation with Lily, when she'd said she would give him space to think. By the time he'd come back into focus, the kids had rotated through the drill three times.

And, of course, he'd thought about Wally Drummer. He found it hard not to think about his old coach when he was in the gym, playing ball. But today's thoughts had centered on the fact that Wally had been a father figure to him.

A father figure.

He'd wanted to go somewhere quiet, somewhere private, to work that one through. But he couldn't abandon the kids. Teaching them basketball was his job, and more important, it was his passion. He refused to let his mind break loose until the last child had left for the day and Jeff had collected the gear.

Watching the lanky teenager scoop the balls into the mesh bag, Aaron recalled when he used to collect the balls for Drummer. The coach used to assign that task to whoever had arrived late for practice, or hadn't run hard enough, or had used bad language. Aaron had spent a lot of afternoons collecting balls.

After a while Aaron had learned that no matter how bad his language, Drummer wasn't going to kick him off the team. If he didn't run hard enough, Drummer would make him run harder. If he arrived late, Drummer would make him stay late. But he wouldn't cut Aaron. "I've got money riding on you," the coach used to remind him. Aaron had assumed Drummer had been referring to the bail he'd posted—but maybe he'd been referring to something else. Those envelopes of cash Dr. Bennett used to bring his mother?

He thought about that as he locked the equipment room and his office, as he washed up in the locker room, as he left the building and climbed into his car. He thought about the kind of commitment a coach made to his players, the kind of commitment

a man made to a troubled boy. The kind of commitment a father made to a son.

Aaron had scarcely come to terms with the news
that Dr. Bennett wasn't his father. To replace Bennett
with his beloved coach in his imagination… It was
too mind-boggling to contemplate.

Whether or not he wanted to contemplate it, the
possibility lurked inside him like a seam in a mine,
glittering with the promise of ore. He had to dig.
Even if the ore turned out to be fool's gold or worse,
something radioactive, he had to excavate it.

He stood at the top of the stairs leading down from
Mary Drummer's kitchen, trying to summon the
courage to join her husband in the basement. Mary
gave him a gentle nudge. "Go on. You won't be in
his way."

"Thanks." He descended the stairs slowly, warily,
wishing he knew what awaited him at the bottom.

Half the basement had been finished into a win-
dowless den, with inexpensive paneling on the walls,
rugged carpet on the floor, bluish fluorescent light
fixtures in the false ceiling, and chunky, indestructi-
ble furniture arranged haphazardly about the room.
Drummer used to invite the team over for pizza
whenever they had a big win. They'd be shepherded
down the stairs, feeling a bit claustrophobic beneath
the low ceiling tiles. Aaron used to sit by himself on
the ugly plaid armchair in the corner, munching on
a slice of pizza and observing the camaraderie of his
teammates. They hadn't ostracized him, but they
hadn't exactly included him, either. Everyone had
seemed aware that he wasn't really one of them.

A door stood open into the unfinished half of the basement. "I'm in here," Drummer shouted.

He found the coach seated on a stool in front of a well-lit workbench that stood against one of the cement walls. A peg-board lined the cement above the bench, with tools neatly arranged on it.

"Hey, Aaron!" Drummer glanced over his shoulder and grinned a greeting. "How are you?"

"Okay." Aaron leaned against the wall, far enough to be out of the coach's way but close enough to study him. Gray eyes, he thought. Wally Drummer had gray eyes. His own eyes were flecked with gray.

But other than that, was there any resemblance? Certainly no more than between Aaron and Julian Bennett. Wally was tall, like Aaron, but huskier in build. His hair was straight, like Aaron's, but Bennett's hair was straight, too. The coach had a sharp chin, but... Damn. Aaron bet half the men in Riverbend old enough to be his father had sharp chins.

Drummer had always been kind to Aaron's mother—but kindness wasn't passion. Aaron had always assumed the coach had treated Evie nicely for no other reason than that he'd invested time, effort and a whole lot more in her son.

That investment was the reason Aaron was in Drummer's basement right now, weighing the odds that the coach's genes had shaped him. He willed his heart not to thump too loudly. He willed his stomach not to twist into yoga-like contortions. He willed himself to smile as the coach set down his screwdriver and lifted the back panel off the clock. "I've got to tell you, Aaron, this is the ugliest clock in the world. Look at it!''

He held it up for Aaron to view. It was shaped like a daisy, the main part of the face yellow, with twelve white petals circling the face, each imprinted with a number. The hands of the clock resembled green stems; the hour hand had a tiny leaf budding off it.

''It's ugly,'' Aaron agreed.

''When it stopped working, I thought my prayers had been answered,'' Drummer said, setting the clock back down and examining the plug and wire extending from the motor. ''Finally, I thought, we can get rid of this monstrosity and buy a new one. But Mary won't hear of it. We got this clock as a wedding present from her aunt. Thirty-two years it's been running. Mary says if I can't fix it, our marriage is over.'' He laughed.

Aaron managed a chuckle as his mind ran through the calculations. If the Drummers had been married thirty-two years, the coach would have been with Aaron's mother *before* he married Mary. But would he have married Mary, knowing another woman had brought his son into the world?

No. Not Wally Drummer. He would have made an honest woman out of Evie. Aaron was sure of it.

Of course, he'd been sure Julian Bennett had been his father, too. The fact was, Aaron wasn't sure of anything anymore.

''I think the problem is a loose connection,'' Drummer continued, tugging on the cord. ''If that's all it is, sorry to say, I can fix it, and then there'll be no escape from the daisy clock. What do you think?''

Aaron leaned toward the bench, wondering if
Drummer was going to ask him to help. "I don't
know much about electronics," he admitted. It occurred to him that repairing broken clocks was the
sort of thing boys learned how to do by watching
their fathers. Basic electronics, basic plumbing, basic
carpentry—little boys were supposed to hang out
with their dads at the tool bench in the basement,
learning the skills necessary to keep a house and its
contents in working order. Aaron had missed out on
that. "Your daughter would probably be a better help
to you when it comes to fixing things," he added.

"Megan is good at this stuff," Drummer confirmed. "She never took much to cooking, but she
loved learning how things go together and how they
come apart." He stripped back the insulation from
the cord, then loosened the screws that connected it
to the motor. "Nowadays, of course, all the girls take
shop and the boys take home-ec. If I recall, they
don't call it home-ec anymore."

"Consumer studies," Aaron supplied.

"That's right. Consumer studies. Boys wouldn't
be willing to take it if it was still called home eco-
nomics. Consumer studies and…what's shop
called?"

"Technology education."

"That's right. It's a good idea, I think, everyone
studying everything. Boys have to know how to cook
and girls have to know how to fix broken clocks.
Even if they're ugly." He pulled a new cord out of
its packaging and separated the wires. "So what's on
your mind, Aaron?"

Aaron scrutinized Drummer's hands as they manipulated the tools and probed the clock's inner workings. His hands were large, like Aaron's. A basketball player needed large hands. "Nothing," he lied, shoving his own hands into the pockets of his shorts so he wouldn't compare them with Drummer's.

"You came over here for nothing?"

"Maybe I came so I could learn electronics from you." Like a son from a father, he thought, then slammed that notion out of his brain with a silent curse.

Drummer glanced at him, smiling wryly. "I may be older, but I'm not that much slower. Now try telling me the truth."

The truth? Aaron wasn't sure Drummer was ready for that. He wasn't sure *he* was ready. But he owed Drummer some sort of explanation. "I guess you could say I'm trying to find myself."

Drummer looked at him again, this time a long, leisurely perusal. "Aren't you a little old for that?"

"When I was the right age for finding myself, all I wanted to do was lose myself," he reminded Drummer.

"Mm." The coach focused back on the clock. "Do you think you can find yourself in my basement?"

Maybe, Aaron thought, the possibility fisting around his soul and squeezing painfully. "I'm thirty-three years old, Coach, and I'm still not sure who I am."

"I know who you are," Drummer said. "You're a smart man, a good man. A responsible man. A man

I'd trust with my life. What more do you need to know?''

Aaron sighed. ''I've just…been going over old times in my mind,'' he said carefully, his voice steady even as his heart pumped like a jackhammer inside his rib cage. ''I'm trying to figure out why my life went the way it did.'' He drew in a deep breath, then pushed out the words. ''Why did you save me, Coach? Why me?''

''*Save* you?'' Drummer gave him yet another probing look, then shook his head. ''I paid your bail. I didn't save you.''

''The charges against me were ultimately dropped because of you.''

''Not because of me. Because of you. Because you kept your nose clean and didn't get into any more trouble, and the judge decided to close that book.''

''My nose stayed clean because of you, Coach. You fed me that morning, and then you made me join the team…''

''I was desperate for a forward, one who could run fast. I'd seen you run. I thought the team would benefit from having you.''

''And I'd benefit from having the team.''

''That, too.''

''You could have chosen some other kid. Lots of kids ran fast.''

''But you had a fire in your eyes,'' Drummer said, laying down his screwdriver and turning to meet Aaron's gaze. ''I didn't want to see that fire burn out, Aaron. I believed in you. Rightly, it turned out. You were a boy who needed only one thing—someone to believe in you.''

"I needed a hell of a lot more than that, Coach," Aaron argued with a laugh.

"Well, you got some of it from me and the rest came on its own. You grew up. You learned self-discipline. It took you a while to get the hang of schoolwork, but you managed to earn yourself a master's degree, so I reckon you figured that out, too. What else did you need?"

Someone to teach him how to fix things. Someone to teach him about love, the kind of love that would drive a man to repair a tacky clock just to make his wife happy. The kind of love that didn't scare a man half to death.

"You need a woman in your life," Drummer guessed, answering his own question.

"I think I've got one."

"Really?" Drummer broke into a smile. A paternal smile? Aaron wondered. "Who is she?"

"Lily Holden."

"Julian Bennett's daughter?" Drummer digested this, then gave a noncommittal nod. "I heard she was still recovering from her husband's death."

"She's pretty much recovered," Aaron said.

"I also heard she inherited a small fortune from her husband."

Aaron shrugged. "I don't know. We don't discuss money."

"She wouldn't by any chance be the source of that out-of-the-blue funding you got for your program, would she?"

Aaron clenched his jaw to keep from blurting out the wrong reply. He didn't want people to associate Lily's generosity with the personal relationship blossoming between them. The two issues were separate. "As I said, she and I don't discuss money," he said.

Drummer eyed him skeptically, then got busy tightening the screws on the back of the clock. "She's a nice girl, and awfully pretty," he said. "Good family, too. You could do worse."

Say something fatherly, Aaron silently pleaded. *Say something that would confirm it for me.* Drummer's interest in Aaron's private life seemed genuine, but Aaron couldn't find in it the proof he needed. Only possibilities. Only maybes.

He wasn't going to get proof from Drummer, not today. Not without building up enough courage to confront his old coach—his good friend—directly. And for that much courage, he'd probably need Lily by his side. "So, that's how you keep a clock going," he murmured as Drummer fastened the back panel into place.

Drummer shot him a grin. "It's how you keep a marriage going," he said.

LILY WAS IN HER STUDIO, seated on a cushion on the floor, a sketch pad propped on her knees and her fingers smudged black with charcoal, when the phone rang. The silky pink light of dusk filled her windows, and the familiar scent of the paint filled her lungs. She'd done several sketches, all of them Indiana landscapes. Her cornfield had been created in a fever of furious inspiration. But in general she preferred to plan her paintings before she applied brush to canvas.

She'd been working all afternoon, mapping out a set of images in her mind: the river, the trees bordering it. The limb from which she and the River

Rats used to jump into the water. The train tracks racing out of town, straight to the horizon. The grain elevator, towering over the edge of town like the last outpost before a frontier.

Riverbend. She wanted to paint her home.

But the rhythmic chirp of the phone told her it was time for a break.

She leaned back against the wall, reached for the cordless extension and pressed the connect button. "Hello?"

"Hi." Aaron.

She smiled. He'd said he would call, and she trusted him, but still, one never knew about guys. But Aaron wasn't just a guy. And last night had been, if anything, even more intense for him than for her. He had much more on his mind than just her. She would have forgiven him if he hadn't called.

Or maybe she wouldn't have forgiven him. Maybe she would have been crushed.

In any case, he'd phoned, and the sound of his voice warmed her. Her bare toes curled, her grip tightened on the handset and she closed her eyes, savoring a sweet, dark memory of the night they'd spent in each other's arms.

"Hi," she remembered to say.

"How are you?"

"Fine." Wonderful. Magnificent. "How about you? How was your day?"

He laughed. "Interesting."

"Tell me."

"Well, I just got home, and there was this letter in my mailbox. From a lawyer."

She opened her eyes and sat straighter. She

reached for the glass of iced tea on the floor a few feet away, then realized her hand was stained with charcoal. She wiped her fingers on her jeans, leaving gray smudges on the denim, and lifted the glass. "A lawyer? Is someone suing you?"

"No. It seems Abraham Steele left me some money in his will."

"Really? You, too?" Her smile returned and she sipped some iced tea. "I also got a letter. From Nick Harrison, right?"

"Same guy. Did Steele leave you money?"

She chuckled. Leaving her money would have been like bequeathing sand to the Sahara. "According to the letter, he left me some paintings. He liked to collect paintings by regional artists. I've seen most of the artwork he acquired over the years. There are a few really nice pieces among them. I'm supposed to go through them with Rachel and Ruth, choose four for myself and help them figure out what to do with the rest. Abraham seemed to think I was some kind of expert."

"Well, he gave you your first box of watercolors."

"Then it's all his fault if I'm any kind of expert. Which I'm not." A tear surprised her, seeping through her lashes and skimming down her cheek. "It was so sweet of him to think I'd like some of his paintings. I know people thought he was gruff and domineering, but there was a kindness in him, a generosity." She wiped her cheek, not caring if she left charcoal on her skin. "And to think he left you money, Aaron! That's really amazing."

"I'm guessing it's for the basketball program."

"Do you think so?"

"I think I told you—before he died, I went to see him, to try to wrangle a donation from him. He wasn't a pushover like you," Aaron teased. "But he said he was interested and he'd get back to me. He never did. I guess life got in the way. Or death." Aaron paused. "I'm figuring maybe he made some arrangements to leave money for the program."

"Is that what the letter from Harrison said?"

"No. It was kind of vague. It claimed there was a monetary bequest and I was supposed to go to this lawyer's office as soon as possible so he could discuss the bequest with me in person."

"Abraham really was generous," Lily repeated. "And he cared so much about Riverbend. It wouldn't surprise me if he left money for a town program like yours. When are you going to see the lawyer?"

"Tomorrow afternoon after work, if I can. I've got to call his office and see if he can squeeze me in."

"That's wonderful, Aaron. I hope it's a lot of money so you can make the program everything you want it to be."

"I'm sure he didn't leave me *that* much money." She could picture Aaron shrugging modestly. She could picture his multicolored eyes, his lean body, his thick straight hair. She could picture his chest, and for a steamy moment she considered painting a portrait of him. Nude. She wondered if he would be willing to pose for her.

If he did, she doubted she'd get much painting done. If she had Aaron naked before her, painting was the last thing she'd want to be doing.

Her yearning surprised her. All day, even as she worked, as she downed half a sandwich, as she drove out to the grain elevator and studied the way the noon light played across its curved surface, a part of her had remained with Aaron. More than a memory, it was a physical sensation, a visceral ache. She had never had such a strong craving for a man before. Before things had gone so terribly wrong in her marriage, she'd enjoyed making love with Tyler—but not like this. Not with a need that pulsed so urgently inside her, so constantly.

"This is stupid," Aaron said, breaking into her thoughts.

She felt a flush of embarrassment at how far her mind had strayed. "What?" She tried to steer her mind back to what they'd been talking about: Aaron's basketball program, Abraham Steele's will—nice, tame subjects.

"Why don't I swing by the Burger Barn and pick up some burgers, and then come to your place."

"I thought you needed time to think," she reminded him when all she wanted to do was scream, *Yes! Come!*

"I do. But..." He sighed. "The only thing I'm able to think about is you. How much I want to be with you."

"I want to be with you, too." Her heart danced, a lively tempo.

"What do you like on your burger?"

"Everything. And, Aaron?"

"Yeah?"

"Bring an overnight bag."

He didn't answer, but she could picture his smile.

WHEN HE ARRIVED at Lily's house, she was fresh out of the shower, her hair still damp and smelling of herbal shampoo, her body wrapped in a silk caftan with a zipper running down the front. All through dinner, as they talked about Mitch's son Sam and Lily's ideas for paintings, he contemplated that zipper, how easy it would be to slide it down, what a fine accomplishment it would be for him if he did. Lust layered every moment in expectation.

"This town needs more art in it," she said after daintily licking ketchup from her fingers. "The library ought to display the work of local artists. Or... You know the front area at the bookstore? Kate could hang paintings there. She could use the space as a gallery for local artists. Not me, but others, like the artists whose paintings Abraham was always buying. What do you think?"

He thought her idea was great. He also thought that if he didn't get his hands on that zipper soon, he'd go mad.

Within minutes of depositing the wrappers from their burgers and the empty cardboard boats from their French fries into the trash, he got his hands on the zipper. And he happily stopped thinking about the letter he'd received from Nicholas Harrison, Attorney at Law, and his visit with Wally Drummer, and everything else that was going on in his life. Everything but Lily.

Her bed was bigger than his, but its width didn't keep them from crowding together at the center. He was exhausted after having gotten so little sleep the night before, but that didn't stop him from waking up several times during the night and brushing his lips against her shoulder, reaching around to caress her breast, luring her awake and making love to her.

He wasn't a kid; he ought to have some self-control. But with Lily, self-control vanished. It simply wasn't there. He wanted her, and having her only made him want her more.

"I'll prepare a nice dinner tonight," she told him when he reluctantly staggered out of bed at seven-thirty the next morning. "And then it's the weekend. We can sleep late on Saturday."

"Thank God," he groaned, although he was smiling.

"Unless you want to have some time alone to think tonight." Her grin was teasing.

"I'd just as soon skip thinking," he told her.

"Then I'll fix that nice dinner. I know you haven't seen any evidence of it yet, but I do know how to cook. You'd be amazed at what I can do with boneless chicken breasts."

His gaze strayed to *her* breasts and he steeled himself against the yearning to climb back into bed with her. "Okay," he murmured. "Amaze me."

She didn't have to cook a chicken dinner to amaze him, he acknowledged as he headed off to the high school an hour later, freshly showered and fueled by a couple of bowls of cereal with skim milk—the woman was going to have to invest in some real milk if she wanted him to eat breakfast at her house. He would pick up a quart of whole milk himself on his way to her house that evening. And a bottle of wine. Maybe some flowers. The flowers in her yard were all in bloom, but the roses growing in her backyard were yellow. She needed red roses, long-stemmed beauties. He'd buy some for her.

His overnight bag contained not just his toiletries but a pair of khakis and a clean shirt, in case he could make arrangements to visit the lawyer that afternoon. He was mystified as to why Steele mentioned him in his will; surely the old man could have made arrangements for a donation to the summer program through his bank, if that had been his intention. Then again, maybe he *had* made arrangements through his bank, and Aaron was going to have to meet with bank officers, as well as the lawyer, so the money could be transferred properly into the program's account.

Lily was right. Despite his crusty demeanor, Steele had been a generous fellow. Aaron had been sure the man would come through with money for the program—and apparently death hadn't prevented him from doing that, after all.

Aaron telephoned Harrison's office while the kids were in the pool. "Three-forty-five would be fine," the secretary told him. "You can meet with Mr. Harrison then."

Great. Aaron would visit the lawyer, then cruise down Main Street and do his shopping—whole milk, wine, roses—and then he'd spend the night with Lily. And in the morning… God, yes. In the morning they would sleep late. He would doze in Lily's arms until noon, and then wake up and make love with her. His definition of bliss.

Energized by the thought of what awaited him, he charged through the day, laughing with the kids, ordering them to sing the birthday song to Jeff, letting them scrimmage with minimal interference from him. When he blew his whistle, they all seemed to hear—even Sam. When their parents started showing up to take them home, they seemed disappointed that the day was over. They all pleaded to come back next week, but next week was reserved for the young teen group—twelve- and thirteen-year-olds.

If Steele came through with enough money for the program, Aaron would hire a couple of more assistants and increase the enrollment so every kid who wanted to participate would be able to, every week for the whole summer.

Once everyone had left the gym, he carried his bag into the locker room, stripped off his athletic gear and took a quick shower. He dressed in the slacks and tailored shirt, brushed his hair, thought about the many different ways Lily might amaze him that evening and took a deep breath.

Nick Harrison's office was in a building a block from the Courthouse Square. Aaron left his bag in the backseat of his car and entered the building. The waiting area was empty and uncannily quiet, a stark contrast to the noisy gym with its vaulted ceiling echoing the laughter, the sneaker squeaks and a chorus of youthful voices warbling, ''Happy birrrrth-day, dear Je-efff!'' A potted shrub stood in a large planter in one corner and a window-unit air conditioner hummed quietly. The furniture looked hardly used, the magazines on the coffee table too smooth to have been read. The receptionist at the desk facing the door smiled at him when his gaze intersected with hers.

''I'm Aaron Mazerik,'' he said.

"Mr. Harrison is expecting you. Please follow me." She stood and led Aaron down a short hall to a door. After knocking, she opened it. "Mr. Mazerik is here," she announced.

"Come in!" Nick Harrison was not much older than Aaron, with black hair, cool blue eyes and the height to have played on the high-school basketball team. The jacket of his summer-weight suit was draped over the back of his chair, his tie was loosened and his shirtsleeves were rolled up. He stood behind a massive walnut desk, smiling enigmatically. At his back a wall of built-in bookcases held ponderous-looking leather-bound volumes. "Come on in, Mr. Mazerik," he said energetically, extending his hand to shake Aaron's. He gestured for Aaron to sit in one of the chairs facing him.

Once Aaron was seated, Harrison settled into his chair and lifted a document from a folder on his blotter. He skimmed it, then lowered it and assessed Aaron. "I'm not sure how well you knew Mr. Steele."

"Not well at all," Aaron admitted. "I mean, I knew who he was. I talked to him a few times. He used to come to all the high-school basketball games. I played for one year on his son's team, when Jacob was a senior."

Harrison nodded. "I thought it would be best if you came into the office to hear about your bequest, rather than my writing you about it in a letter. It just…well, it may surprise you."

"It's money, right? You said in your letter—"

"Yes, it's money."

"Steele and I had talked about his contributing to

a summer basketball program I'm running. I figured that's what this is about.''

''He left you one hundred thousand dollars,'' Harrison said.

Aaron blinked. Coughed. He glanced toward the window overlooking the square, then turned back to the lawyer, who continued to gaze steadily at him. There was no sign the guy was joking, no evidence he was delusional. No reason to believe this was anything but reality.

''Excuse me?'' Aaron asked. He must have misheard. It made no sense that Steele would have left him—

''One hundred thousand dollars.''

''For my summer basketball program?''

''For you, Mr. Mazerik. To do with as you wish.''

''One hundred thousand dollars?''

''That's a one with five zeroes after it.''

''I...'' Aaron sank back in his chair, too stunned to find that number anything but preposterous. ''I don't get it.''

''It was Mr. Steele's wish that you receive this.'' Harrison opened the folder, pulled out a check and handed it to Aaron. ''There may be some tax ramifications to a bequest this large, so you'll want to discuss it with your accountant.''

Aaron didn't have an accountant. He hadn't needed one—until now. He stared at the check lying before him on the desk. It was made out to him, all right, ''Mazerik'' spelled correctly, and the figure on it was just as Harrison had described it: a one followed by five zeroes.

''I don't get it.''

"There's nothing to get, Mr. Mazerik. Mr. Steele made some unusual personal bequests. Yours was one."

"Who else got an unusual personal bequest?" he asked. Lily obviously hadn't. Being left a few paintings from Steele's collection made perfect sense. Being left *anything* made sense, since her family had a relationship with Steele. She'd gotten her first paints from him as a four-year-old.

Aaron had never gotten anything from the man. Now, Steele was dead and... Something cold nipped the length of his spine. Something cold and eerie and ominous.

"Mr. Steele included many Riverbend citizens in his will. He was very close to this town, and he left a lot of people bits and pieces from his estate."

"A hundred thousand dollars isn't bits and pieces. It's a small fortune."

"He obviously had a special feeling about you," Harrison said, shrugging. "I assumed he was close with your family. Your mother picked up her bequest this morning."

"My mother?" Aaron struggled to breathe, to remain in his chair as suspicion closed in on him. "Evie Mazerik?"

"She is your mother, isn't she?"

"What did Steele leave her?" Suspicion closed in on him.

Harrison must have read the change in Aaron's mood. His manner changed, as well, transforming from amiable to uncomfortable. "Money," he said quietly.

"How much?"

"I think you'd better discuss that with her."

A deeper chill gripped Aaron, an icy bite at the base of his skull. He stared at the check for another moment. It seemed malevolent to him, tainted, the multicolored anti-forgery printing of the numbers, the double signatures on the bottom line, Aaron's name across the center of it: Pay to the Order of Aaron Mazerik… It scared the hell out of him.

Without taking the check, he shoved out of his chair, spun on his heel and stalked out of the office. By the time he reached the front door, he was running.

CHAPTER FOURTEEN

ARMED WITH HIS OWN KEY, he didn't bother ringing the doorbell. He unlocked the front door, charged up the flight of stairs and jammed his key into the door at the top. His mother opened it before he could twist the knob.

"Aaron!"

He couldn't tell if she was surprised or dismayed to see him. To decipher her enigmatic expression would have taken more time and patience than he had at that moment. He simply stared at her fluffy red hair, her surprisingly delicate lips, the creases fanning out from the corners of her eyes and etching the skin of her throat.

"How much did he leave you?" Aaron asked.

Evie averted her eyes. "You come barging in, you don't even say hello—"

"How much?"

She sighed and stepped away from the door, a tacit invitation for him to enter the apartment.

As usual, the dim babble of the television came from the living room, roiling the cigarette-scented air. As usual, dirty dishes were heaped in the kitchen sink. A thick porcelain mug filled with tea stood steaming on the table. He could have pointed out that the late afternoon was too sweltering for hot tea. But when he saw the sheet of thick creamy stationery lying unfolded next to the mug, he forgot about her choice of beverage.

Two long strides carried him across the small kitchen. Her letter was essentially the same as the one he'd received from Nick Harrison yesterday—that there'd been a bequest and to please make arrangements to come into the lawyer's office....

"How much?" he asked her again, lowering the letter to the table and turning to her.

"How dare you come in here and ask me these questions?" she shot back. "This is my home, Aaron. You haven't lived here for fifteen years. You can't just come in here and act like—"

"He left me a hundred thousand dollars," Aaron said.

That shut her up. She limped past him and sank into her chair, her gaze still avoiding him. With trembling hands, she shook a cigarette out of the pack on the table and lit it.

"How much did he leave you?"

"He was a very generous man," she said wearily, facing the window, aiming her smoke at the screen. "We should just be grateful that for whatever reason, he decided to remember some of the people he met along the way. It's a kindness, Aaron. I'm not going to question it."

"I am." He leaned over her, resting his fists on the table and glowering down at her, even though she stubbornly refused to look at him. "I'm going to question it. Why would a man like Abraham Steele leave me a hundred thousand dollars? Tell me, Mom."

She shrugged unconvincingly. "How should I know?"

"Did he leave you a hundred thousand dollars, too?"

"Of course not."

"What do you mean, 'Of course not'? There's no 'Of course' about any of this. He left me all that money for a reason. He left you money for a reason, too. What were you to him? The lady who refilled his coffee cup when he went to the Sunnyside for breakfast? How much was that worth to him, Mom? Eighty thousand? Seventy-five?"

"Stop it, Aaron." He heard a plea fraying the edges of her voice. Staring at her profile, he saw tears glimmering in her eyes. "He was a good man."

"Tell me," Aaron demanded.

"Tell you what? He left me a much smaller amount. It doesn't matter." A few tears escaped and slid down her face, leaving shiny streaks. Not bothering to wipe her cheeks, she took another drag on her cigarette.

"He was my father," Aaron said, because she wasn't going to say it. He hadn't even realized *he* was going to say it until the words came out—and then there they were. Spoken. Almost tangible, four cold, solid links in a chain of truth.

Hearing them astonished him. Hearing her silence, her inability to deny them, astonished him even more. He sank into the chair opposite her and struggled to breathe.

Abraham Steele. The town patriarch. The richest, most powerful man in Riverbend, direct descendent of the town's founder, bank president, erstwhile mayor, mover and shaker. Abraham Steele, who'd sat on the bleachers at every damned home game Aaron played in, even after his son Jacob had graduated from high school and the basketball team. Steele had sat through the games, well-groomed and quiet while all around him people were screaming and cheering, flirting and fooling around. He'd come to the games to watch his other son play.

Abraham Steele. Who had never acknowledged Aaron, never come to his house, never waved to him on Main Street. Who had never smiled at him, never touched his arm, never ruffled his hair. Never taught him how to dribble a ball or repair a clock. Never bailed him out of jail or any other kind of trouble. Never sat beside him in the living room and asked him what he was learning in school.

One hundred thousand dollars. Was that the price of an unwanted son? Was that the money Steele had paid to bail himself out of fatherhood?

"I loved him," Evie murmured, her tears falling freely now. "I loved him, Aaron. Okay? The rest doesn't matter."

"It matters," he retorted, shock and rage constricting his throat, making him hoarse. "How could he buy us off like this?"

"He didn't buy us off. He left you money because you're his son. He left me money because I'm your mother."

"He left you money because you kept your mouth shut all these years. You protected him. You let him off the hook."

"I loved him," she repeated, her voice dissolving into a moan, her hand still shaking as she lifted the cigarette to her lips. She inhaled, then shook her head. "Don't you see? He was a gentleman. He was good to me. He talked to me. He told me I was beautiful, treated me like a lady."

"You weren't a lady. You were his whore."

His mother slapped him. He heard the blow more than felt it, a sharp clap of sound in the stuffy kitchen. "Don't you ever say that. He loved me!"

One slap wasn't going to stop Aaron. The agony inside him was so bad the sting of her fingers went forgotten. "Sure he loved you. He loved you enough to abandon you when you got pregnant. He paid you to keep your mouth shut. What is this inheritance supposed to be? A final thank-you for staying out of his life and leaving me in the dark? He could have done anything he wanted! He was Abraham Steele. This town revolved around him! If he loved you, he would have accepted you into his life. And accepted me, too."

"He was married! How could he have accepted me?"

"He accepted you just fine when he was having an affair with you. Then what? You told him you were pregnant and he took a powder? Or did he tell you he'd give you some money to go see a special doctor in a distant city and have 'the problem' taken care of? Was that what he asked his beautiful lady to do? Or was he a real gentleman, saying you could go ahead and have me, as long as you went to that distant city and put me up for adoption? Let me guess—you were a lady until you decided to stay in town and have me here. Then you just became an expense. A cheap woman who threatened his nice, comfortable existence.''

''It wasn't like that!'' She was sobbing. ''He loved me! If I hadn't got pregnant, he would have kept seeing me.''

''I ruined it for you, huh?''

''What could he do? He was married! He was a good man, Aaron.''

''He was a son of a bitch. He used you and he discarded me like a piece of trash.''

''He was the best thing that ever happened to me.'' She cupped her hands over her eyes as she wept, her grief deeper than Aaron could comprehend.

But he comprehended this: Abraham Steele was the best thing that had ever happened to her. Aaron was not. No wonder she had protected Abraham from him. In all the years since Abraham had deserted her and her bastard son—*his* bastard son—she still believed her affair with Abraham had been the best thing in her life. If his will hadn't slapped Aaron in the face even harder than his mother's hand, she would have kept Abraham's secret forever. She never would have told Aaron.

She loved Abraham. Their son had never mattered to either of them.

He shoved away from the table, knocking his chair over from the force of his anger. Not bothering to right it, he stalked out of the kitchen. The muted sounds of his mother crying followed him out the door.

BY EIGHT O'CLOCK Lily gave up. The coq au vin had been done an hour ago, the rice steamed and cooled.

She wrapped everything, put it in the refrigerator and tried to keep from panicking.

He'd given her his phone number that morning, and she'd dialed it four times in the past hour. No answer. She'd tried his office at the high-school gym. No answer. She considered phoning the police and asking if there had been any accidents—but if there had been, if Aaron had been hurt, her father would have contacted her. He was the doctor with seniority in town. He'd know if someone had been injured in a car accident, and if Aaron had been injured, her father would have gotten word to her.

So Aaron hadn't been in an accident, at least not in Riverbend. Had he left town? Why would he? And why without telling her? Just that morning he'd cuddled up with her in bed, holding her as if she was precious to him, as if their love was the most precious thing in the world. She'd told him she was going to make an amazing chicken dinner for him, and she had. He'd promised to sleep late with her tomorrow.

He'd told her he loved her, and she understood that *love* was a word that didn't come easily to him. He wouldn't have said it if he hadn't meant it.

So what had happened? Where was he?

Standing in the doorway of her dining room, she pressed the redial button on her cordless phone's handset and lifted it to her ear. While it rang, she surveyed the beautifully arranged table, the candles waiting to be lit, the elegantly folded napkins and silverware, the empty crystal wine goblets. She'd wanted tonight to be festive, a treat for them both, a celebration of their love.

At the tenth ring she pressed the disconnect button.

She wasn't going to cry. She wasn't going to fall apart. Something was wrong, but until she knew what it was, she saw no point in becoming hysterical.

Instead, she carried the phone back to the kitchen, gathered her purse and keys, and left the house.

The late-evening air was cool, but she kept the top down on her car. She wanted the dark breezes to press against her face. She wanted to hear the distant chatter of irrigation systems spraying the fields. She wanted to smell the damp earth and the green of flourishing crops. She wanted the night to envelop her.

She drove to River Road. Loose pebbles bounced against the underside of her car. She would check Aaron's cabin first. Perhaps he'd slipped in the shower and was lying unconscious on his bathroom floor. Or he'd gotten stuck somehow—a bookcase had fallen on him, pinning him—and he'd been going nuts, unable to reach his ringing phone. She would rescue him. She'd save his life. They'd eat the chicken another night.

His cabin was nearly dark; she almost drove past it before catching sight of the unpaved driveway in the beam of her headlights. She coasted slowly to the end by the shed where he stored his firewood and shut off the engine. His car was there. She wasn't sure if that was a good sign or a bad one.

Night sounds settled gently around her—crickets, frogs, wind sifting through the trees—as she got out of her car and walked the path to the house. Through the front window, she spotted only a single lamp burning inside, one small amber dot of light in the house. Pushing past her anxiety, she knocked on the front door, then twisted the knob. Locked.

She shielded her eyes and peered through a window. All she saw was the glow of that one lamp, which stood on the counter separating the front room from the kitchen. No sign of life in the house.

But his car was in the shed. Had he gone off somewhere in someone else's car?

Sighing, she turned back to her own car. If she got into it, she wouldn't know where to drive, where to look. She swallowed the worry crowding her throat. What if he'd hiked to the river and fallen in? Surely he could swim, but what if he'd banged his head? She knew the perils of hitting one of the rocks that jutted up from the riverbank.

Aaron, she thought, her heart thumping. *Aaron, where are you?*

She strode around his cabin. Dead twigs and mulch crunched under her sandals; underbrush tugged at her shins and knees. The stairs to his deck beckoned. She climbed them, not sure what she hoped to find at the top.

So little light reached the deck it took her a minute to make out the motionless body on the hammock. A minute longer, and she discerned one long leg dangling over the side of the canvas, the bare foot reaching the floorboards. An object was propped on his stomach, held in place between his hands.

"Aaron?"

He slowly turned his head toward her, then pulled the object toward his mouth. As her vision adjusted, she saw that it was a bottle. She heard the scrape of metal against glass as he unscrewed the cap, and the gurgle of him drinking. She caught a whiff of alcohol, pungent, much stronger than the refined smell of Tyler's martinis.

What crowded her throat was no longer worry. It was bile.

"Aaron, what are you doing?"

His eyes seemed to take their time focusing on her. He pushed himself higher on the hammock so he was halfway between reclining and sitting. Then he took another swig from the bottle, meticulously screwed the cap back on and shoved himself higher. "It's been one hell of a lousy day," he said.

Oh, God, please don't let him be drunk, she prayed, although it was probably too late for prayers. *Please, don't let him be like Tyler.*

"You were supposed to come to my house for dinner," she reminded him, cringing at the shrewish undertone in her voice.

"I forgot."

Obviously. "What happened?"

"I found out who my father is." He toyed with the bottle cap, loosening it, tightening it. She closed her eyes and sent another prayer heavenward that he wouldn't open the bottle all the way, that he wouldn't drink any more. "It's not Coach Drummer."

No, it wouldn't be. He wouldn't try to climb into a bottle of whiskey over Wally Drummer. "Who is it?"

"You don't want to know."

"I asked."

"I asked my mother for thirty-three years, and she refused to tell me."

"All right." Anger mixed with nausea inside Lily.

The combination made her feel light-headed, but she refused to sit. If she sat she might lose what little strength she had. She might cry or implore him to stop, to transform himself back to the strong, disciplined man she loved. "Don't tell me."

"Then I'd be as bad as my mother, wouldn't I?"

"Don't play games with me, Aaron. If you want to tell me, tell me. If you don't, don't. If you want to get drunk—"

"I want to get drunk," he said, raw pain lacing his tone. "Goddamn it, that's what I want."

A shiver gripped her. She couldn't believe she was in love with a man who wanted to get drunk. What could he have learned, who could his father be, that the truth turned him into this weak, defeated wretch?

"She loved him," he said, seeming to struggle with the words. "All these years, my mother loved him. He tossed her aside and got on with his life, and she carried a freaking torch for him. And she hated me because I spoiled their love affair. I made it impossible."

"Aaron, I know you're hurting, but—"

"You don't know," he cut her off, his bitterness scalding her. "You can't begin to know."

He was right. She couldn't begin to know the rejection he was suffering. But that didn't make getting drunk an acceptable response. Nothing justified getting drunk.

She ventured forward one step, two. If she moved quickly, she might be able to snatch the bottle from his hand. Once she had it, she'd be able to think about what to do, how to save him. Whether to save him. He was bigger, stronger, faster, but if she could just get the bottle away from him…

He was opening it again, tipping it to his lips, swallowing. The sight repulsed her so much she had to close her eyes.

"Life is ugly sometimes," he said harshly, obviously aware of her disgust. "I warned you I wasn't easy. This part—this part is hard."

"You're self-destructive," she muttered, resorting to the terminology he'd taught her.

"Oh, I'm trying, Lily. I'm trying to destroy myself." He tilted the bottle away to gauge its contents. "This might not be enough."

No way could she grab the bottle. It might go flying, breaking and hurting them. Or Aaron might hurt her. She knew from experience with Tyler what happened when a woman came between a man and his attempt at self-destruction.

"Please stop," she said. "Put the bottle down, Aaron."

He shot her a stony look, then raised the bottle and drank some more. Maybe he was self-destructing, but he was also aiming at her, telling her without words that her concern for him didn't matter, her love didn't matter. Nothing mattered but his own private despair.

"If you don't stop, I'll leave."

"Then you'd better leave," he said, the words so clear and pointed she could hardly believe he'd consumed more than half the bottle. If he truly wanted to get drunk, he had a long way to go, a lot of drinking left to do.

She wasn't going to stick around and watch him achieve his goal. She'd spent ten years with a man who'd attempted to solve his problems—or run from them—by drinking himself into oblivion. She'd tried to salvage him and he'd hated her for it. She'd tried to help him and he'd blamed her. She'd tried to love him, and her love had shriveled and died.

She would not go through that again. Not even for Aaron.

She spun around and crossed to the stairs. She was afraid of what she'd say if she spoke, so she pressed her lips together. She was afraid she would start to cry, so she kept her eyes open, letting the air keep them dry. She was afraid that if she slowed down, she would lose her resolve, run back to him, urge him to stop drinking, give their love a chance, let her fix everything enough that he wouldn't want to do this to himself. So she didn't slow down.

His voice reached her when she was halfway down the stairs. "Abraham Steele," he said—quietly, but she heard him.

She faltered and clutched the railing to keep from stumbling. Abraham Steele?

Oh, God. *Abraham Steele.*

The name came at her like a punch, nearly doubling her over. Abraham, the stately, silver-haired gentleman, an image of propriety, of rectitude, of all the solid values of Riverbend. The man who had introduced her to art. Who had golfed with her father. Who had supported the town and its people in so many ways.

That Abraham Steele was Aaron's father shocked her, but it wasn't enough to justify Aaron's behavior. He might be drinking over Abraham, but the true target of his rage was his mother, the mother who'd loved a long-ago lover more than her own son.

Lily's heart broke for Aaron. But she couldn't stay. She couldn't let herself love a man who fled from love and looked to the bottle for solace. She'd done that once, and she couldn't do it again.

CHAPTER FIFTEEN

LILY WASN'T SURE how the word got out—maybe Nick Harrison had mentioned it, or his secretary, or somebody else—but by Sunday everyone in church was buzzing about Abraham Steele and Aaron Mazerik. Milling around outside the entrance to the Riverbend Community Church, people whispered, murmured, shook their heads and clicked their tongues. Riverbend, as always, was the Land of No Privacy. What astonished most people was that this secret had been kept as long as it had.

Aaron wasn't at the church, of course. Lily had no idea where he was. For that matter, she was having trouble figuring out where *she* was. At church, yes, but drifting. Floating. Disconnected from the world around her.

Oh, Aaron. Why couldn't you have been strong enough to get through this without drinking? Why, of all the ways you could have dealt with this, did you have to choose the bottle?

Her father stood with her while her mother chatted with Mary Drummer and Gloria Hoff, ostensibly about garden-club business but most likely about Aaron. "So, the secret's finally out," Lily's father said. "I'm glad I wasn't the one to tell. Abraham had made me promise. Doctor-patient confidentiality and all that. How is Aaron bearing up?''

"Not well," Lily said, then cleared her throat in an effort to dislodge the lump of tears in it. What an understatement. Aaron wasn't bearing up at all. He was going down.

"Everyone was talking about it at the golf course yesterday," her father informed her. "No one wants to believe it. Abraham Steele was such a pillar in this community."

"He was a human being," Lily said. "He made a mistake."

"He made a son out of wedlock. Quite a mistake."

His real mistake had been in refusing to acknowledge that son. What would Aaron's life have been like if Abraham had taken responsibility for him? Aaron would have grown up as Jacob's half brother. He might have seen himself as more a part of the town. He might have become a River Rat.

Instead, he'd grown up feeling rejected, not just by the town but by both his parents—the father he never knew and the mother he lived with. He'd become a renegade, someone who broke the law. What was truly amazing was that he'd matured into such a fine man.

A man who dealt with shocking news by getting himself stinking drunk, she reminded herself with a shudder.

"Look at your mother," her father said, angling his head at Eleanor Bennett, standing several yards away. "Doesn't she look fabulous? The hairstyle really suits her."

"Nice of you to notice," Lily said, managing a grin.

"Oh, I'm noticing. I'm noticing." He looped his arm around Lily and gave her a squeeze. "Thank you."

A fresh lump of tears took up residence in her throat. She was thrilled that her parents were once again connecting, communicating, nourishing their relationship, and she was gratified that she had helped them mend the damage before it became irreparable.

She wished someone would come along and mend the damage between her and Aaron. But it couldn't be mended. Whenever she missed him—and that had been pretty much constantly since Friday night—all she had to do was close her eyes and picture him in his hammock, reeking of booze and hostility. She reaffirmed her vow. She couldn't go through that again. Not even for him. Not even for love.

The church bell began to chime and the doors swung open. Lily's mother left her friends with a farewell wave and rejoined Lily and her father as they climbed the front steps, entered the church and took seats about halfway down the aisle. All around her Lily heard the continuing hum of voices.

"Can you believe it? Evie Mazerik's kid. The one who got into all that trouble as a teenager..."

"The poor sisters. I can just imagine what Ruth and Rachel must be feeling right now..."

"Think of the irony. Jacob disappeared, and Abraham never recognized Aaron. He fathered two sons and wound up with none..."

"I can't picture Abraham with Evie Mazerik, of

all people. I mean, she's just…you know. Evie Mazerik.''

Lily was almost grateful when the organist stopped playing and Lynn Kendall stepped up to the pulpit. She was tired of hearing people gossip about Aaron and his mother, tired of being reminded over and over about the scandalous circumstances of his conception. She hated them all—Abraham Steele for choosing appearances over integrity, Evie for not giving her son the love he needed, and Aaron for deadening himself with drink.

A hymn was sung, a reading done, and the congregation sat forward as Lynn began her sermon. Did they think she would talk about Abraham's sins and secrets? If everyone else in Riverbend knew the hottest gossip, surely Reverend Kendall knew it, too.

''Forgiveness,'' she said, then paused.

A long pause. Lily heard pews creaking as people shifted in their seats. She heard the scuffing of shoes against the floor, a cough, a rattle of paper.

Finally she resumed. ''Forgiving is one of the hardest acts we're called upon to do, one of the greatest challenges we're ever faced with, because forgiveness requires the ability to open our hearts fully. And opening our hearts that fully scares us. A heart open to forgiveness is also a heart vulnerable to pain and fear. If we forgive a person for what he has done, what if he does it again? Here's my heart, wide open. He can wound me another time.''

Lily leaned back in the pew as a wave of sorrow washed over her. She recalled the ocean in Massachusetts, its surf curling in and rolling over her, the undertow wrapping around her ankles and tugging hard. Riverbend had its river, but that wasn't the same. The river flowed smoothly. It might carry a person away, but it couldn't suck her under.

Lily had been sucked under once. It had taken all her strength—and Aaron's help—to swim back to the surface, to fight her way back to air and sunshine and life. And last night, seeing him drinking to get drunk, she'd felt the waves crashing over her again, pulling her under.

She couldn't go through it again. She just couldn't.

From the pulpit Lynn related a story about a woman who couldn't forgive. A cranky loner, the woman remembered every slight, every offense, every injury she'd ever suffered. She was determined never to be hurt again, and she protected herself by not forgiving those who had hurt her before. And instead, she wound up hurting herself, wounded by her own loneliness. "The person most hurt by a lack of forgiveness," Lynn Kendall said, "is the person who is unable to forgive."

Lily ruminated. What had she said to her father about Abraham Steele? *He was a human being. He made a mistake.*

Aaron was a human being, too. Friday night he'd been suffering, and he'd tried to anesthetize himself. And instead of helping him, instead of forgiving, Lily had stormed away, determined to protect herself from the kind of hurt she'd endured once before. She'd gone home, shut herself in her house, gone at another canvas with wild aggression and painted something unrecognizable, ugly, dark slashes and splatters, a reflection of some wretched nightmare. Her own night-

mare. A woman locked tight, imprisoned by her inability to forgive.

She'd been alone since that night. Protected from
hurt, and hurt by her own lack of forgiveness.

"I have to go," she whispered to her parents, rising and edging past her mother's knees. The rest of
the people in the pew stirred and murmured as she
eased past them. No doubt the next hot topic of gossip in town would be her abrupt departure from
church in the middle of Reverend Kendall's sermon.

She hurried up the side aisle and out the door into
the bright sun. Not stopping to think, she climbed
behind the wheel of her car and pulled out into the
road.

Riverbend was empty. Sunday mornings found
most people in church and the rest either at the golf
course or in bed, sleeping late. The sidewalks were
vacant, the stores closed, the streets clear of traffic.
The sun glazed the clock tower of the courthouse on
the square. It threw trees and bricks and blades of
grass into sharp relief.

Lily had never felt more alone. Even in her disastrous marriage, she hadn't felt this alone. Right
now, in the stillness of downtown Riverbend, she
might have been a visitor to a ghost town, an ex-
plorer on a strange planet, a wanderer in the wilder-
ness—utterly alone, because she'd been afraid that
loving someone like Aaron could hurt her.

Love always brought with it the risk of being hurt.
But only someone afraid to take that risk, someone
determined to keep herself safe, would run from a
love that could also bring great joy, a chance to heal.

He was a human being. He made a mistake.

Aaron could forgive his father, if he wanted. And she could forgive Aaron—if she was willing to take the risk.

She drove down River Road to his cabin. His car wasn't in the shed, but she walked to the front door, anyway. In the sunny morning, he would not need to leave a lamp on as he had last night, and when she cupped her hand over her eyes and peeked through the window, she didn't see him. She knocked. No response.

As she had last night, she picked her way around the house to his deck. She had to hold her skirt up to avoid snagging the hem on the underbrush; she had to watch her footing in her low-heeled leather pumps as she made her way to the deck stairs. Even though his car was gone, even though she knew he was undoubtedly gone, as well, she almost expected to find Aaron passed out in his hammock, a pile of bottles lying empty next to him. She wasn't sure exactly what she'd do if he was in that condition. She would try not to berate him. *Forgiveness,* she reminded herself.

He wasn't on the deck. The hammock was empty. No bottles.

Where could he have gone?

Anywhere, she realized with a sigh that felt suspiciously like a sob. Distraught about his father and his mother, angry with her, he might have pocketed his inheritance and left town. Why not? The people who should have loved him had all turned their backs on him. Especially her.

No. He wouldn't leave town, not with his basketball program flourishing. He might feel abandoned by her, but he would never abandon his kids.

Perhaps he'd gone to the one person who had never walked away from him: Wally Drummer. Except that Wally and his wife had been at church. Aaron hadn't been with them.

Stumped, she climbed down the deck stairs, lifted her hem and made her way back to her car. She would go home, change out of her church clothes and then figure out how to find him. If he was truly gone...

No, she wouldn't even entertain that possibility. She was going to be strong and brave and optimistic. She was going to find him, and when she did she would tell him she loved him. She'd tell him the sight of him drowning his problems in whiskey had terrified her, and the possibility that he might do such a thing again terrified her even more. But she would brave that terror to find him, to see if she could forgive him, to see if she could ever trust him with her heart.

As she approached her house, she saw his car in her driveway and Aaron himself sitting on her front-porch steps. He wore jeans, a T-shirt and sandals. In his hand he clutched a bouquet of wildflowers, blue and red and yellow blossoms on thin green stalks.

She pulled into the driveway behind him and got out of the car. He watched her, the multitude of colors in his eyes glinting like sparks.

At the steps to the porch she halted. He rose to his feet. His mouth was set in a grim line and a muscle ticked in his jaw. "I'm late for dinner," he said.

She drew in a deep breath. Standing next to him ignited a throbbing heat inside her. She remembered the romantic dinner she'd prepared, the hopes she'd had for Friday night, before everything had gone wrong.

His eyes looked surprisingly clear, considering. His body looked surprisingly pain-free. If he was hung over, she saw no sign of it. "How do you feel?" she asked.

"Like hell."

"Aspirin helps."

A smile seemed to threaten his mouth, but he resisted it. "I feel like hell here," he said, poking his thumb into his chest. "I blew it, Lily. I did the one thing you could never accept. And I feel like hell." He glanced down at the flowers, then pressed the small bouquet into her hands. "I was going to bring you roses Friday night. This was the best I could do on a Sunday morning. Anyway…I'm sorry." He held her gaze for less than a second, then lowered his eyes and moved past her, as if he intended to leave.

She grabbed his wrist to keep him from going. The feel of his skin sent a fresh surge of yearning through her. She did her best to ignore it. She couldn't think about what sleeping with him had been like, and waking up with him, and loving him through the night. Aaron was about to walk out of her life. She had to stop him.

"I just came from your house," she told him. "I went there to apologize."

Surprise flickered across his face. "What do you have to apologize for?"

"Judging you. Leaving you. Hating you for what you were doing to yourself."

"Of course you hated me. Why wouldn't you?"

"But it wasn't up to me to approve or disapprove of you. You went through a horrible experience, Aaron, and there I was, deciding you should have reacted differently. I had no right to do that."

"I was drinking to get drunk, Lily."

"I know."

"Not just because of Steele and my mother. Because…" He swallowed. "Because of who I am. You need to know this about me, Lily. I'm a punk. An outsider. The town bastard. That's who I am. I drank in front of you deliberately, so you'd see that." Gazing past her, he let out a long breath. "I'm not the kind of man you deserve. You're a princess. I'm no prince."

The spicy scent of the wildflowers drifted up between them. It made her want to cry. Aaron's determination to make her reject him made her want to cry even more.

"I don't want a prince," she said. "I want a man. I don't care if you make mistakes—God knows, I make more than my share. You're not a drunk, Aaron. You were trying really hard to get drunk Friday night, but that doesn't make you a drunk."

"Friday night you wouldn't have said that."

"Friday night I was too selfish to realize what kind of pain you were in." Her fingers softened against his wrist but didn't let go. "I hated it that you were drinking, Aaron, but I wasn't even thinking about you. I was thinking about what I'd been through with Tyler. That wasn't fair to you." She stroked the skin of his wrist with her thumb, searching his face for a sign that she was getting through to him, that he believed her, that he knew how much she loved him. "You're not a punk, Aaron. You're a strong, brave man. I don't ever want to hear you say such things about yourself again."

At last he turned back to her. His gaze met hers, testing, measuring. "What would you do if you saw me drinking like that again?"

"I'd shake you till your teeth rattled. I'd scream at you. I'd wail. I'd beg. I'd tell you I loved you and wanted you to stop. I don't know." She offered a hesitant smile. "Would any of that work?"

"The last strategy might." He remained solemn, even as her smile expanded. "Lily, I mean it. I'm not just the town bastard. I'm Abraham Steele's bastard." He shook his head. "My whole past is so screwed up—"

"That's not important. I mean, of course it's important, but it's not as important as your present. And your future. You're a teacher. A counselor. A coach. A role model. And a pretty decent art critic, too."

Another smile, faint but promising, flickered across his lips at that last description.

"You know, I don't even like hard liquor that much."

"Good." She skimmed her hand up his arm to his shoulder and pulled herself up to kiss his cheek. "Do you forgive me?"

"There's nothing to forgive."

"There's plenty. I want your forgiveness, Aaron."

He studied her upturned face. His eyes were so intense, so full of need, so desperately hopeful. "Anything you want, Lily. If I can give it to you, I will."

"I want you," she murmured.

"I'm yours," he said. Plain, blunt, lacking eloquence, but they were the two most beautiful words she'd ever heard.

She closed her arms around him as he lowered his mouth to hers. They kissed, with forgiveness and love, all the love they had to give, all the love they would ever need. Later they would talk about what Aaron had been through, how he was going to deal with it. They would figure out how a man who had grown up believing he was an outsider could accommodate the knowledge that he was, in fact, the son of the ultimate insider. They would work it out.

But for now, they had already worked out the most important truth. She and Aaron loved each other. He was hers and she was his. And there was more than enough forgiveness to share.

* * *

Look for the next story from Riverbend,
That Summer Thing *by Pamela Bauer,*
available next month.

SILHOUETTE® SUPERROMANCE™

AVAILABLE FROM 16TH AUGUST 2002

SHELTERED IN HIS ARMS
Tara Taylor Quinn

Shelter Valley

When Sam returns to his home town—and his ex-wife, Cassie Tate—with a seven-year-old child, it's a shock. When he'd left he hadn't even known she was pregnant. Or that she had lost their baby. They've both changed. Can Sam be the man Cassie needs now?

THE LISTENER Kay David

The Guardians

Marie's latest case is the hardest she's ever had. No patient has walked closer to the edge than SWAT team cop Ryan Lukas, despite the fact that he thinks he's fine. But how can Maria allow herself, and her teenage son, to need Ryan when he doesn't know what he needs for himself?

THAT SUMMER THING Pamela Bauer

Riverbend

Everyone thinks that Charlie Callahan is the original good-time Charlie, especially his ex-wife Beth Pennington. But when an inheritance is left to them both, they are forced back together to settle the strange bequest...and to deal with a troubled boy.

HER SISTER'S BABY Janice Kay Johnson

9 Months Later

When Colleen Deering agreed to be a surrogate mum for her sister Sheila and her husband Michael she never dreamed that Sheila wouldn't survive to see the baby. Or that in turning to Michael in sorrow, she would discover a dangerous attraction...

Diana
Palmer

WEDDINGS IN WHITE

A fabulous collection of three
irresistible wedding stories

On sale 20th September 2002

Available at most branches of WH Smith,
Tesco, Martins, Borders, Eason, Sainsbury's
and most good paperback bookshops.

THE COLTONS

FAMILY PRIVILEGE POWER

*Look out for our fabulous brand
new limited continuity series*
THE COLTONS,
*where the secrets of California's
most glamorous and talked about
dynasty are revealed!*

Available from 16th August

FREE!

2 Books
and a surprise gift!

We would like to take this opportunity to thank you for reading this Silhouette® book by offering you the chance to take TWO more specially selected titles from the Superromance™ series absolutely FREE! We're also making this offer to introduce you to the benefits of the Reader Service™—

- ★ FREE home delivery
- ★ FREE gifts and competitions
- ★ FREE monthly Newsletter
- ★ Books available before they're in the shops
- ★ Exclusive Reader Service discount

Accepting these FREE books and gift places you under no obligation to buy; you may cancel at any time, even after receiving your free shipment. Simply complete your details below and return the entire page to the address below. **You don't even need a stamp!**

YES! Please send me 2 free Superromance books and a surprise gift. I understand that unless you hear from me, I will receive 4 superb new titles every month for just £3.49 each, postage and packing free. I am under no obligation to purchase any books and may cancel my subscription at any time. The free books and gift will be mine to keep in any case.

U2ZEB

Ms/Mrs/Miss/Mr ....Initials ....
BLOCK CAPITALS PLEASE

Surname...

Address...

....

....Postcode ....

Send this whole page to:
UK: The Reader Service, FREEPOST CN81, Croydon, CR9 3WZ
EIRE: The Reader Service, PO Box 4546, Kilcock, County Kildare (stamp required)

Offer not valid to current Reader Service subscribers to this series. We reserve the right to refuse an application and applicants must be aged 18 years or over. Only one application per household. Terms and prices subject to change without notice. Offer expires 29th November 2002. As a result of this application, you may receive offers from other carefully selected companies. If you would prefer not to share in this opportunity please write to The Data Manager at the address above.

Silhouette® is a registered trademark used under licence.
Superromance™ is being used as a trademark.